Outstanding Praise for the Novels of T. Greenwood

Where I Lost Her

"A spellbinding tale about finding what we most want in the places we least expect. I loved everything about *Where I Lost Her*."
—Mary Kubica, bestselling author of *The Good Girl* and *Pretty Baby*

"Greenwood crafts believable relationships with searing, heartbreaking realism. This mysterious, suspenseful exploration of the human psyche will keep readers turning pages and losing sleep."
—*Publishers Weekly*

"Greenwood's fascinating tenth novel is sure to have readers riveted, as a distraught Tess struggles to learn the truth."
—*Library Journal*

"*Where I Lost Her* will not disappoint."
—*The New York Journal of Books*

"This intoxicating blend of women's fiction and psychological thriller is the perfect platform for Greenwood's exquisite prose and masterful storytelling."
—*RT Book Reviews*, 4.5 Stars Top Pick

The Forever Bridge

"Greenwood deftly captures the complicated and subtly volatile situations of three women at three very different stages of their lives with sensitivity and a stark honesty that makes for a compelling read."
—Tawni O'Dell, *New York Times* bestselling author of *Back Roads*

"T. Greenwood adds another enticing, lyrical novel to her body of work."
—Miranda Beverly-Whittemore, *New York Times* bestselling author of *Bittersweet*

"I loved *The Forever Bridge* from its first beautiful sentence to its breathtaking final one."
—Ann Hood, author of *The Knitting Circle* and *An Italian Wife*

"T. Greenwood's latest is her best. Written with acute humanity and depth, the beauty of the novel is in its complex story and, ultimately, its heartbreaking and redemptive end."
—Michelle Gable, author of *A Paris Apartment*

"Full of palpable emotion: both the pain of unbearable losses, and the indomitable human connections that somehow allow us to bear them. This lyrical and poignant novel will appeal to fans of Caroline Leavitt's *Pictures of You* and Jonathan Evison's *The Revised Fundamentals of Caregiving.*"
—Gina Frangello, author of *A Life in Men*

Bodies of Water

"A complex and compelling portrait of the painful intricacies of love and loyalty. Book clubs will find much to discuss in T. Greenwood's insightful story."
—Eleanor Brown, *New York Times* bestselling author of *The Weird Sisters*

"A wrenching look at what happens when two people fall in love in the wrong place at the wrong time . . . Beauty and tragedy at the same time, darkness then light—those are Greenwood hallmarks."
—*The San Diego Union-Tribune*

"*Bodies of Water* is no ordinary love story, but a book of astonishing precision, lyrically told, raw in its honesty and gentle in its unfolding. A luminous, fearless, heart-wrenching story about the power of true love."
—Ilie Ruby, author of *The Salt God's Daughter*

"This compassionate, insightful look at hope and redemption is a richly textured portrait. This gem of a story is a good choice for those who enjoy family novels."
—*Library Journal*

"By turns beautiful and tragic, haunting and healing, I was captivated from the very first line. And Greenwood's moving story of love and loss, hope and redemption has stayed with me, long after I turned the last page."
—Jillian Cantor, author of *Margot*

Breathing Water

"A poignant, clear-eyed first novel . . . filled with careful poetic description . . . the story is woven skillfully."
—*The New York Times Book Review*

"A poignant debut . . . Greenwood sensitively and painstakingly unravels her protagonist's self-loathing and replaces it with a graceful dignity."
—*Publishers Weekly*

"A vivid, somberly engaging first book."
—Larry McMurtry

"An impressive first novel."
—*Booklist*

"*Breathing Water* is startling and fresh . . . Greenwood's novel is ripe with originality."
—*The San Diego Union-Tribune*

Grace

"*Grace* is a poetic, compelling story that glows in its subtle, yet searing examination of how we attempt to fill the potentially devastating fissures in our lives."
—Amy Hatvany, author of *Best Kept Secret*

"This novel will keep readers rapt until the very end . . . Shocking and honest, you're likely to never forget this book."
—*RT Book Reviews*

"*Grace* amazes. Ultimately so realistically human in its terror and beauty that it may haunt you for days after you finish it."
—*The San Diego Union-Tribune*

"Exceptionally well-observed. Readers who enjoy insightful and sensitive family drama (Lionel Shriver's *We Need to Talk About Kevin*; Rosellen Brown's *Before and After*) will appreciate discovering Greenwood."
—*Library Journal*

"Greenwood is an assured guide through this strange territory; she has a lush, evocative style."
—*The New York Times Book Review*

"T. Greenwood writes with grace and compassion about loyalty and betrayal, love and redemption in this totally absorbing novel about daughters and mothers."
—Ursula Hegi, author of *Stones from the River*

"A lyrical investigation into the unreliability and elusiveness of memory centers Greenwood's novel . . . The kaleidoscopic heart of the story is rich with evocative details about its heroine's inner life."
—*Publishers Weekly*

"A complicated story of love and abuse told with a directness and intensity that packs a lightning charge."
—*Booklist*

"A remarkable portrait of resilience. With clarity and painful precision, T. Greenwood probes the dark history of Indie's family."
—Rene Steinke, author of *The Fires* and *Holy Skirts*

"Deft handling of a difficult and painful subject . . . compelling."
—*Kirkus Reviews*

"Potent . . . Greenwood's clear-eyed prose takes the stuff of tabloid television and lends it humanity."
—*San Francisco Chronicle*

This Glittering World

"T. Greenwood demonstrates once again that she is a poet and storyteller of unique gifts, not the least of which is a wise and compassionate heart."
—Drusilla Campbell, author of *The Good Sister* and *Blood Orange*

"Swift, stark, calamitous. Her characters confront those difficult moments that will define them, and Greenwood paints these troubled lives with attention, compassion and hope."
—Jerry Gabriel, author of *Drowned Boy* and winner of the Mary McCarthy Prize in Short Fiction

"Stark, taut, and superbly written. This haunting look at a fractured family is certain to please readers of literary suspense."
—*Library Journal* (starred)

Undressing the Moon

"This beautiful story, eloquently told, demands attention."
—*Library Journal* (starred review)

"A lyrical, delicately affecting tale."
—*Publishers Weekly*

"Rarely has a writer rendered such highly charged topics . . . to so wrenching, yet so beautifully understated, an effect . . . T. Greenwood takes on risky subject matter, handling her volatile topics with admirable restraint . . . *Undressing the Moon* beautifully elucidates the human capacity to maintain grace under unrelenting fire."
—*The Los Angeles Times*

The Hungry Season

"This compelling study of a family in need of rescue is very effective, owing to Greenwood's eloquent, exquisite word artistry and her knack for developing subtle, suspenseful scenes . . . Real, complex, and anything but formulaic."
—*Library Journal* (starred review)

"A deeply psychological read."
—*Publishers Weekly*

"A wonderful story, engaging from the beginning that gets better with every chapter."
—*The Washington Times*

Two Rivers

"Ripe with surprising twists and heart-breakingly real characters, *Two Rivers* is a remarkable and complex look at race and forgiveness in small-town America."
—Michelle Richmond, New York Times bestselling author of *The Year of Fog* and *No One You Know*

"This novel is a sensitive and suspenseful portrayal of family and the ties that bind."
—Lee Martin, author of *The Bright Forever* and *River of Heaven*

"Greenwood is a writer of subtle strength, evoking small-town life beautifully while spreading out the map of Harper's life, finding light in the darkest of stories."
—*Publishers Weekly*

"T. Greenwood's writing shimmers and sings as she braids together past, present, and the events of one desperate day. I ached for Harper in all of his longing, guilt, grief, and vast, abiding love, and I rejoiced at his final, hard-won shot at redemption."
—Marisa de los Santos, *New York Times* bestselling author of *Belong to Me* and *Love Walked In*

"*Two Rivers* is a stark, haunting story of redemption and salvation. A memorable, powerful work."
—Garth Stein, *New York Times* bestselling author of *The Art of Racing in the Rain*

"A complex tale of guilt, remorse, revenge, and forgiveness . . . Convincing . . . Interesting . . ."
—*Library Journal*

"In the tradition of *The Adventures of Huckleberry Finn* and *To Kill a Mockingbird*, T. Greenwood's *Two Rivers* is a wonderfully distinctive American novel, abounding with memorable characters, unusual lore and history, dark family secrets, and love of life. *Two Rivers* is the story that people want to read: the one they have never read before."
—Howard Frank Mosher, author of *Walking to Gatlinburg*

"*Two Rivers* is a dark and lovely elegy, filled with heartbreak that turns itself into hope and forgiveness. I felt so moved by this luminous novel."
—Luanne Rice, *New York Times* bestselling author

"*Two Rivers* is reminiscent of Thornton Wilder, with its quiet New England town shadowed by tragedy, and of Sherwood Anderson, with its sense of desperate loneliness and regret . . ."
—*Bookpage*

The
Golden Hour

Books by T. Greenwood

The Golden Hour

Where I Lost Her

The Forever Bridge

Bodies of Water

Grace

This Glittering World

The Hungry Season

Two Rivers

Undressing the Moon

Nearer Than the Sky

Breathing Water

The
Golden Hour

T. GREENWOOD

KENSINGTON BOOKS
www.kensingtonbooks.com

KENSINGTON BOOKS are published by

Kensington Publishing Corp.
119 West 40th Street
New York, NY 10018

All Kensington titles, imprints, and distributed lines are available at special quantity discounts for bulk purchases for sales promotion, premiums, fundraising, educational, or institutional use.

Special book excerpts or customized printings can also be created to fit specific needs. For details, write or phone the office of the Kensington Sales Manager: Kensington Publishing Corp., 119 West 40th Street, New York, NY 10018. Attn. Sales Department. Phone: 1-800-221-2647.

Kensington and the K logo Reg. U.S. Pat. & TM Off.

eISBN-13: 978-0-7582-9058-8
eISBN-10: 0-7582-9058-6
First Kensington Electronic Edition: March 2017

ISBN-13: 978-0-7582-9057-1
ISBN-10: 0-7582-9057-8
First Kensington Trade Paperback Printing: March 2017

10 9 8 7 6 5 4 3 2 1

Printed in the United States of America

Acknowledgments

Sometimes writing is a struggle. This was one of those times. With gratitude to those who gave me the necessary fortitude: Amy Hatvany, Jillian Cantor, Henry Dunow, and Peter Senftleben.

Thanks as well to Neal Griffin and to Amy Morrissette McGarry for their invaluable advice and professional expertise.

For Sally Mann, Diane Arbus, Susan Meiselas, Vivian Maier, and in memory of Mary Ellen Mark, in appreciation for their painfully beautiful and true work, which continually informs my own.

For their endless patience, love, and comic relief, thanks to Patrick and the girls.

And lastly, I am grateful to my Grampa Craig, whose magical *Epitaphs and Prophecies* box inspired this story.

Palette

*I*f this day were a painting, if I were asked to fill my palette with all the colors of that afternoon, you might be surprised by the ones I'd choose: grasshopper greens and cerulean blue. It was June, I might argue, the last day of school. Of course, the grass was green, the sky blue.

But what color is thirteen? Is it the cinder brown of wide eyes, the crimson flush of hot cheeks? Maybe a dollop of peach for the chipped nail polish on ragged fingernails, that same fleshy pink for thin legs as they run across that endless green. A cadmium shirt, and the washed-out cobalt of denim cutoff jeans. Add blue to black for the hair, tied back, a horse's tail swooshing side to side like a pendulum with each stride.

If this day were a painting, there would be trees at the edges of the canvas: the familiar woods that bordered the impossible green of the school's lower playing fields. White and gray for the birches, with their bleached and ragged bark, but also the viridian of fir and pine. An infusion of white for the spot of sunlight illuminating the path, the shortcut home. A foyer of leaves and sunshine.

But what is the color of breathlessness, of a sudden quickening of the pulse? What color could I coax from the palette to illustrate the pounding of feet, the crush of brush? What color would the shadows be? And what color, what shade, could I select for this moment when I stopped, breathless, heart thrumming, and almost turned back instead of taking that shortcut through the green? What color is hesitation? What color fear? The blue is easy, but what about the moment when I stepped into those woods and lost the sky?

I am haunted by the birches. By what lives beyond the edges of the canvas. By those things for which there are no colors to paint.

The Golden Hour

The Google alert about Robby Rousseau came while I was painting. I was at home, in our duplex in Queens, working on a commission job. It was late afternoon, that single gilded hour when the dingy corner of my living room where I worked was imbued with a sort of magical light. The Chet Baker station was playing on Pandora. Liquid amber sunlight was pooled across my paint-splattered hands. *The golden hour.* That's what photographers call it.

My four-year-old daughter, Avery, was next door with Gus, my ex, and I was alone and lost inside those painted trees. I stepped away from the easel, tilted my head, studied the canvas. It was one of my Etsy shop paintings, my craft fair paintings: the quirky birches, the frazzled, skittish sky. Over the years, I'd come to realize this was what people wanted: thick white branches, sturdy, steady limbs. The predictable, slightly comical, green of leaves. A painting you could just as easily hang in a child's room as a dentist's office. The kind of painting you buy to match your sofa or blinds.

And while I was grateful for the work (and trust me, I was grateful to be making money making art), commission jobs pulled me away from my own projects. Between this and taking care of Avery, there was little time or energy left for much of anything else. But now that Gus and I had split up, I couldn't rely on him anymore to put food on the table, for his paychecks from the sign shop to cover the minimum payments on my maxed-out credit cards or my staggering student loans. Thankfully, he'd agreed to keep me on his health insurance plan since we weren't legally divorced yet, or even officially separated for that matter. He paid the tuition at Avery's preschool, and the "rent" I paid to live in the other half of the duplex was simply a gesture on my part. For the first couple of months, Gus didn't even cash my checks. "Focus on your work," he'd insisted, but I wasn't a fool. I knew my real paintings (the ones stacked in the closet like a pile of dirty secrets) would likely never see the light of day, golden or otherwise. And the birches brought in decent money. It was either accept commission work or go back to bartending, and the mere thought of even one more shift pouring drinks at El Cortada was unbearable. I'd worked at bars off and on for the last decade, but after Avery was born I'd sworn I would never go back. I was thirty-three years old, too old for that backbreaking, heartbreaking sort of work.

As the sun slipped behind the building across the street, breaking the ephemeral, twilit spell, I set my brush down and went to my laptop to check my e-mail. And there, amid the Michaels ads and bill notifications, was the e-mail:

RE: Google Alert—"Robert J. Rousseau"

I hesitated before clicking on the link. It had to be a different Robert J. Rousseau. It had happened before. He shared his name with a French philosopher, after all. And a plumber upstate. But I knew the moment the page began to load that it was *him*. My Robert J. Rousseau. Because it was the header for my hometown newspaper, *The Haven Gazette,* that appeared above the article.

I held my breath and scrolled down to the headline.

Local Activist Solicits Help from New Hampshire Innocence Project—Former Social Worker Insists Robert J. Rousseau Falsely Accused in 1996 Crime.

I studied the photo of the woman in the article. *Jan Bromberg.* She wore the same long, thick braid, round glasses, and denim skirt. She'd aged, of course, but I remembered her. She sat through the whole trial. She called my parents practically daily for almost a year until they got a restraining order, changed our number.

But now here she was again. Twenty years later.

The headache began at the base of my skull and bloomed like a flower upward, filling my head. I scanned the article, which provided an interview with Ms. Bromberg, claiming her team at the Innocence Project expected new evidence would ultimately exonerate Robert J. Rousseau.

Ms. Bromberg argued that despite Robby's "confession" (their quotes, not mine), for the last two decades he had maintained his innocence. Apparently, six months before (unbeknownst to prosecution, unbeknownst to me) the Innocence Project's legal team had petitioned to get the rape kit, taken that night in 1996, tested for DNA. There had been no need back then. They'd caught Robby red-handed (he'd *confessed*). But now, with the DNA results expected shortly, Ms. Bromberg was confident this new evidence would provide definitive proof that Robert J. Rousseau was, indeed, *not* guilty.

Trembling, I clicked out of the e-mail, as though I could make the news go back into the ether from which it came, and went to the kitchen. Every one of my ribs ached with the effort of keeping my heart contained within my chest.

He wasn't supposed to ever get out. He was going to rot in prison. That's what my family's lawyer had promised. What the small New Hampshire community where I grew up demanded. And what I'd foolishly believed. I'd been a kid then, though. I'd trusted adults. Even after my entire world was shattered, I somehow thought promises meant something.

I picked up my phone from the rubble on the counter and trembled as I realized that while I'd been painting, basking in that amber light, everyone I knew had found out about Robby Rousseau. Ten missed calls. My mother. My father. My little brother. My mother again. A few numbers I didn't recognize. The cycle repeating.

I put the phone on speaker and listened to each message.

Hi honey, it's Mom. Please don't worry about all of this. That woman is batshit crazy. He confessed. They convicted him. You have nothing to worry about.

It's Dad. Listen, just wanted you to know Larry is already on this. It's a bunch of hoo-ha. Same song and dance as when they tried to appeal before. A DNA test isn't going to change anything. Do not worry.

Hey Wyn, it's Mark. Listen. Just wanted you to know I'm thinking about you. This sucks. Sorry. Call me.

Hi honey. It's Mom again. Maybe you can come home for a little bit? I don't like the idea of you being alone right now. Daddy and I could drive down and get you and Av if you want.

The next two calls were hang-ups. The media, I assumed. Somehow they always managed to get my number. I deleted all of the calls and then picked up the phone to call my best friend, Pilar.

Pick up, I willed. *Pick up.*

Voice mail. Unlike me, Pilar never answered her phone when she was painting. I imagined her in that beautiful room, the floor-to-ceiling windows I coveted. Her own paint-splattered hands. And those gorgeous, *true* paintings she made.

I worried my voice, like my legs, would fail. But when she implored me to "Leave a message . . . or else," instead I felt chilled with an odd calm.

"About Maine," I said. "If you still want me to come with you? I think I'm ready." I hung up before I could change my mind.

Grey Gardens

"It was a steal," Pilar had said when she first showed me pictures of the cottage.

We were sitting at a coffee shop halfway between our two houses. She'd just cut her bangs, and they were crooked—like the time Avery got ahold of my good scissors and cut her own hair. Pilar had recently bought a pair of 1950s reading glasses, which she wore tethered around her neck by a beaded chain. She was the kind of person who hid her beauty behind homemade haircuts, cat's eye glasses, and thrift store housedresses. But her homely outfits had the opposite effect of calling attention to her striking face: golden skin, freckled nose, high cheekbones and almond eyes, her beauty the alchemical result of Colombian, Japanese, and Scottish ancestries.

We huddled together at the wobbly bistro table, shielding the phone's screen from the bright autumn sun, and she thumbed through the photos of the crumbling clapboard cottage that sat atop a rocky cliff on Bluffs Island, a remote islet far off the coast of Maine. She'd bought the house on a whim that summer after she sold a triptych of paintings for a high five figures.

"I had to buy it as is. No inspection. It's a *mess.*"

It was hard to tell from the photos on her phone, but it was clearly dilapidated. She wasn't exaggerating.

"Isn't it a beautiful disaster? Like a mini Grey Gardens? I mean when Big Edie and Little Edie were living there," she said.

"It is." For Halloween one year, she and I dressed as Big Edie and Little Edie (Jackie O's eccentric relatives). Gus had dressed up like one of the feral cats that lived with them in their wrecked mansion in the Hamptons.

"But it's right at the edge of the ocean. It's on two acres. And I figure I can rent it out when I'm not using it."

I'd nodded, feeling tears welling up in my eyes, though I wasn't sure if I was upset because this meant Pilar might move away or if it was just envy. I'd been finding myself experiencing a nasty sort of jealousy around Pilar lately that made me feel awful inside.

"And you can come stay with me. It'll be like when we were at Rizdee."

Pilar, Gus, and I had all gone to art school together at Rhode Island School of Design fifteen years before. And while I had eventually resigned myself to painting those happy birches, and Gus used his skills to make metal signs, Pilar's career had moved at a slow but steady pace. Then last year a collector fell in love with her work, and suddenly she was an artist with a capital *A*. A profile in the *New York Times* and a show at the Pace Gallery had cemented this, and suddenly, everything was changed.

"I'm going to spend a few months there this winter. Try to get some work done. Make sure the pipes don't freeze. That raccoons don't move in."

"Or squatters," I said.

We both knew what it meant to live someplace that didn't belong to us. I'd slept on more couches and shared more bare mattresses than I could count. Gus and I once spent a year living in a teepee in Colorado. I pretended a gypsy life was what I wanted, who I was. But a free spirit was exactly the opposite of the truth. I was afraid. I'd been afraid and running away for twenty years.

Pilar had eventually grown out of this nomadic life and decided to stay in the city about six years ago. And when I got pregnant with Avery, Gus implored me to settle down too, though every inch of me resisted. Gus's grandmother had owned the duplex in Queens since the 1980s. When she passed away, his father had offered it to us, explaining we could rent out the other half for extra cash. Suddenly we had utility bills in our names. Public records. A landline. The duplex made me a real person.

When we split up, I became the tenant, living on the other side.

The idea had seemed to make sense when we first separated that spring. Especially when it came to Avery. It would be a transition, we thought, with a literal wall between us replicating and solidifying the chasm that had been growing between us for the last few years. But now I knew it had been a foolish thought that we could somehow live our separate lives together. That Avery might not even notice as she passed between the doorway that connected our separate homes.

"You could come with me to Maine," Pilar had offered. "It would be good for you, Wynnie. To get away."

Pilar called back an hour after I left her the message and said, "I'm coming over."

"No, it's okay. Everything's fine."

"I don't believe you," she said.

As I waited for her to arrive, I took inventory of what I might need to pack in order to leave. Gus and I had lived in the duplex for five years. But I'd only been on this side of the house for five months. I had most of Avery's toys: the puppet theater that hung suspended in the bedroom doorway, the wicker basket filled with stuffed animals, plastic Little People, and dolls. A bookshelf brimming with board books, and the easel Gus had given her for her birthday.

The apartment was furnished, and I hadn't bothered to hang up any art. That would have meant I'd somehow accepted this was permanent. But how could living on the other side of the wall from an ex be permanent? It was crazy. I could hear every step he took in the other room, the music he played, the muffled conversations he had. Snoring, sneezing, dreaming. All the intimacies of our marriage were now just beyond my reach. And even as

I knew this was the right thing, the best thing, I longed for what we'd lost. Or what I'd somehow squandered away.

Pilar only lived four blocks away, but still her *knock-knock-knock* startled me.

She rushed past me to put the beer in the fridge, turned the knob on the old gas oven, and unwrapped what appeared to be a pan of enchiladas. Pilar was a better mother by far than I was, and she didn't even have any children yet.

When the beer was uncapped and the enchiladas were warming in the oven, Pilar motioned for me to sit on the couch next to her, where she was already sitting, tucking her long legs under her like a child.

"Is it Gus?" she asked, because lately, it was always Gus.

I shook my head. Gus, for the first time in ages, seemed to be the very least of my problems.

She cocked her head. She was wearing a Rosie the Riveter–style bandana today, her bleached blond bangs poking out in all their uneven glory from beneath.

"Because, you guys really need to work this shit out. It's killing me. And *this* is crazy," she said, motioning to the hideous couch she was sitting on. The blank walls.

"I know."

"Where's Av?" she asked. "Nap?"

"With Gus," I said. Gus worked ten to twelve hours a day at the sign shop, so Avery only spent the weekends on his side of the wall.

I took a long pull on my beer. It was bitter. Hoppy. One of those expensive craft beers she liked.

"Tell me what's going on," she said. "You can't just say you want to exile yourself to Bumfuck, Maine, and then clam up."

I stared out the window at the tree whose last leaves had withered and fallen a week ago. The branches looked skeletal, exposed. Raw.

"I just need some time away, to clear my head. To focus on

my painting. I can't keep living like this," I said. Now *I* was the one motioning to the ratty couch, the bare walls, the peeling linoleum. The thin wall that divided Gus and me.

"Okay," she said. "But what about Gus? And Av? He'll never let you take her."

I took a deep breath.

"Robby Rousseau might get a retrial," I said.

Her face drained of color, making her bright red lipsticked lips look like a stain on her face. She shook her head. "That can't be. You said he was in for life."

I shivered and the ancient radiator clanged and hissed as it kicked on. It was October, and winter would be here soon.

"The Innocence Project is getting involved," I said. "They tested the rape kit for DNA."

She winced perceptibly at the word *rape.*

"So?" she said.

I shook my head, felt my throat thicken. My voice was damaged that day; afterward, I was left with the crackling rasp of a heavy smoker, the raw hoarseness I've had guys (ones who had no idea) tell me is sexy. And this voice, this reluctant, faulty voice, sometimes completely fails when I am under stress, the wound made fresh. Decades of healing suddenly undone.

"I'm just worried," I managed. "This lady, Jan Bromberg? She's obsessed. Convinced he didn't do it. Apparently, she tried to get the DA to test the kit for DNA, but it was denied. So she went to the federal district court and they gave her access. Six months ago. Depending on the results, she plans to petition for a retrial. What if he gets another trial? What if a new jury lets him go?"

"Wait. Didn't he confess, Wyn?" Pilar asked.

I nodded, squeezed my eyes shut. I could almost hear the crackling recording playing in the courtroom. His high, uncertain voice, describing what he'd done to me.

"Okay," Pilar said, nodding her head, likely formulating a

plan. Pilar had always been a problem solver. The logical one. "When is this all supposed to happen?"

"I don't know. They're expecting the results any day now, the newspaper said. And then, if the DNA is messed up . . ."

"What do you mean messed up?"

"God, I don't know," I said, my body prickly. "Like if the lab screws up or something . . ."

"Shit, Wynnie," she said, then more softly, "Are you safe? I mean, if he somehow manages to get out . . . would he . . . you're not going to Maine because you think he might . . ."

My skin buzzed, and my heart started to race. I shook my head. There was no way to explain.

"Okay," she said, still nodding. "We'll go. It'll be okay. We'll figure out what to do. But what about Avery?"

"She'll come with me. I mean, she'd have to. We don't really have a choice with Gus's job. He can come up on the weekends. It'll be okay." Even as I began to formulate my argument, I could anticipate his response to this plan.

"Do you think it's smart to be so far away while all of this is happening? It's an *island*," Pilar said. "It's totally remote."

It sounded perfect. I wanted nothing more in that moment than to be on an island far away from everyone on the other end of that phone line. From Gus. I wanted, *needed*, to take a flying leap off the grid.

"I mean, what if they need you to, like, testify or something?"

"That wouldn't happen unless he was granted another trial. Seriously," I said, feeling frustrated now. "I thought this is what you wanted. You said you wanted me to go with you."

Pilar sighed and reached out, grabbing my hands. Her fingernails were painted like shiny ladybug shells. "That was before all of this. Don't you think Gus is going to want to help you too?" she asked. "Be there for you?"

I swallowed hard, pushing the lump that often rendered me mute down again.

"It's really fine. I'm sure everything's going to be okay," I said.

But I knew that nothing was okay. Because no matter what Robby had said to the police back then, when we were both just a couple of terrified thirteen-year-olds—no matter that a jury had convicted him on all counts—the DNA test could change everything.

Playing House

After Pilar went back home, my side of the duplex felt too quiet, too empty. I could hear Avery squealing in oblivious delight on the other side of the wall, and it nearly brought me to my knees.

It was Sunday, time for me to pick her up and bring her back "home." I decided to take the remaining enchiladas over to Gus. I'd never be able to finish them all on my own, and they were too spicy for Avery.

I went outside onto the sagging porch and knocked on his door, an odd formality that hadn't gotten any less odd in the last five months. The streetlights were coming on outside, and the chill in the air had gone from crisp to bitter.

Avery answered the door. "Mama Llama!" she squealed and rushed at my legs. She was wearing her pajamas already, the red union suit I'd bought her to wear as part of her devil costume for Halloween in a few weeks. Her hair was a tangled mess of dark auburn curls. She wouldn't let Gus near her with a brush, but she also wouldn't let me cut her hair.

"Hi, cutes," I said. "Where's Daddy-O?"

"He's making dinner," she said. "It stinks." She plugged her nose dramatically and twirled on one dirty, bare foot before skipping through the cluttered living room to the kitchen, where I could see Gus standing at the counter.

Something thumped hard in my chest.

"Hey," I said awkwardly. "I brought some of Pilar's enchiladas."

"I already started dinner." He gestured to the pot. It smelled like curry, but looked like vomit. The rice cooker steamed on the counter.

Gus had grown a beard since we broke up. Shaving was the only demand I'd ever made about his appearance, and it was more practical than aesthetic; I couldn't stand the gruffness of it on my face when he kissed me, the abrasiveness like steel wool. And now his beard was like the wall that separated us, ensuring neither one of us would slip up and cross over to the other side.

Tonight he also had his pajamas on—a pair of plaid flannel pants I had bought for him a few Christmases ago and a faded Yankees T-shirt. I willed myself not to look at his tattooed arms, muscles straining against the sleeves. He, like Avery, was barefoot.

"You sure?" I asked, motioning to the dish.

"Keep 'em," he said, nodding. And, as if to prove his point, he ladled some of the goop out of the pot and took a tentative bite. He wrinkled his nose a little and then smiled. "So what's up?"

My mouth twitched. I knew if I didn't say it now, I wouldn't. And there was no reason to drag this out any longer than necessary. I glanced behind me quickly to check on Avery. She was occupied with a house Gus seemed to have fashioned out of a giant cardboard box he must have brought home from work.

"I'm going away for a few months. To help Pilar out with her house in Maine," I began. "And to work."

He stopped stirring the disgusting concoction and looked at me. His eyes, steel blue and intense, made me blink and look away.

"Wyn?" he said. "What happened?"

I had hoped he would think this was just the next logical step. That inevitably, one of us would have to leave this peculiar arrangement. That I was just the one who finally called attention to how unhealthy all of this was. But he had always found me transparent. The walls I'd built were impenetrable by others, but never by Gus.

"Av and I need more space," I said vaguely. "And *this* isn't

healthy. It isn't working. It's weird, Gus. We can't live like this forever."

He took a deep breath and waited for me to tell him the
truth. This was his way with me. He knew if he were patient, I
would eventually stop talking around the truth (or at least part of
the truth) and offer it up like a ripe peach in an open palm.

"Also, they're reopening Robby Rousseau's case," I said, the
cat hissing and clawing its way out of the proverbial bag.

"*What?*"

"Apparently, they tested the old evidence kit for DNA. They're
arguing that if this DNA evidence had been available during the
first trial, he wouldn't have been convicted," I said, forcing a smile,
shrugging my shoulders.

"What does that mean? Why?"

"I have no idea," I said, my throat feeling swollen. "The defense wants a retrial."

"That's insane."

I nodded. "I know. But if this happens, if the court grants the
motion, and he actually gets a new trial, I may have to testify. I
need some time to think about it. To clear my head and figure out
what to do. Pilar's place in Maine is empty. I can work and help her
get it cleaned up. If he goes back to trial, things are going to get
crazy."

"You said he was in for life. What the hell? Have you talked
to your folks? Jesus Christ, Wynnie." He stooped down to my
height, clutched my elbows in his hands.

And suddenly I was eighteen years old again, peering up into
his sweet face, the black freckle below his eye making it impossible to do anything but love him. When I'd first told him about
Robby Rousseau, I'd dismissed it in the same way. As if it were
only something I'd read about somewhere. I recited the story I'd
created, the only one I could tell without breaking down in tears.
The one I'd been rewriting in my head for five years. And that
night, as we sat on the precarious rooftop of the group house in
Providence where we all lived, he'd taken his finger and touched

the thin scar that traversed my damaged throat. I remember closing my eyes and concentrating on the rough pad of his finger as it
traced the place that divided my life between *Before* and *After*. Between childhood and adulthood. Between truth and lies.

His eyes had gotten glossy that night, but he didn't cry.

Now Gus rolled his head, cracked his neck. Threw his shoulders back almost imperceptibly. I could see his bicep muscles
twitch. And I knew what he was thinking. He was thinking about
Robby, the ghost who had haunted our lives for the last fifteen
years, who suddenly wasn't a ghost at all. But a real man. A thirty-
three-year-old man who had spent the last twenty years in prison
because of me.

"I need you to let me go," I said. "I promise it will be okay.
I just need to get away for a while. And I'm sure, if he actually
gets another trial, if I testify, there will be no chance they'll let
him out. . . ."

"*If* you testify?"

"Look, Mama!" Avery said. She was peeking out through the
window Gus had made in the box. The window even had panes.
He had stapled two of my old scarves I'd left behind, fashioned
them into curtains. Affixed a sort of window box filled with tis-
sue paper flowers.

"Come see my new house."

Tears stinging in my eyes, I went to the living room and
squatted down on the floor next to the box. Her arms reached
out through the window, her hands wriggling toward me. I knelt
and peered in, and she cupped my face in her chubby hands. She
smelled like paste.

"Play house, Mommy? You be the mommy, Daddy can be
the daddy, and I'll be the honey."

"The honey?" I asked, my throat aching.

"You know," she said, cocking her head and picking a baby
doll up off the floor. "The *baby*." She cooed to the baby doll, "*Oh,
honey.*"

"In a minute, sweetie. Daddy and I are talking. Okay?"

Back in the kitchen Gus whispered, "What about Av? Who's going to take care of her while I'm at work?"

My heart plummeted. How could he think I'd leave her behind? What kind of mother did he think I was?

"I'll take Avery with me, and you can come see her on the weekends. I can come down too. It's not that far." But even as I said this, I knew I'd been foolish to even entertain the idea. Gus would never let me take Avery away.

He shook his head. "It's too far, Wyn."

"It will just be a few months."

He shook his head, rubbed his face, his temples, and then ran his hand through his hair. He peered at me, his eyes filled with both frustration and a sort of reluctant sympathy.

"Think about Avery," he said. "This is going to mess her up."

"Please don't do this," I said. "Don't do this to me."

He snorted a little, sighed, and I felt myself seethe.

"What?" I asked.

"Yeah, you're right. *I'm* the one doing this to you. To us."

I looked at the cardboard box house Gus had made, at Avery, sitting cross-legged on the floor, humming softly to her baby doll. My eyes filled with tears.

"You can't always just run away," he said.

I swallowed. Hard.

"I'm not," I tried. I *lied*. "I just need time to think everything through. Please, can you give me this?"

I brought Avery and the enchiladas back over to my side of the duplex. Avery washed her face, brushed her teeth, and fell asleep halfway through the book I was reading to her.

In the living room, I ate the leftover enchiladas straight out of the pan, dipping each bite into a cold vat of sour cream. I watched the last forty-five minutes of *Stand by Me* on TV and then plopped into bed. On the other side of the wall, I listened for the familiar sounds of Gus, but was met with silence. I looked at the clock: midnight.

I got up, went to my painting corner, and stared at the canvas. The tidy rows of birches were like the bars on some of the windows in our neighborhood. I couldn't bring myself to work, but I knew I wouldn't be able to go back to sleep. Sitting down on the paint-splattered stool by my easel, I absently pressed my hand against the wall that divided us.

Maybe he was right. Our living arrangements were crazy, but running away to Maine was crazier. Instead of creating clarity, it might just make everything even more confused. Especially for Avery. Maybe I should stay here for a while longer. Decide what to do about Gus, about *us,* after this business with Robby was more certain.

When the landline phone began to ring, I jumped. Nobody but my parents and Gus knew the number. I'm not even sure why we had it. I figured it must be Gus. With time for my idea to sink in, I was pretty sure he'd formulated his argument.

I clicked the TALK button. "Hello?"

Nothing.

"Gus?"

Then there was the faint sound of someone clearing his throat.

"You and me got a deal. Remember?"

My body felt molten, heat flooding my veins, my flesh melting. Another cough, a sickening smoker's cough.

"I know you got a little girl. I bet she's pretty like you were."

I hit the OFF button again and again. I barely recognized my own hand as it gripped the phone and hurled it across the room. It landed on the couch, its face glowing brightly in the now dark shadows. It rang again.

I paced back and forth, trying to figure out how he'd gotten my number here. How he knew about Avery. Did this mean he knew where I lived too?

I thought about running back over to Gus's house, telling him everything. Finally. He'd know what to do. But helping me wasn't Gus's job anymore. And he could never, ever know the truth.

I needed to get the hell out. Now.

Inquiry

"**D**id you know him? Robert Rousseau. He was your class-mate?"

"Yes, sir."

Robby Rousseau moved to Haven in the fifth grade. He was tall and quiet and his clothes didn't fit right. He carried his lunch in a greasy paper sack. His older brother, Rick, showed up after school to pick Robby up in a rusted-out Camaro blasting AC/DC from the speakers, the bass making the earth tremble. If there were a group of us girls lingering out-side, Rick would roll the passenger window down and lean across the seat, leering, licking his lips at us. If we ignored him, he'd make a sort of growling sound and snap his teeth together again and again like a dog, and then he'd laugh, smashing his palms against the steering wheel like he'd just heard a hilarious joke. We'd giggle nervously, close our circle in tighter, breathe a collective sigh when Robby came out of the school and ducked into the car and Rick peeled away from the curb. People said Ricky liked to set fires, that he almost burned down the old roller rink two summers ago. And that Robby's older sister, Roxanne, who was in high school, had gotten pregnant in the seventh grade and had an abor-tion. I didn't really know what that meant. It was the stuff of late-night sleepover conversations. Everything I knew about sex came from a book my mother gave me and information dispensed by Hanna Lamont, a self-proclaimed expert. My understanding of this, and most things grown-up, was obscured in a sort of lovely haze then. Some of my friends, like Hanna, were determined to clear that fog, but I was content to stay in the mist.

Robby was tall and pimply with terrible posture and an overbite that made him look a bit cartoonish. He was awkward and always stared too long at people. I'd catch him looking at me sometimes, and because I was not yet a girl that boys looked at, it disarmed me.

At recess he hung out by himself, back against the brick wall of the school, one knee bent, foot against the wall, watching the endless violent games of "Smear the Queer," my school's version of dodge ball.

He was just a weird boy from a bad family who never had enough in his lunch bag and lived somewhere far enough away his older brother had to give him a ride.

"Did he ever speak to you? Before that afternoon?"

"A couple of times."

"And what did he say?"

"Well, one time the teacher made him, the one on recess duty."

"I don't understand."

I was on the swing, alone, soaring, legs pumping, my cheeks burning with the cold air.

Even my teeth were cold. To their roots.

"What happened?"

The bell rang, and I stopped pumping my legs, came to a slow stop. The next thing I remember is something hitting me from behind. I fell forward onto the sandy ground beneath the swings, and I couldn't breathe. When I looked up, I saw the teacher marching toward the swing set. She asked me what happened, but I couldn't speak. It was as if he'd knocked my words out of me. I almost thought I might look down and see them scattered on the ground.

"She made him say it."

"Who?"

"The teacher. She made him say *I'm sorry*."

Haven

It took three weeks and three separate conversations with Gus to convince him to let me take Avery with me to Maine. I couldn't tell him the real reason I was leaving; I couldn't tell anyone about the call. I only knew I needed to do whatever was necessary to get away and to take Avery with me.

And so I tried a pragmatic approach first, arguing a two- or three-month reprieve from the cost of her preschool tuition alone could make a huge difference for us financially. I should have known this wouldn't work; Gus had never been motivated by money, never crippled by the lack of it.

"But, it's *school,* Wynnie," he'd said. "You can't just yank her out. I know it's just pre-K, but she's learning important stuff. She's got friends."

"I can homeschool her. We'll do art projects. We'll work on her reading. Pilar will be there. You know how much she adores her. And Maine is beautiful. She'll be so close to nature. It's a great opportunity, if you think about it. Once she's in kindergarten, we won't be able to do something like this anymore."

Gus shook his head.

"Without the tuition, we could actually get ahead," I added.

"What *we?*" he said, sitting, defeated, at the edge of the couch, hands in his hair.

I sat down next to him, leaned my head on his shoulder. I didn't know how not to be with him; his body had been a place of safety for me for fifteen years. When he shrugged me off, I knew I'd need to come up with something more compelling.

"You were right," I said softly. "About the commissions."

His mouth had twitched then, likely recalling the argument that had set this disaster into motion.

Gus and I had split up over the tree paintings.

It's ridiculous, I know. Those stupid tree paintings had been nothing but trouble from the first one I sold.

Of course there were a hundred other small grievances that piled up, as things will in any marriage. He was impulsive, for one thing. And while it was something that made him exciting and fun when we first started dating, it became exhausting and unpredictable after Avery came along. When it was just us, in our twenties, he could talk me into eating magic mushrooms on a Monday night, taking the subway into the city and exploring. He'd blow every dime he had on tickets to a concert we'd dreamed of seeing. Everything about my life with Gus was thrilling. But those same instincts, that restlessness, that impetuousness, grew tiresome. And so later, while I stayed home and took care of Avery, he continued to flit about like some sort of fidgety moth, always seeking a brighter light. It made him a fun dad though. He'd pull Avery out of preschool and take her to Central Park. He'd make lasagna for breakfast on the weekends. He'd stay up all night with her watching cartoons and blowing bubbles.

And not only was he impulsive, but he was irresponsible. He had a good job at the sign shop, and at work he was very dependable. But when it came to our personal lives, he was a nightmare. He forgot to pay bills. Our credit was shit. Once, the lights went out just as I was finishing up one of my commissioned paintings, and somehow I knew nobody had blown a fuse. That it was Gus who'd blown it; the electricity had been turned off because he'd failed to pay the last three bills. But instead of dealing with it right away, he bought a bunch of candles, got Chinese takeout, and made a candlelit dinner in the dark dining room.

He never did his own laundry. He was loud in the morning when I was trying to sleep. He listened to music at full volume even after the neighbors complained.

And he hated the tree paintings. With a passion.

In the spring, I'd been working on a commission for a particularly difficult client. The woman had asked me to incorporate a fox somehow, because *foxes are so cute, aren't they?* And so I had sketched out my usual rows of trees and then drawn the pointy face of a fox peeking out playfully from behind one of them.

Gus was playing Go Fish in the other room with Avery. He'd been uncharacteristically taciturn all night as I worked, though he was slamming cabinet doors and clanging the pots and pans around more loudly than usual.

I had been bitching at dinner about the fox. "She showed me a T-shirt with a fox on it, asked me if I could make it look like that fox. What the hell?" I'd said.

"Then don't do it," Gus had said.

"What?"

"Don't do it."

"Don't paint the fox?" I said.

"The trees. The fox. Any of it."

"That's what she's paying me for," I said. "That's what she hired me to do."

I was baffled. I'd always griped about the commissions. It's what I did. I griped, we joked, and then I sucked it up and painted. He never complained when checks came in.

He sat back in his chair then.

"You've sold out, Wynnie," he said. "And it sucks."

I felt my face go hot.

I looked at Avery, who was trying to fan her Go Fish cards in her little hands. She didn't seem to be paying attention to us.

"Seriously," he said. "You haven't painted anything but those goddamned trees since Avery was born. It's like they've taken over your life."

I could feel the anger welling up inside of me.

"I'm painting the goddamned *trees* so we can have goddamned *food* on the table," I hissed. "So the goddamned *electricity* stays on."

His back stiffened.

"Av," he said. "Can you find me my slippers?"

"Okay," she said and hopped down off her chair, disappearing into our bedroom.

"You've just gotten so *bitter*," he said. "Did you know that? Don't you realize it? You used to be so happy."

"I *was* happy," I said, my eyes filling with tears. And he was right. Despite everything, I had been happy. Gus had made me happy. "But seriously, Gus. *Happy* doesn't pay for preschool. Or shoes. Or paint even."

"I feel like you sold your soul," he said, looking at me with nothing but sheer disappointment. He had never looked at me that way before. "And I miss it."

What I should have done is gone to him, leaned my forehead against his, let the tears that were welling up inside of me fall. I should have told him everything he said was true. I should have curled up in his lap and let him stroke my back.

But instead I stood up from the table and said angrily, "What about you? You work in a *sign* shop." I said this with such tremendous disdain, the words tasted bad in my mouth. Bitter. Bilious.

"I work at the sign shop to *support* us. To support Avery," he said softly, as if this particularly low blow had knocked the wind out of him. "I never gave up who I am as an artist."

I knew this was true. The vibrant, gorgeous work he made hadn't changed one bit. Every minute he wasn't working or spending time with our family, he was making art. It might only be a few hours a month, but those hours were dedicated to something honest. True. He may have vended his *time,* but he hadn't abandoned his vision, hadn't *sold his soul.*

My nerves felt raw, exposed. Everything hurt. And I wanted him to hurt like this too.

"I'm done. I can't take this anymore," I said. "I want out."

It was the truth. I wanted out. I wanted out of fake forests with cute foxes ripped off from Urban Outfitters T-shirts. I wanted out

of this duplex with its crappy linoleum and rust-stained sinks. I
wanted out of my own head at night when I couldn't sleep.

But I didn't want out of *us*.

"You mean *this?*" Gus said in disbelief.

"Yeah," I said. "I mean this."

Then he'd gotten angry. And silent. Which only made things
worse. It wasn't fair. So I stood up, found Avery still in the bedroom hunting under the bed for Gus's slippers, and like some sort
of petulant child, started packing my things.

"I'm going to Pilar's," I said. "Can Avery please stay here with
you tonight?"

Gus looked at me in disbelief but nodded, threw his hands up
as if he didn't know what else to do with me, and I walked the
four blocks to Pilar's apartment still not breaking down, still not
crying. Still not knowing how to rewind everything back to that
moment when I broke everything. When I broke *us*.

I had thought, hoped, that when I returned the next morning, I could apologize, go to him. But none of what I'd said could
be unsaid now. I had set into motion something bigger and more
powerful than either one of us. He was pissed. And rather than
pining and waiting for me to end my tantrum, he simply began to
disentangle me from his life. Two weeks later, when our tenant
moved out, I moved my things across to the other side of the duplex. That crack I'd started had become a full and unforgiving
chasm between us. And we were both too stubborn to try to fix it.

"Maybe if I can just get away for a while, I can get back to
the work that matters to me," I tried to explain now. And while it
wasn't the main reason for leaving, it was a good one. A true one.
Part of me knew if I could actually do this, then Gus and I might
even stand a chance. "Please, Gus. I need this. And I need you to
let me go."

He'd sighed hard, his eyes wide and sad.

"I'll take good care of Avery. Pilar will be with us. You can come whenever you want. And you can have Avery over Christmas. It'll be *okay*." I was pleading now, desperate.

Gus's eyes filled with tears, and this time when I leaned against him again, he didn't pull away. "Wyn, I can only do this for a few months. Just until March. I need you to promise." These words he spoke into my hair, his breath warm. Gentle. My breath hitched.

I held up my hand, pinky finger extended, and he linked his finger with mine.

We left New York on Saturday, Halloween. Gus let me take our old Honda; the sign shop was just a couple of subway stops from our house, so he wouldn't really need the car. I hadn't wanted to stop in Haven, where my folks still lived, but they had pleaded with me to bring Avery to see them before we went to Maine. I knew they also wanted to talk about Robby, about what it might mean if he was granted a retrial.

I had avoided going home except for major holidays since I moved out at seventeen. Everyone in Haven knew what had happened to me. I couldn't seem to go anywhere without a thousand eyes on my back, never mind that Robby's family reportedly still lived there, in that house way out on Route 9.

My plan was for us to spend the night with my parents and then drive to Maine on Sunday morning. Pilar was finishing up some things in the city and would fly into Portland to meet us on Sunday afternoon. We'd take the car ferry to the island together. If we could just get to the island, everything would be fine.

Avery was very excited about trick-or-treating in my parents' neighborhood. She'd never been trick-or-treating before. Last year, Gus and I had thrown a costume party at our house; our neighborhood in Queens was not the kind of place you take your kids and go around knocking on doors for candy.

As I pulled into my parents' driveway, I could see my mother had pulled out all the stops. Every house on the street was decked out from top to bottom. Their neighborhood, once full of young families, was now filled with retired grandparents. In the last few years, it had garnered a reputation for having the best holiday decorations (both Halloween and Christmas) and the best Halloween candy. They bused kids in for this. Last year my mother said she counted fifteen hundred trick-or-treaters. She started buying candy on clearance the day after Halloween to stock up for the next year.

Filmy ghosts hung from the trees that lined the drive. A pair of harvest dummies dressed up like the *American Gothic* couple were propped up on the porch. Cobwebs laced every shrub, every mum. A virtual pumpkin patch filled the front yard. The plaster of paris tombstones she'd carefully crafted were interspersed between. In deference to my father, they were all for literary figures: Emily Dickinson (*Because I could not stop for Death—He kindly stopped for me*—), Edgar Allan Poe, Thoreau.

Our house had been, at one time, a beautiful Queen Anne like all of the other Victorians on this street. But by the time my parents bought it in the early eighties, its beauty had faded. They'd always intended to revive it, to give it a face-lift. But there was never the time nor the money required, and it had settled into looking like the scary haunted mansion of its reputation. I think they actually enjoyed it now.

My mother was in the yard wrestling with a giant piece of chicken wire when we pulled up. Avery unbuckled herself from her car seat and threw open the door, running toward my mother like an offensive tackle. My mother stumbled backward.

"Careful!" I warned as I got out of the car and reached into the backseat for our overnight bag.

"What are you making?" Avery asked.

"*Ghosts,*" my mother said to Avery, wiggling her fingers and widening her eyes. To me, she said, "I saw it on Pinterest. Are you on there?"

I shook my head.

"You should be on there; it's great for artists. Anyway, you use chicken wire to make the shapes of ball gowns and then you spray paint them with glow-in-the-dark paint. At night, it looks like there's a ghost ball on your lawn."

"Cool!" Avery said. "Can I help?"

"Sure thing, sweet bean, but let's have some tea first."

My mother came to me, pulling off her work gloves and holding out her arms. She was wearing paint-splattered overalls and a gray mohair sweater that scratched against my cheek. Her silvery hair was piled up on top of her head in a sloppy bun. She had metallic butterfly barrettes holding the loose hairs in place.

My mother was a high school art teacher until two years ago, when she retired. Now she'd taken on *kooky lady who lives in the haunted house* as a full-time job.

"Where's Daddy?" I asked, pulling away from her.

"At the library."

My father retired from his own teaching job a year ago. He had been a beloved English teacher at the high school for thirty-five years. When he retired, they built a new library and named it after him. Now he volunteered there, running a chess club after school.

"Is this a new one?" my mother asked, squinting at the new tattoo on the inside of my wrist. She stroked it with her thumb, frowning.

"Yeah," I said.

For the last ten years, I'd been slowly illustrating my left arm. It had started as a way to mask the scars. I started at my clavicle with a night-blooming cereus, a moonflower. But eventually the garden grew to include a sea of forget-me-nots, wild roses, snapdragons, ivy creeping between them. Before I left the city, I had my friend, Gino, who is responsible for most of the more recent flowers, add a small pinecone on the inside of my wrist. We usually worked in trade, but this one was on the house. A going away present.

"It's Maine's state flower," I said.

"A pinecone? Is that really considered a flower?"

"Apparently."

"I can't say I'm happy about any of this," she said, touching the pinecone absently.

"The tattoo?"

"Maine," she said.

Inside, my mother made tea and put three teacups and saucers on the table. She got Daddy's work stool from his office and adjusted it so Avery was able to sit with us at the table. She'd made the raspberry linzer cookies Avery loved and bought some fancy pink paper napkins with butterflies on them too.

"One at a time," I said to Avery as she reached for the plate of cookies. "How's Mark?" I asked my mother.

Mark was my little brother. He was a firefighter. For a long time he was a part-time weed smoker and full-time gamer, but in the last two years or so he'd come around. He still lived in Haven.

"He's good. He'll be here for supper," she said.

The tea was peppermint. Avery carefully poured the cream from the little china pitcher into her own teacup.

"Careful, baby," I said as the liquid threatened to spill over.

"I spoke to Larry again this morning," my mother said. Our lawyer.

I glanced at Avery. My mother was a firm believer that children should not be shielded from, nor silenced around, adult conversations. As a kid this was great, but as a mom, I was no longer so sure I agreed.

When I didn't respond, she continued, "He's not worried. So they tested for DNA. Big deal. Worst case, and I mean absolute worst case, his DNA isn't anywhere in the sample or whatever, he gets another trial. Larry says your testimony should be more than enough."

I shook my head. My hands were sweating, my heart flip-flopping.

"What?" she asked.

"I'm just not sure I'd want to testify."

Her eyes widened. "That's ridiculous," she said. "Of course you would. They can't let that monster out of prison."

This was a conversation I'd anticipated. I knew from the minute she'd found out about the petition she'd been speculating and planning what our next steps should be. And so I'd planned my counterargument. How my testimony hadn't been necessary to *put* him in prison, why should it be necessary to keep him there? Every other bit of evidence pointed to him. Never mind his confession. It took the jury a whopping hour to convict him on all counts. *On all counts.* And even if they assembled a new jury, my case was the stuff of legends in these parts. There wasn't a single person in a hundred-mile radius who didn't know the story of what happened to me.

Running through my argument point by point, it was almost enough even to convince myself. That I was safe. That none of this mattered.

I remained silent, occupying myself with the teapot lid.

"Of course we'd find a way to appeal," she said. "If they actually granted him another trial."

"Too expensive," I said. I knew this argument wouldn't work with her, even though it was true. Too expensive. My parents had mortgaged this house three times in the last twenty years to cover legal expenses. If not for their pensions, they'd never have been able to retire.

"Who fucking cares about money?" my mother hissed. When Avery looked up at her from her tea, my mother said sweetly, "Pardon my français."

"I'm sure Larry's right. It'll be fine," I said, forcing myself to smile. "And in the *meantime,* Avery and I are going to Maine. I'm going to paint. Get my head together and figure out what to do . . ." I started, looking at Avery to see if she was paying attention. She was absorbed in twirling her honey on a wooden honey stick. ". . . about Gus."

"So what does Gus think about this?"

You can't always just run away.

"He's being a grown-up," I said. "He knows this is my choice."
"He'll kill him, you know," she said. "If he gets out."

Avery looked up again. "Daddy won't even kill spiders," she said. She was always, always listening. "Really. I found one in my room and he carried it outside. It was in the middle of the night even."

"Daddy is not killing anybody," I assured her. "And I am not talking about this anymore."

My father came into the kitchen like a storm, dressed in blue jeans and a soft flannel shirt, olive green rubber boots and suspenders.

"Well, if it isn't Miss Avericious Alouiscious!" he said.

"Poppy!" she squealed, tipping over her tea. I used the pretty pink napkins to sop it up.

"How about we go see what Lucy is up to?" he said, winking at me. At least *he* knew she shouldn't be a part of this conversation.

"Yay!"

Lucy was my parents' pig. They'd bought her several years ago at the same time they bought their chickens. She was intended to be an Easter ham, but wound up being an adored pet.

He lifted Avery up, threw her over his shoulder, and marched out the door.

"Are you guys talking about divorce?" my mother blurted.

"God. I don't know, Mom. Let me just deal with one thing at a time, please."

She stood up, picked up Avery's plate and empty teacup. I noticed her hands trembling. She took the dishes to the sink.

"There are fire ants in Maine," she said. "Just so you know. They'll eat you alive."

I sighed.

My brother came for supper and I could tell he was in love before he even opened his mouth. He was practically glowing. He'd also lost weight. At one point he'd been close to two hundred fifty pounds. But not anymore. He looked fit. Healthy. I could always tell how happy he was by the size of his waistline.

After supper, while my parents took Avery out trick-or-treating, Mark and I sat outside on the porch handing out candy. They'd left us with ten bags and strict instructions about how much to divvy out per kid to make it last. I'd found an old roach in the glove box of the Honda and now surreptitiously lit it. I hadn't smoked pot in years, but I was antsy, needed something to calm me down. I thought Mark might want to share.

"So who is she?" I asked.

"Who?" he said, grinning.

"The *girl*." I smacked his arm and peered down the street to make sure no kids were coming before taking a quick drag on the joint. "Who is she?"

"Veronica."

"Veronica from high school?" I asked, coughing. Smoke blew out of my nose. Veronica Smith was the first girl who broke Mark's heart. I'd had to talk him down from a few rooftops over this stupid girl before.

"She's different now," he said. "She's got a daughter. Her husband died."

"Shit," I said.

Mark was twenty-three years old, which made Veronica twenty-three as well. Widowed with a kid at twenty-three didn't seem fair, even for her.

I offered him the joint, but he shook his head. "Can't," he explained. "Random testing."

I nodded and took his puff.

"It sucks about Robby."

"Yeah," I said.

He was only three when it happened. He says he doesn't remember anything except Grandma coming to stay with us for the summer. He barely remembers who I was in the land of *Before*. I remember him though. A mop of dark hair, big brown eyes. He was quiet and shy, sweet and pudgy and gentle. I also remember he had nightmares every night that summer. It was as if on some primitive level he was sympathizing with me. Kids know shit. They know when the world isn't good.

"I worry about you," he said, and suddenly I felt stupid sneaking a joint on my parents' porch. My baby brother looking at me with such pity.

"Well then, we're even," I said.

While I was thrilled he'd found something he was good at, could make money at without breaking the law, I worried about him every time he went to work. Just a year ago one of the fires he was fighting caused the building to collapse, and two of his coworkers died.

"Are you ever scared?" I asked him.

"All the time."

"Seriously, who runs *into* a burning building?"

He shrugged. "Sometimes, running into a burning building is the only way to save it."

"Trick or treat!" A little girl dressed up as an Egyptian princess stood with her plastic jack-o'-lantern bucket outstretched. I quickly stubbed the joint out in one of my mom's mums.

"Trick or treat!"

One family after another arrived: Disney princesses and superheroes, homemade costumes and plastic masks. So many kids. It was unbelievable. And every time a mother and father came up the walkway holding their child's hands between them, I felt an ache deep inside my gut. *Was I doing the right thing leaving Gus? Was I crazy?*

By the time Avery came back, skipping up the sidewalk with my parents close behind, the candy was gone; we'd snuffed out the jack-o'-lanterns and turned out the porch lights to signal we were closed for business. Only my mother's ghosts remained, dancing across the yard in the darkness.

My father had to carry the pillowcase Avery had used for her candy. He disappeared into the bathroom and came out beaming. "Ten pounds!" he said.

"She can't eat all that!" I said.

"Oh, they're just baby teeth," my mother said, smiling.

I couldn't sleep in my old room, which had been converted into my mother's studio five minutes after I left the house. Even though it no longer resembled my childhood bedroom, the shadows were the same. The daybed she'd put in there for guests was lumpy, and the Windsor chimes kept going off every fifteen minutes. *Ding, dong, ding, dong.* I yanked the battery out of the clock and still tossed and turned for nearly an hour. Finally, I crept downstairs and hung out on the couch in the living room while Mark watched *SportsCenter* and I ate up all of my mother's leftovers and pilfered Reese's Cups from Avery's stash.

In the morning, I woke to eyelashes brushing my cheeks. Butterfly kisses from Avery. I felt thick and droopy. A weed hangover. I also had eaten way too much candy.

"Morning, sweet bean," I said, and she curled up under the blanket with me. Her body was small, her skin hot. "So are you ready to go to our new house today?"

She nodded and burrowed in deeper.

"Pilar will be there, and Daddy will come to visit in just a couple of weeks," I said, feeling that pervasive sense of unease, of uncertainty.

She was quiet for so long I figured she'd fallen back to sleep.

"Maybe he'll want to come live with us," she said softly.

And I just held her. What else could I do?

As we were both dozing off again, my mom's voice rang out from the kitchen. "Wynnie?"

"Yeah, Mom?" I said, slowly extricating myself from Avery. I tucked her back in under the blanket and sat up. I stretched and rolled my head, my neck cracking.

I padded into the kitchen, where she was making coffee. She

was wearing a huge, puffy, hot pink robe and Cookie Monster slippers.

"What's up?" I asked, grabbing a mug from the cupboard.

"Pilar called earlier while you were still sleeping. She said something's come up—something with a TV program? An interview?"

"What?" I said.

"I don't know exactly. She just said she's sorry and she can't leave New York yet. She's going to have to meet you guys in Maine in a few weeks. Thanksgiving, I think. You need to call her to get instructions for getting into the house. She said she already gave you the key though, right?"

Beautiful Disaster

This wasn't the way it was supposed to be. I needed Pilar. We were going to Maine *together;* I would never have agreed to do this alone. Part of me considered just getting in the car and driving back to New York. But then I thought of his voice on the other end of the line and I knew I had no choice. We weren't safe in New York. Not anymore. I worried a little he would call the house again, but unless I answered what could he say? Besides, he'd made his point. He'd delivered his message. We had a deal, he and I. An understanding. His call really was just a friendly reminder, wasn't it?

Avery and I left my parents' house just after noon. I calculated it would take four hours to drive from Haven to Portland, not including pee stops, of which I was sure there would be many. In the off-season, the ferry that would deliver us from Portland to the island ran only a few times a day. We couldn't make it for the noon ferry, so we'd have to plan on the evening one. While it did seem strange to be arriving at the house after dark, we didn't really have any other choice.

There was only one main road heading east toward Maine. In order to get to Portland, I had to take Route 9 out of town. There simply was no other way. But that meant driving right past the Rousseaus' house. Of course, I didn't know how many of them still lived there. Robby's father had been in and out of jail. Roxanne had been removed from the home not long after Robby went to prison. But Rick likely still lived there.

I gripped the steering wheel with both hands as I saw the small yellow farmhouse in the distance. I glanced quickly in the rearview mirror at Avery, who was babbling to her stuffed donkey, having an animated private conversation.

This was the road where the police had found Robby walking home that night as the sun fell. I had often imagined what they would have seen as they approached him from behind. His gangly, bowed legs, his high-water pants. Chin to chest, gaze at the ground, hands shoved into his pockets. When they pulled up next to him, rolled down their windows, did he know what would happen next? Did he understand this was the beginning of the end for him?

Son? You hurt? they might have asked.

Did he shake his head?

You get yourself in a fight or something?

How long did it take before they realized it was not his own blood that drenched his shirt?

I was jarred back to reality by something dashing in front of the car. A dog, a Doberman, I think. It was chasing the Honda, forcing me to slow as the Rousseau house came into focus. The dog was barking, jumping at the driver's side door.

"Go away," I hissed, tears filling my eyes. I glanced up quickly and looked at the house. There were several cars in the driveway. The screen door was hanging by one hinge. The yard was overgrown and littered with rusted barrels, old tires, and some sort of wire coop. There was a washing machine sitting out on the porch next to an old recliner.

The dog finally moved to the side of the road, standing erect at the edge of the yard, still barking. I pressed my foot on the gas and accelerated as quickly as I could. I glanced back only once, certain the dog was chasing us again. In the rearview mirror, as the house slipped into the distance, I saw the door open and someone come outside.

Feeling like I might vomit, I raced forward, intent now on reaching our destination.

Avery fell asleep as we crossed over from New Hampshire into Maine, and slept almost the whole way to Portland. My heart finally settled back into its regular rhythm, and when Pilar called, I put her on speaker, so grateful to hear her soothing voice. We talked for over an hour. She said she felt just awful she wasn't able to be with us, but *CBS Sunday Morning* had called and wanted to do a feature on her. Since she would still be in town, her manager had set up several interviews with gallery owners over the next few weeks as well. She wouldn't be able to come until Thanksgiving.

"So you still have the keys?" she asked for the hundredth time.

"Yep," I said. Thankfully, she had made sure I had a set of keys before we left. It was pure luck.

"The electricity is connected, but you'll need to turn on the breakers. The panel is outside on the left side of the house. The oil tank is full, and the furnace should be working. Don't use the fireplace yet, because the chimney still needs to be cleaned. I'll have somebody come out when I get there. What else, what else . . ."

"Is there a hot water heater that needs turning on?"

"Yep. That switch is in the downstairs bathroom. And just a heads up, the water smells like rotten eggs. It's sulfur. They say you get used to it."

"Okay," I said. When Gus and I lived in Colorado, we used to go to the hot springs, soak our naked bodies in the steaming, sulfurous baths.

"You have groceries with you, right? The basics?"

"Yep."

My mother had taken me shopping earlier that morning the way she used to when I was in college. She'd filled a cart with all the essentials: milk, eggs, flour, and oats. Then bread, fruit, vegetables, canned soups and sauces, boxes and boxes of pasta. I'd tried to pay at the register but she'd shooed me away like she would have an annoying bug. I was embarrassed but grateful. At thirty-three years old, it would be nice to be able to afford my own groceries, but the $200 receipt had caused me to catch my breath.

"There's a very small main street on the island, with shops where you can get some things, but it's a total rip-off. For the tourists mostly, and for emergencies. You'll want to go to the mainland and do a big trip after you get settled in. There's no Wi-Fi. But there's cell service, so if you have your phone, you can go online, deal with your e-mails and stuff."

Frankly, I was looking forward to being disconnected. The idea of a world without the Internet seemed like something out of a storybook.

"I know you'll say no, but I'm going to pick up another iPad."

"I don't need an iPad," I said.

"Since there's no Wi-Fi, I'll get a data plan. I'll use it too."

Pilar has always been terrifically, terribly generous. Even when we *all* had nothing, she was the one who would show up at our house with giant jars of spaghetti sauce she got at Costco. She'd spend an entire paycheck taking us all out for drinks. She'd maxed her only credit card when I'd found out I was pregnant with Avery, buying us a stroller, a car seat, and a drawer full of onesies. And now that she actually had money, *real* money, the gifts had become more frequent and more extravagant. For Avery's fourth birthday, she'd bought her a bicycle. When Gus and I split up, she came over with a cashmere floor-length robe and ten pints of Cherry Garcia ice cream. She'd also bought me an Apple TV to stream movies into my side of the house and gave me a brand new box of paints so I didn't have to keep slicing open the existing tubes, scraping out the precious little bits of color left inside.

"Pill?" I said as I drove past a very large Paul Bunyan statue.

"Yeah, hon?"

I could hear Avery stirring in the backseat. I looked in the rearview mirror and watched as her eyes flickered open and she slowly oriented herself.

"Is this crazy?"

She paused. And I could picture her, thinking about how to answer this.

"A little bit," she said. "But the good kind of crazy."

"Thank you for letting me do this," I said. "I'm really sad you aren't going to be there with us."

"You'll be fine. And I'll be there before you know it." I could practically hear the swelling in her throat. "Love you, hon. Kiss that baby girl for me. And I will see you in like three weeks, okay?"

I nodded.

"Is that Auntie Pill?" Avery asked sleepily from the backseat.

"Hi, sweetness!" Pilar said loudly. "Call me when you get there."

I followed the Google Maps directions my father had printed out for me to get to the ferry docks in Portland. And we followed a long line of cars onto the deck of the boat. The ferry would stop at two other islands before Bluffs Island.

Avery was straining against the straps in her car seat to see.

"We're driving onto the boat?" she asked in disbelief.

"I know. Isn't it crazy?" I smiled at her in the rearview mirror.

We parked the car on the parking deck and then got out with all the other passengers, careful to lock the doors. Everything we owned was in the backseat of the Honda or strapped to the roof. I hadn't felt this *portable* for so long. Living in the duplex with Gus had domesticated both of us. Like turtles, or hermit crabs, we'd always been able to carry our most precious belongings on our backs. But having a house to live in, a house that belonged to us, somehow made the accumulation of possessions obligatory. It seemed the more space we had, the more things we needed to fill it. I thought of the closets and attic stuffed now with clothes and books and boxes. It felt liberating for our lives to be unencumbered again, to have pared things down to just the essentials.

"Let's go see if we can get some snacks," I said. Pilar told me there was a small café on the ferry.

As we climbed the narrow stairwell to the second story of the boat, Avery clung to my hand, oddly nervous. She was normally the kind of child who greeted life head-on, without reservation or fear. A kid who simply lacked caution—to the point I sometimes worried about her common sense. She was the kid who, after leaping into the deep end of a pool and nearly drowning, came up sputtering, "Again, again!" Gus and I joked she would be the death of us if she was still like this in high school. We'd already been to the emergency room at least a half dozen times with her for stitches and concussions. I seriously feared the next trip to the ER would result in a visit from CPS.

When she was only a year old, she fell down the stairs at Pilar's house. I remember watching helplessly as she tumbled head over heels down the steep steps. In just a few breathless moments, it was over. Then there was only the heart-crushing sensation, the helpless, horrific fear that filled my body like something liquid. And I stared down at her still body at the bottom of the stairs, paralyzed. She had curled herself into a ball like some sort of pill bug, and when my legs finally complied and I raced down the stairs after her, she slowly uncurled and opened her eyes before squealing a blood-curdling scream. An egg had already risen up on her forehead by the time I reached her, turning black and blue before my eyes. But she was okay.

She later fell off of monkey bars, cut her chin open going face first down a slide at the park, shut her fingers in doors thrown open too wide, and broke her arm when she was jumping on the bed and fell onto the wood floor. In four years, she'd lived her life with a wild sort of abandon that both thrilled and terrified me.

But now, suddenly, she was tentative. Cautious. As we watched the city behind us recede in the distance, as the world around us turned to water, she clung to my hand and wouldn't let go. It was as though she sensed my terror. But she was only four years old, how could she know? How could she possibly understand?

We stood in line in the little café, and I ordered a cocoa for Avery and a coffee for me. I got us each a sugary donut. Hardly a proper dinner, but I knew I wouldn't be able to stomach much else. We sat together at a little booth, a Formica tabletop between us, and Avery silently sipped her cocoa and stared out through the glass at the dark, still water.

And while we were finally headed away, leaving everything behind, I felt a bit queasy, uneasy, but I wasn't sure if it was from being on the water or something else. I'd only gotten seasick once before. When Gus and I were still in Providence, we had a friend at school whose family had a sailboat. He took us out during the jazz festival, and I thought I'd die. I spent the whole day holed up beneath the deck in the cramped bathroom, spilling my guts out. Everyone assumed I was just drunk. But for three days afterward, I still felt like I hadn't quite gotten my equilibrium back.

"Mama," Avery said. Her mouth was ringed with chocolate.

"Yeah, sweets?"

"Isn't Daddy going to be lonely?"

My heart stuttered.

"The loneliest of lonelies," I said, reaching across the table to swipe a bit of whipped cream from her nose. "He is going to miss you so much, he'll probably cry himself to sleep." I knew the image would make her laugh. "And the tears will soak through the sheets, and the mattress, and fill up like water in the bathtub."

"Like Alice!" she said, her eyes widening. Pilar had bought her a beautiful illustrated *Alice in Wonderland* pop-up book. "The Pool of Tears" chapter was her favorite.

"And he'll have to swim to the bathroom and the kitchen," I said. "He'll have to wear his swim trunks and goggles every day, just to make a sandwich."

She was giggling now.

"But he won't drown," she said.

"No, no, of course not. He's a very good swimmer." I reached across the table and plucked one long, spiraling curl from her cocoa.

"Tell me about my room again?" she said softly.

Pilar had told me to feel free to make ourselves at home. It had four bedrooms. She said to paint the walls if I wanted. To settle in. "Consider this *our* house," she had said.

"Your room will be purple," I said to Avery.

"*Sparkly* purple."

Of course. We had stood together at the hardware store back in Queens and selected the shade of purple from the spectrum of chips. Violet Surprise, it was called. I had a hard time envisioning it on a wall, but Avery was determined. We'd also gone to the craft store and bought every bit of purple glitter they had in stock. I figured I'd just mix it into the paint.

"And there will be a swing?"

"Maybe. When Daddy comes we'll see if he can put one in."

"And a big pillow on the floor."

"Sure," I said.

"Can there be stars?" she asked.

"On the ceiling, like at home?"

"No," she said. "On the floor. I want it to be like I'm walking on the sky. Upset down."

"*Upside* down?"

She nodded.

"Done," I said. I would do anything for her. This was the truth. I would turn the world upside down for her.

It was getting dark by the time we drove off the ferry, and I could see Avery was struggling to stay awake, despite the excitement. I reached behind me and squeezed the small knob of her knee, more to comfort myself than to comfort her.

I followed a small line of cars off the boat. Some passengers would stay on to the next, even more remote, island in this bay. According to Pilar, Bluffs Island was the second least inhabited of this archipelago. Most residents were lobstermen and lobster-women. With a few eccentrics thrown in, she'd promised.

Just when I thought Avery had fallen asleep, as my headlights bobbed and dipped along the winding road that led away from the docks, I heard her small voice from the backseat. "Will there be other kids there?"

I glanced up to try to see her in the rearview mirror, but the headlights of the car behind us blinded me. My heart started to race. *Don't be ridiculous,* I thought. *It's just someone else who lives here. Calm down.*

"I don't know," I said. "Pilar said she doesn't really know her neighbors yet."

"Will there be a playground?" she asked.

Avery was a true city kid. Even with my parents living in New Hampshire, her frame of reference involved city blocks, conveniences, and concrete. The idea of a place without parks, without bodegas, without sidewalks, without *people* was likely in-comprehensible to her.

"There will be plenty of places to play," I said, smiling for her benefit although she couldn't see my face. But I wondered. It was already November; would we be housebound for the next four months? I hadn't thought to ask if it snowed here (though I knew it must). Did the ocean freeze over? I had taken Avery to see *Frozen,* and I suspected the house, the island, might exist in her imagination like Elsa's castle of ice.

"Can we go sledding like at Poppy's house?" she asked. Last winter my father had bought two aluminum flying saucers and taken Avery sledding for the first time.

"If there's snow, we will *definitely* go sledding," I said.

I could hear the sleep in her voice, the way it took over. She was fighting and losing against it.

"And my room will be purple?" she asked.

"With stars on the floor."

Then there was silence. When she was a baby, I coveted this peace. The only time I could paint when she was an infant was when she was sleeping. But now, the silence, the quiet rasps of her ragged breath, made me anxious. When the headlights that had been shining through the rear window disappeared as the car behind me turned off one of the narrow roads that branched off this main one, I felt completely alone.

Pilar had said the house was easy to find. That I wouldn't even need a map.

"Just take the main road from the ferry until it stops. It curves around the island and dead ends at the driveway. There's a giant rock at the entrance, a rope tied between two tall pine trees. Just undo the rope and drive on in." And suddenly, as if this were a dream somehow becoming manifest in real life, there were the rock, the pines, the rope. I stopped the car but left it running, threw open the door to the cold night air, got out, and untied the rope from one tree. I glanced down the empty road behind us and took a deep breath.

I went back to the car and glanced in the backseat at Avery. Her head lolled to the side, her curls spilling across her face. "We're here," I said softly, but she didn't stir.

I got back in the car, shut the door as softly as I could, and pulled up the long dirt drive to the house.

It *was* a beautiful disaster. Crumbling, listing to the side, beaten and battered and worn, yes, but *magnificent*.

Like something from a Wyeth painting.

I willed my mind to remember it this way, the way I saw it now before it became familiar, before I grew blind to its beauty. In that brief moment, I had already thought of the exact colors I would need on my palette. The brushes I would use in order to capture the grayed cedar shakes, the peeling paint on the porch banisters. The ivy that wound around the porch railings and encircled the chimney.

"Wake up," I said to Avery softly. I got out of the car, leaving my headlights on to illuminate the walkway. "Av," I repeated, louder.

"Mama," she whined.

"*Look,* Av."

I opened the car's back door, unfastened her from her car seat and hoisted her onto my hip, noting she seemed to have grown in the last few hours. She rubbed the sleep from her eyes and squinted at the sight before us.

"It's like that painting, Mama," she said. "The one at Daddy's house."

The Wyeth. I smiled.

"Are you ready for an adventure?" I asked.

"I'm ready, Mama."

I set Avery down. "Stay on the porch," I said and headed around the side of the house, searching for the electrical panel. Shivering, my fingers numb, I clicked each of the breakers on, and as I did, the sconces on either side of the front door clicked on. I joined Avery on the porch and dug through my purse for my phone. I opened a new text, entered in Pilar, my mom, and then Gus and quickly typed a group message: **Got here, safe and sound. Will call tomorrow. It's beautiful. XO.** The signal was a bit weak, but the text sent. And before I could even use the key to unlock the front door, both Pilar and my mom wrote back. Pilar: **Love you, honey.** Mom: **Call me in the morning.**

I wiggled the knob, which stuck a little, and pushed the door hard with my hip. Inside, the house smelled like mildew, like the murky pond near my parents' house. I fumbled around, looking for a light switch, and finally found it awkwardly placed on the opposite wall. A bare bulb overhead illuminated the foyer.

"Holy shit," I said.

The floral wallpaper was peeling like sunburned skin, the

floor was covered with mounds of sawdust (likely made by ter-
mites or carpenter ants), and the stairwell was missing both banister and balusters.

"Don't go up the stairs," I cautioned Avery, thinking about
how accident-prone she was and the very real fact that the closest hospital was at least an hour-and-a-half ferry ride away.

I moved slowly from the foyer into the kitchen, clicking on
lights, trying not to trip over the boxes that littered the floor,
which seemed precarious. It was soft in some spots and just off-
kilter enough to make me wonder if the whole thing might be
trying to shrug me off.

The kitchen looked like it had never been renovated, the
knotty pine cabinets with hammered iron cabinet hinges and
drawer pulls likely original. The only "update" appeared to be a
1970s-era refrigerator, which hummed loudly. The linoleum on
the floor was filthy and curling away from the walls.

"I should put our food away," I said. "Want to help?"

We carried the bags of groceries into the kitchen and I set
them down on the counter. I put the few perishables in the refrigerator, leaving them in the Styrofoam cooler until the fridge
got cold. The kitchen would be the first thing I'd need to tackle.
I was too afraid to even open the cupboards.

"I'm thirsty, Mama," she said.

I'd bought some juice boxes, knowing there likely weren't
any dishes or glasses in the cupboards. Somewhere in the trunk of
the car was a box holding a complete set of four dishes, bowls,
cups, and silverware. But for now, I poked the straw into the apple
juice box and handed it to her.

"This place is dirty, Mama," she said.

I nodded and started to feel tears welling up in my eyes. Pilar
had warned me, but I still had somehow vastly underestimated
the amount of work that would be required to make this house
into some sort of home. I'd dreamed we'd do some cleaning up:
wiping down counters, mopping floors, making beds, and that
within a couple of days, I'd be set up in my studio painting. That

Avery would be at my feet happily playing with her dolls or coloring in her coloring books. That it would be clean and bright.

The reality was this house was falling down. Smelly. I turned the faucet, heard the pipes groan in protest, and (as promised) the noxious scent of rotten eggs filled the air. I turned the handle to the left and noticed there was a fairly bad drip. I cranked the handle harder, thinking maybe I just hadn't turned it off all the way, but the handle came off in my hand.

Trying not to cry, I picked up Avery and said, "Let's go find your room."

I lifted her onto my hip and made my way up the broken stairs, every step as cautious as if I were walking through a land mine–riddled field. At the top of the stairs, there was a long hallway with doors to four bedrooms, most of them small and dormered with slanted ceilings. Some had beds in them. Others were empty.

Finally, I found a small room with a twin bed and child–size bureau.

"Is this *my* room?" Avery asked, already delighted. Her expectations, like mine, lowering with every second.

"Yes, it is," I said. I knew if I cracked, if I wavered, she'd be onto me.

"I love it," she said. "Even if it smells bad."

"I'm going to sleep in here with you tonight, okay?" I asked.

"Okay. Just this one night," she said seriously.

I went to the car and grabbed the bag of old sheets my mother had given me and Avery's little backpack, which was stuffed with her blanket and plush animals. I had her brush her teeth and slipped her nightie over her head. When she was ready, we lay down together. She fell immediately to sleep, and I curled around her. I pressed my cheek against her back, listened to her breaths, to her heart, to her sighs, and wished myself into my own fitful slumber. But just as I was drifting off, my phone buzzed next to me, pulling me out of that deep, dark cocoon of sleep.

I reached over like a drunk to the phone on the floor next to the bed.

Heat spread through my body, electric. It couldn't be. He didn't have my cell number. We were safe here. I blinked hard, my eyes struggling to focus.

It was just a text from Gus: **Sending kisses for my girl.** And for just one delirious moment, I thought he meant me.

The Box

Avery woke me up crying.

"I'm wet, Mama," she wailed. She was standing next to the bed in the dim light of dawn, her nightgown soaked. I slowly felt the cold dampness of the sheets against my legs and sighed.

"Crap," I grumbled.

I climbed out of bed and went to her. She raised her arms up, and I peeled her wet nightgown off. Shivering, she stood there naked while I searched for something to put on her. Finally I peeled off the sweatshirt I was wearing, which was, thankfully, still dry, and pulled it over her head.

Avery hadn't wet the bed in over a year. She was one of those kids who refused the potty until one day she suddenly gave up the diaper. She'd been the same with her bottle, then her pacifier.

She was crying loudly now.

"It's okay," I said, though it really wasn't. Her little pink rolling suitcase with all of her clothes was still in the car. I glanced at my phone and saw it was only six o'clock. It would be cold outside.

"I'm wet," she wailed.

"I know, cutes," I muttered.

The house was cold, freezing. Pilar had said to set the thermostat at sixty-five, and the furnace should just kick on, but when I put my hand near the vent, it was bone cold. I could see Avery's breath as she shuddered and exhaled one last whimper and sigh.

I stripped the wet sheets off, pulled the blanket from the foot of the bed, wrapped it around her, and ushered her to the next room over, where at least the mattress was dry.

"Stay here, baby," I said. "I'm going to see if I can get the heater going."

She curled up into a little ball on the bare mattress, clutching her threadbare donkey (Donk, she called him) to her chest.

I grabbed a sweater from my suitcase and pulled it over my head. I pulled on a second pair of socks. The wood floor was like an ice rink.

The house looked different in the dim light of day, less ominous. Now it simply felt run-down and shabby. *Run-down and shabby* I could deal with, had dealt with my whole adult life. Gus and I had lived in places a lot worse than this. And we'd been happy. And while Gus wasn't here, he was *here,* cracking jokes and making light of everything that scared me. *Remember that place we lived after graduation? The time we used the garbage disposal and our salad wound up in the bathwater? At least there aren't any crack addicts living in the hallways. Bright side, Wynnie, bright side!*

I remembered to be cautious on the stairs—no small feat given the missing railing. The last thing I needed to do was plummet to my death, leaving my four-year-old child alone. I'd need to teach her how to call 911, I thought.

I made my way through the cold house, located the door to the basement. She said the cellar was partially finished on one side; that's where I would find a washer and dryer, she promised, the hot water heater, and the furnace. I groped around in the darkness for the cord that would bring light and pulled.

"Finished" was a very optimistic word for this. It was like some sort of underground hovel. The "walls" were made of brick on one side and earth on the other. The floor, as far as I could tell, was some strange, crumbling hybrid of cement and dirt. It smelled like earth and, again, the pungent scent of sulfur was ubiquitous.

I quickly found the utility room where the furnace sat, or rather slept. Like the vents it serviced, it was still and quiet. Cold to the touch. Defiant. I had definitely clicked the thermostat up-stairs to "on," so I had no idea what could be wrong. I looked, hopefully, for some sort of switch.

Nothing.

I turned around, as though the answer might be somewhere else in that room. In the exposed galvanized pipes that ran across the ceiling in a complicated network. In the hot water heater I prayed would not defy me (I wanted nothing more than to give Avery a nice warm bath after this).

I wondered if maybe there was some sort of master switch somewhere that would just turn everything on. I knew it was magical thinking at this point, but I was desperate. Gus and I had lived in one apartment where there was a light switch that con-trolled the electricity for an entire side of the house. Anything was possible. I glanced quickly at each of the walls: nothing. And so I moved to a small tower of boxes, which obscured the back wall.

The boxes were mostly empty, but some were filled with old magazines, miscellaneous papers, dusty books, and newspaper-swaddled breakables. It was as if someone had never finished un-packing, or maybe had just begun. I moved the boxes away, still looking for that mysterious switch, and a recessed area in the earthen wall was revealed. It was about one foot by one foot, a strange little cubbyhole, just big enough for the shoebox sitting there.

I brushed a thick layer of dust and dirt from the top. The box was sealed shut. On the lid, written in careful script, it said *Epi-taphs and Prophecies*.

How strange. I picked up the box and shook it. Something rolled around inside.

Curiosity, as it was wont to do, got the better of me, and I picked at the packing tape, which crisscrossed over the lid. It took me several minutes to wriggle it free and to get the lid off.

Film canisters.

Roll after roll of 35 mm film. I hadn't seen these in ages, since

I was in college. I'd taken photography for one semester in art school before focusing on painting. I'd always been inept at processing and printing film; it took a patience I didn't have. I liked the immediacy of paint on canvas. The certainty of it, the control. Photography seemed like such a crapshoot. So many factors at play. And even if you were to take a brilliant photo, a simple, careless error (an open door, a sliver of light) could destroy it.

I plucked one of the canisters from the box and studied it. There was no film sticking out, nothing to thread through the spools of a camera. Which meant it was used up. Spent. *Undeveloped.* I grabbed another and another; every one of them. There must have been fifty rolls of film in the box. *Damn.* Who takes fifty rolls of film and doesn't get them developed?

There were either twenty-four or thirty-six exposures on each roll. I quickly calculated this meant there were likely close to fifteen hundred pictures trapped inside those canisters.

A gust of cold air came from somewhere, and I shivered, remembering why I was down here. The dead furnace.

"Mama?" Avery's voice brought me back to reality.

"I'm down here, honey," I said. "I'll be right up."

I grabbed the box of film and took one last glance at the useless furnace before I made my way back through the dingy basement to the stairwell. Avery was waiting at the top, swimming inside my sweatshirt.

"Hey, baby girl," I said. "I thought I told you to stay in bed. Those stairs are really dangerous."

"I peed again," she said.

I sighed. How many beds were left? I hoped there was some vinegar, some bleach, something in the kitchen cabinets. And I forgot all about my discovery as I pulled off my now-wet sweatshirt from Avery and replaced it with the sweater I was wearing.

The sun came up bright and luminous, and by eight o'clock I could see why Pilar had fallen in love with this house. Every room was filled with gorgeous light. My amber spot in the duplex living room seemed pathetic compared with the honey-dipped floors here.

The east-facing windows also faced the ocean, and the view from the kitchen table was nothing short of spectacular. I unloaded the small stash of kitchen stuff from the car and made French toast stuffed with cream cheese and raspberry jam, Avery's favorite. She sat on my lap, and we drank from apple juice boxes, looking out at the rocky shore below us.

"Can we go swimming today?" she asked.

"It's too cold for swimming, but we can go down to the beach later if you want," I said.

My brain was buzzing with all of the things I needed to do to make the house habitable. First on the list was getting the furnace working. The warm glow of the sun was nice, but by the time the sun went down, it would be freezing cold again.

The hot water, thankfully, worked, and after I washed the dishes and ran the soiled sheets and blankets through the washing machine, I called Pilar about the furnace.

"It's probably the pilot," she said. "Do you know how to light a pilot?"

"I can figure it out," I said.

"Usually there are instructions somewhere on the furnace itself. There should be matches in the cupboard. Are you freezing?" she asked.

"It's a little nippy," I said, smiling.

"I'm so sorry."

"It's not your fault. I signed up for this, remember?"

On her end of the line, I could hear the familiar sounds of the subway, the rattle of the tracks, the voice announcing a train's arrival. I felt a pang of homesickness.

"Hey, who owned the house before you?" I asked.

"I don't know. It was in probate. Why?"

"When I was in the basement I found a box . . ."

"What?" The train had arrived, the dinging and shuffle and hustle too loud to hear over.

"Nothing," I said. "I'll talk to you later."

"I'm losing you. Call me if you can't get the pilot lit."

"Okay," I said, but her phone had already cut out.

I searched the drawers for the matches.

"Oh my God!" I screamed. A dead mouse was curled up inside the one where our silverware would go.

"What's the matter, Mama?" Avery stood up, and I slammed the drawer shut.

"Nothing. It's just really dirty in here. Do *not* open any of the drawers."

One catastrophe at a time.

"You stay right here," I said. To make sure she wouldn't go wandering, I found the coloring book and box of stubby crayons I kept in my purse.

I located the instructions on the side of the furnace, just as Pilar had promised, and felt like an idiot for not noticing them before. I read through them twice before starting with step one. I turned the pilot valve to OFF. Counted five minutes in my head, waiting for any residual gas to clear, turned it to PILOT, located the pilot, and lit my match. I said a prayer, closed my eyes, and reached the flame in. The *whoosh* startled me, and my eyes sprang open, my heart whooshing along with the flame. I did it! I then turned the knob to ON and the furnace shuddered and rumbled to life. I felt ridiculously proud of myself, but mostly relieved to have not blown myself, or the house, up.

Upstairs, air blasted hot through the vents, and wonder of all wonders, began to fill the rooms with the smell of burning dust, but also with heat. I could do this. We would be okay.

I spent the morning cleaning the kitchen and the bedroom Avery had chosen for herself. By lunchtime, I'd managed to unpack our meager kitchen supplies and had made a list of everything we'd need to pick up the next time we went into Portland. I figured we'd only need to go onto the mainland once to refill our cupboards before Pilar arrived at Thanksgiving. I really hoped we could find what we needed until then on the island.

Avery had grown tired with coloring, and so I waited until she was occupied with her toy ponies in her room (a prenap ritual) before extricating the dead mouse from the drawer. I used a pair of salad tongs I'd found in a cupboard and dropped it into a plastic bag. "Sorry, little guy," I offered and carried it outside to look for a place to throw it away.

I circled the perimeter of the house, studying my surroundings for the first time. The back and sides of the house faced a thick patch of woods. The front of the house sat perched at the top of a cliff (one of the island's namesake bluffs, I supposed) that led down to a rocky cove. There wasn't another house in sight, though Pilar had said there were neighbors. I figured they must be down the road a ways, or on the other side of those woods.

I thought about tossing the mouse down the cliffs; I'd aim for the sea. But the tide was low, and it would likely just land on the sand. Some unsuspecting sap might go out for a walk and step on it. And so I went around the back of the house and walked to the edge of the woods. There seemed to be a path, or at least a clearing there, and I smelled the faint but distinct scent of wood smoke. I looked up, and sure enough, in the distance I could see smoke billowing out from an invisible chimney. I hurled the mouse as hard as I could into the dark thickness of trees and backed away from the woods, feeling my heart clattering around in my chest like those used-up rolls of film inside that box.

The Birches

When Avery went down for her nap, I unloaded a large canvas from the trunk and brought it into the bright, empty dining room, which was now flooded with light. I had already committed to this commission, but I figured as soon as it was done, I could start to work on my own projects. My goal was to finish before Pilar arrived.

My client had seen one of my paintings, "fallen in looove" with my "work," and asked me to paint one of my signature tree paintings, making sure to incorporate plenty of rust and gray to pick up on the colors in her throw pillows. She had actually sent me, express mail, paint chips of her wall color and fabric swatches from said pillows. This painting was to be situated, ultimately, above a slate fireplace in her ski lodge in Aspen.

I'd started painting birches years ago. I was pregnant with Avery, Gus and I were renting a shitty basement apartment that had rats ten times the size of the mouse I had just chucked into the woods, and neither one of us had a regular paycheck. There was a coffee shop around the corner that periodically offered wall space to local artists, and I had brought in a painting I'd made as soon as I found out I was pregnant. It was of trees, of course, because I had not yet wearied of their bark and branches. I had meticulously crafted each trunk, the bark nearly photo-realistic, but the spaces between the trees were where the energy was, where the danger was. I had been sweating, my heart racing as I painted those shadows. The painting, in many ways, terrified me.

And I remember thinking even then how strange it felt to

hang it up on those exposed brick walls, to slap a truly arbitrary price on it ($500, I recall, which seemed a ridiculous figure, foolishly optimistic), to have it hanging above a battered wooden table where people slurped overpriced coffee and choked down dry scones.

I'd done shows in art school, of course, but the only people who came to those exhibits were other students and teachers. Sometimes family, friends. If there was buzz around a particular student, then there was an occasional critic. But the pristine white walls, the nodding heads—they were all of the same world. We were *all* exposing ourselves. *Exhibitionists.* Putting those dangerous trees in my local coffee shop, where a homeless man once sat in the corner picking the dead skin off his feet, where babies wailed and tired mothers commiserated, where couples courted and split up, where exasperated waitresses cleaned up spilled milk, spilled coffee, and so many crumbs, felt like I'd torn my heart from my chest and hung it there with a price tag affixed to it.

But we were living hand to mouth, and that hand was sometimes empty. I figured if I could sell just one painting then I could cut back on my shifts at the bar. Staying awake until 3 A.M. had been hard enough when I wasn't pregnant, but nearly impossible now that I was. Gus had just started working at the sign shop. He was making barely above minimum wage, but they let him use the space after hours for his own work. We did what we needed to do. And I knew I needed to do this.

And so when the call came from the coffee shop manager that someone wanted the painting, it wasn't uncertainty I felt at all, but relief. Our cupboards were empty. I couldn't even afford the prenatal vitamins I knew I needed, never mind vegetables. Thank God, my parents still paid my health insurance, which, while considered catastrophic, thankfully included maternity care—though I suppose other people like us might classify that as a catastrophe. Five hundred dollars would pay the rent on that crappy apartment for a whole month. We might even be able to get ahead.

But when the same man who bought the painting asked me

to do another, but this time, maybe "just the trees," I felt that awful unease setting in. "I love the birches, my wife loves the birches, but there's something a bit dark about the background. If you could just make it a bit, I don't know, cheerier?" He'd had a mustache, with crumbs of a blueberry scone clinging for dear life as he talked to me at one of those rickety tables.

I'd nodded my head even as my heart resisted. He said he'd pay me a thousand dollars if I could make this one bigger. "Twenty-four by thirty-six," he'd said. "I'm looking to fill a space in the waiting room at my office." He was a psychiatrist with a practice on the Upper East Side. (I still have no idea what he'd been doing in Queens that day.) Countless wealthy patients would walk by my trees every day. He promised I could put out business cards, postcards. That dozens of wealthy housewives who came in to get their heads shrunk (my words, not his) would pass by my trees every day. That legions of anxious, anorexic, depressed, disgruntled, or simply lonely women would be exposed to my art. And so, I said yes.

By the time Avery was born, I had opened my Etsy shop with greeting cards, giclée prints, and original commissions made to the customer's color and size specifications, which was my real bread and butter. And those shadows? They disappeared. I pushed them out of the margins of the paintings; they resided off the canvas, lingered at the tips of my fingers, and finally receded into my imagination.

This latest commission, this one I'd dragged my feet on and then dragged with me all the way to Maine, was for Ginger Hardy, one of Dr. Holder's patients. (My guess was narcissism with a touch of anxiety.) Her husband knew some bigwig art publisher. She'd alluded several times that she could imagine my work being licensed and mass-produced. Sold at Crate and Barrel or Pier 1. Bed Bath & Beyond. She'd winked and said, "Make this one a good one and you never know . . ."

I laid the canvas out on the floor in a pool of sunlight. I

spread the swatches of fabric, the paint chips, next to it and stood over it, staring at my sketches. I'm not sure what people liked so much about the birches. I suspect it's that they are such innocuous trees. Pale, thin, almost fragile-looking. Nonthreatening. I'd thought so once too, of course. I'd also been fooled to believe those shadows didn't exist.

Night Pictures

I *was taught in art school that an artist must pay attention not only to the light, but also to the shadows; it is in the contrast between light and dark where the beauty lies. Da Vinci used a technique called sfumato (after the Italian* sfumare, *"to evaporate like smoke"). In this technique, colors are blended together softly, the contrast between light and shadow a gentle thing. A nebulous one. Think of the* Mona Lisa. *That ethereal flesh, that ambiguous smile.*

However, to achieve a more dramatic effect, the other Old Masters used chiaroscuro, *which in Italian literally means "light dark." It is a technique that relies on the contrast between darkness and light to create a dramatic effect. Rembrandt used it. Caravaggio. De La Tour.*

Tenebroso is an extreme style of chiaroscuro, *with dramatic, even violent, illumination. In these seventeenth century paintings, figures are often illumed by a single light source, with all else left in darkness. Painting this way was referred to as the "dark manner," these portraits, "night pictures."*

If this day were a painting, it would be like this. The focus drawn to the violence by a solitary spot of light (sun piercing through the trees, illuminating that spot inside the dark woods). A "night picture" so shocking and startling, you need to look away.

Da Vinci said, "A painter should begin every canvas with a wash of black, because all things in nature are dark except where exposed by the light."

And so, perhaps, if this day were a painting, I would begin with black.

Mermaid Tears

By the time Avery woke up, I was sick of painting. I'd made progress on only a single trunk. Each one required a sort of manic attention to detail; my hand cramped up after only a couple hours of work. I never thought of painting as manual labor until I started working on commissions.

"How about after you have some lunch we go exploring?" I said as she rubbed the sleep from her eyes and nestled into the crook of my arm.

The climb down the cliff was a bit more precarious than it looked. I held her hand as we walked from one craggy rock ledge to the next. It was really, really windy. My hair whipped around my face violently. I wished I'd worn a hat to keep my ears warm; they ached and itched from the cold. Avery's cheeks looked like they'd been slapped.

By the time we reached the sand, I was already thinking about what a nightmare it was going to be to get back up again. There had to be a way up that didn't require mountain climbing equipment.

The stretch of beach was small, but beautiful. As soon as we reached the sand and Avery was sure-footed again, she began to run, gleefully squealing into the wind. She chased the waves and then backed up, her little feet bicycling so she wouldn't get wet.

"The water is cold, Mama!" she said, but her face was joyful.

As she played, I walked slowly along the sand, when I suddenly spotted a sliver of something blue and picked it up. Sea glass. There had been tons of sea glass in Providence. Sally, one of my friends from school, wound up opening a shop that sold jewelry made from the treasures she found along the shore. She'd made me a bracelet once; I still had it somewhere. I'd have to find it, maybe give it to Avery when she was older.

I kept scouring the sand, sure this was just a fluke, but soon I saw another cobalt piece, an emerald shard, a fleshy pink marble.

Avery was about a hundred feet ahead of me. "Av," I hollered, "look!"

She came running back to me, and I held out my open palm. She peered down at the smooth, colored glass with wide eyes.

"What are they, Mama?"

I remembered Sally telling me a story once. A myth. "I think," I said, quietly, conspiratorially, "they're *mermaid* tears."

"Mermaid tears?" she repeated, cocking her head and considering the possibility.

"Yes," I said. "This means there's a mermaid living somewhere near here who has been banished to the sea. When she cries, her tears wash ashore and turn into colored glass."

"What's *bamished?*"

"*Banished*. It means she's not allowed to leave the sea, ever again."

"That's sad. Who bamished her?"

"Neptune," I said. "The god of the sea."

"Sage doesn't believe in God." Sage was a preschool classmate with a terminally runny nose.

I had no answer for this, and it wasn't really a question anyway, so I just kept walking, picking up the sea glass, which I gave to her piece by piece.

"She must be *really* sad," she said.

"Yep," I said.

We collected the pieces and made a pile of gems on a flat rock a safe distance from the waves crashing angrily against the jetty that divided us from our neighbors' beach.

"Let's go see what's over there," I said, motioning to a patch of sea grass that further divided Pilar's property from whoever owned the house with the smoking chimney next door.

She shoved all of the glass treasures into the pockets of her sandy jeans and took my hand as we made our way to the jetty, where I helped her climb up the rocks. We peered at the beach beyond.

"Can we go over there?"

I shrugged. "I guess."

"It's a free country," she said, nodding knowingly. This was something else she'd picked up at preschool. She used it pretty much any time she wanted to do something we didn't want her to do. And then some.

We climbed to the opposite side of the jetty. On this side was a pristine beach as well as a boathouse and, sure enough, a set of stone steps leading up the rocky face of the cliff. We climbed up to the top, where there was a giant, grassy clearing, and in the distance I could see the source of the smoke.

There was the *real* Grey Gardens, a massive, *colossal* really, house: a Tudor mansion, very Kennedian.

"Wow!" Avery said. "That's a big house."

"That is a very big house."

"Who lives there?" she asked.

"I have no idea."

"Probably a movie star. Maybe Taylor Swift."

"I don't think so. But you never know," I said. I wasn't sure how she even knew who Taylor Swift was. I blamed the preschool.

"Can we go see if they have kids?" she asked.

I doubted there were any children living beyond those manicured hedges. But I didn't have the heart to crush her dreams of a playmate.

I shook my head. "Not today."

"But maybe they have a little girl."

"I need you to help me paint this afternoon," I said.

"Trees?" She scowled.

"No, silly, your *room*."

"Oh," she said, as if I'd offered her a bran muffin in place of a piece of chocolate cake.

"There's a shortcut to our house," she said. "Look."

And she was right, there was a pathway that led away from this sprawling lawn to the small forest dividing our properties.

"Can we go that way?"

I felt my chest constrict. I shook my head.

"No," I said. "We should go back the way we came."

"Why?"

But how do you explain? How do you ever explain that to a child? That the world is a dangerous place, that there *are* monsters that live under your bed. That the bogeyman is *real*. I figured it was my job as a mom to keep my daughter somehow both happily oblivious and safe. So I said, "It's trespassing. That means we have to stay on our side until we've been invited."

"Oh," she said. At least I could also thank preschool for teaching a bunch of arbitrary rules regarding possession and sharing.

"Here, can you carry the sea glass?" I asked.

"What's sea glass?"

"I mean the *mermaid's tears*," I corrected myself. "Put them in your pocket so we can climb back up."

Halfway up the rocky cliff, I was thinking I should have just sucked it up and taken the path through the woods. These bluffs were more dangerous.

Avery got bored with "helping" me paint after only a few minutes, and so I set her up at the kitchen table with a plastic box of children's watercolors and some paper. I had brought along the baby monitor I couldn't seem to relinquish, and put it unobtrusively on the kitchen counter. I listened to her happy babble and singing as I painted around the windows, edged along the ceiling, and rolled the violet color across the walls.

I ran out of paint just as I finished the fourth wall and the sun was beginning to set. I had only brought a gallon, thinking that would be enough to cover a small bedroom. But the walls were porous, and it took two coats for the color to become the shade Avery had wanted. I didn't have blue paint for the floor/sky yet since I wasn't sure if the floors would even be amenable to being painted. Luckily, they were made of wide pine boards. I figured a good sanding and a coat of primer would be all they'd need before I painted the "sky." I'd need to either buy some glow-in-the-dark stars online or just use some of the glow-in-the dark acrylic paint I had in my stash of craft paints.

After I put her to bed, I checked my Facebook and e-mail on my phone. I also realized I hadn't checked my business e-mail account since we left the city. I had set up an address just to receive my Etsy orders, messages sent via my miserably out-of-date Web site. Usually, I'd get a few a month. Things generally picked up before the holidays; I had created a line of Christmas cards with a snowy version of the birches.

There were a couple of inquiries about commissions, one order for a small print (thankfully, I'd packed some of my inventory). And then an e-mail with the subject line: *looking for you.*

I clicked to open the e-mail, trembling as I read:

> I need to talk to you bout some things. You no
> what. If you think you can just ignore me, that's
> not very smart. Cuz I no where you been living
> in New York city. And I also no where your
> parents live.

I felt my stomach turn, bile burning at the back of my throat. Tears burning in my eyes, I clicked out of the e-mail. I thought of my Etsy page, the profile picture of me. Gus had taken the photo right after I'd had Avery. In it, my cheeks are as full and pink as the knit cap on my head. It was late spring, and I was holding Avery, kissing her forehead. Under my profile picture, it said *Wyn Davies, Queens, NY.* And my stupid bio. I'd read online how important it was to personalize this page, to make yourself *likeable.* Friendly, accessible artists sold more work than elusive ones. All anybody had to do was click on this page and learn that I lived in Queens, that I was a mom, that I'd grown up in New Hampshire and studied art at RISD.

Quickly, I went to Google's home page and searched "Wyn Davies Queens, NY." For under five dollars you could have my current address, phone number, address history. For thirty bucks, you could get everything shy of my dental records.

I thought about deleting everything: social networking accounts, my Etsy account, my Web site. I wanted to systematically destroy the platform I'd spent the last several years building. But the damage was done.

An image search of my name revealed the same photo from my Etsy shop as well as the one head shot Gus had taken of me ten years ago when I had my first and only solo show, at a small gallery in Durango. There were maybe a dozen of these same images of me as I scrolled down the page, but most of the photos were of Robby Rousseau: the mug shot taken that night after they arrested him, his face acne-riddled, bearing scratch marks, downcast eyes, and the faintest hint of an adolescent mustache. The photo of him being led to the courthouse in shackles, chin to chest.

I reread the message, trembling, and tried to comfort myself with the fact that at least it seemed he had no idea I'd left Queens, that I was here on this remote island. I was safe here. Avery and I were safe here. That had been the whole plan, hadn't it?

That night I curled up with Avery in "my" room. My back

ached from painting, and I couldn't get comfortable. I tossed and turned, sleeping fitfully. When I did sleep, I dreamed of trees, of that dense and terrifying forest. But then the leaves and green gave way to water, waves crashing against the sand, the tide creeping closer and closer, climbing up the cliffs, depositing the tears of a sorrowful mermaid held prisoner by an angry god.

Inquiry

"Do you recall anything different about that day? Anything at all out of the ordinary?"

"No. Only that Carly Noone got . . . um . . . sick. During algebra. I went with her to the nurse during last period. We were still in the nurse's office when the last bell rang."

Mrs. Valencia had me walk Carly down to the nurse's office, my sweater tied around Carly's waist to hide the red splotch blooming on the back of her white capris. I was squeamish, and the idea of bleeding like this made me feel faint. I didn't have my period yet. The nurse sent her into the bathroom with a pad. When the bell rang, she told her she could wait there, she'd call her mother to come get her so she wouldn't have to walk home.

"And you?"

"I stayed with her until her mom showed up. She asked me to. I was bummed because I wanted to go hang out with my other friends."

"Who? What did you normally do after school?"

"Hanna Lamont. Sara Richards. Usually, we would be gossiping, playing with somebody's Tamagotchi toy."

Talking about the new boy who'd just moved here from North Carolina. Hanna said she'd blow him, if he asked her. I didn't know what she meant, but I acted like I did. But not that day.

"But not that day?"

"No. Everybody had gone home except for me."

Her white jeans ruined, the red burst right at the center of her. When she gave me back my sweater, I saw some of the red had seeped onto it. Like spilled ink. Like a contagion.

"Did you see Robert? Was he outside the school?"

"It's Robby. Nobody called him Robert."

"Yes. Robby. Were you aware of him being on the campus?"

The pounding of the bass always preceded the car. I remember I could feel it in my jaw, the pavement throbbing like a heartbeat. I didn't need to look up to know he was rolling the window down, leaning toward us like a flower toward the sun. We were so bright, weren't we? All of us, such shining girls?

"Miss Davies?"

I could feel the bass in my throat, in my shoulders.

"Let me try this again. Did you see Robert—Robby—on campus after school? Or had he already left?"

Before he had time to roll down the window, before he could hiss and lick his lips, make those sounds at me, I crossed the street and started down the road that would take me to the lower playing fields. Teeth clacking, jaw snapping, like a dog growling.

"Miss Davies, when did you realize he was following you?"

"Who?"

"Robert. *Robby* Rousseau."

Bluffs Island

I put him out of my mind. I had no choice. I wasn't going to engage him in whatever conversation he wanted to have. I needed to focus on making our life here. On just getting settled in. I'd worry about all of this after the court made its decision about the retrial.

I would paint Avery's room. I would paint the birches. I would get the house ready for Pilar. Everything would be okay if I could just stay focused on these simple things.

While it was unlikely this little island would have its own hardware store where we could get the paint, I thought if we went into town we might find some of the other things we needed. It would also be a chance to check in with civilization.

I made a quick mental list (excluding the paint), in the off chance there might be some sort of general store, a la *Little House on the Prairie,* where we could find the things I'd forgotten: toilet paper, ibuprofen, bleach.

After breakfast, I bundled Avery up into a thick Aran sweater she hated but my mother had knitted for her and made her look like the little Irish girl on the cover of the knitting pattern. Chestnut hair, green eyes and all.

As we were headed out the door, I remembered the *Epitaphs and Prophecies* box, which I had put on the kitchen counter earlier. What I hadn't noticed before was each roll of film had a date marked on its side in ballpoint pen. How strange. I lined them up in date order, finding the oldest one first: *7/12/76.* I grabbed that one and the next one, labeled *7/13/76,* on the highly unlikely chance there was someplace in town that could develop film.

I took the same road we'd driven to get to the house from the ferry, noting it was just as desolate as it had seemed in the dark of night. I counted only five turnoffs, all of them marked PRIVATE. And it only took a few minutes to get to the place where the main road split. Going straight would take you toward the water, toward the docks (where the ferry was notably absent). Turning left would, apparently, take you into "town." A hand-painted sign hung on the side of the road announcing BUSINESS DISTRICT with an arrow to lead the way.

I put my blinker on, though for whom, I have no idea. There didn't seem to be another soul out today. The road hugged the rocky shore and did, indeed, eventually arrive in a small village with one main street populated with both people and a few shops and restaurants. Civilization! My heart sang at the sight of a small market and a drugstore. A post office, and an old phone booth now filled with books and marked PUBLIC LIBRARY.

I angle-parked the car and almost gleefully unbuckled Avery from the backseat. It was pathetic; I'd only been away from the city for a few days. But something about these signs of commerce, of life, was such a relief. How I planned to make it through an entire winter here suddenly baffled me. I thought of Jack Nicholson's character in *The Shining,* slowly going mad inside the old hotel while his family could do nothing but try to survive. At least Pilar would be here soon.

As I locked up the car, no fewer than four people nodded their heads at me, mumbled hello, and tried not to stare at the New York plates on the Honda. They probably figured I was just a tourist. Pilar had told me in the summertime, the island's population grew upward of two thousand people. But in the winter, there were only a few hundred. I figured these shops and restaurants were likely designed to cater to the summer residents, a sad fact confirmed as we made our way down the street only to realize more than half of them had signs saying CLOSED UNTIL MEMORIAL DAY hanging in their doors. Memorial Day was six months away! My singing heart went silent.

"Oh, look, Mama!" Avery said, stopping in front of a tourist shop where there was a display of stuffed lobsters, fishing buoys, and nets. Brightly colored T-shirts and plastic sand buckets. "Can we go in?" she asked. But again, CLOSED FOR BUSINESS announced the hand-written sign on the door.

Three restaurants, a coffee shop, and a high-end jewelry store with empty display cases (as if a burglar had come and pillaged the velvet necks and hands) were also closed. I was about to give up when we got to a small drugstore near the end of the block and saw people moving around inside.

"Come on, sweets," I said, motioning for Avery to come. She had her hands pressed against the cold glass of an abandoned candy shop, her eyes forlorn.

I pushed open the door to the drugstore, and the sleigh bells hanging on it jingled. There was a man behind the counter, busy ringing up an elderly woman's purchases. I smiled. Avery skipped down the aisles, which were sparsely stocked. I managed to find a few things we needed: a plunger, for one (none of the toilets seemed to be fully operational), as well as toilet paper, some bleach, ibuprofen, a couple of postcards to send home, and, from a dusty display near the back of the store, some sand toys for Avery. I brought our items to the counter and noticed a Kodak kiosk. I rummaged through my purse for the rolls of film and said to the man behind the counter, "Excuse me?"

He turned away from what he was doing and offered a sort of half smile. "Aftah-noon," he said, his accent as thick as the dust on those sand buckets.

"Hi," I said, realizing this was the first adult conversation I'd had in a couple of days. "I saw you guys have a photo, um, *department?*" I gestured to the enlargement kiosk. "I was wondering if you also developed film?"

"Film?"

"Yeah," I said. "Camera film. 35 mm?" I looked at the canisters to verify.

"Used to have a one-hour shop set up, but don't nobody use film no more."

I nodded, still smiling. "But can you send it away or something?"

He shrugged his shoulders. "I got some envelopes. In the back."

"Okay?" I said as he continued to look at me quizzically. "Envelopes to mail away film?"

"Ayuh," he said, slowly turned around and looked back over his shoulder, as if worried I might rob the till if he left it unattended, and then disappeared into a back room.

He emerged again with a handful of large preprinted envelopes. "You might want to check on the computer and make sure these addresses are still good," he said. "These must be fifteen years old."

Online. Of course. What an idiot I was. There must be places you could send your film to get it developed. Still, I took the envelopes from him and studied them. "Do I just bring these here? Or do I need to mail them myself?"

"The post office is the next block o-vah," he said.

After we'd paid for our things, I sat in the car, checked via my phone to confirm this was still the address for film processing, and popped the film canisters in one of the envelopes along with my credit card number, hoping my most recent payment would free up enough credit to cover the cost. Then Avery and I made our way to the post office.

I explained to the postmistress that I had just moved into the house on the bluffs and that I was wondering if there was mail delivery. The woman raised her eyebrow.

"You mean the house up to Bluffs Drive?"

I nodded, smiling.

She scowled and her mouth twitched, and she looked down at Avery, who had been collecting handfuls of green certified mail receipts and change of address kits.

"Av," I said. "Just one of each."

"Mail trucks don't go up there," the woman snapped. "You gotta rent a box, hon." And she pointed to a wall of bronze boxes, each with their own spinning lock.

I filled out a form with my info and wrote a check for twenty-five dollars I hadn't planned on spending, but I figured I would likely need to be able to receive as well as send mail. I had no return address to put on the film envelope otherwise.

Avery was getting antsy and whiny after running all these errands, and so I said, "Do you want some cocoa?" I'd found in my brief history as a mother that I wasn't above bribery.

We found a small restaurant open on the opposite side of the street and went through the heavy doors. Inside it was dark, more bar than restaurant, and for a minute I worried Avery wouldn't be allowed inside. But a young woman ushered us in and put us at a table near a window that looked out at the incredible view of the ocean.

The other patrons were mostly men, fishermen, I supposed from the looks of them. Flannel and beards here were practical necessities rather than hipster fashion statements. Just as Avery's cocoa and my coffee arrived, one of the older men hobbled over to us. He had to be nearing eighty. He had a vague sort of limp and wispy hair that blew about in the forced-air heat coming through a vent over our table, liver-spotted hands, and pale eyelashes.

"You the one who bought the house up on the bluffs?" he asked.

Well, I guess it was obvious we weren't locals. But not quite tourists either.

I thought about explaining it was actually Pilar's house, that she was just letting us stay there, but it all seemed so complicated and unnecessary to explain this to a stranger, so I just said, "Yep."

"Glad somebody finally moved in. House's just been sittin' there for the last thirty-five years," he said.

Thirty-five years? Well, that explained the state of things.

"I remember her," he said, nodding.

And I thought again of Pilar. But that made no sense. Pilar had been on the island a whopping two times, once to look at the house, and once when she closed on it.

"Who's that?" I asked.

"What was it, back in '80, '81?" He rubbed a hand across his freckled head as though he were trying to conjure up some distant memory.

I was getting more and more confused.

"Never fit in here, ya know. Kept to herself mostly. Didn't talk to nobody." He was caught up in some sort of distant reverie now. "'Course folks like that don't last long here. Still, the way she just disappeared. Very strange."

He wasn't talking to me, not really, but it felt like an accusation.

"What happened?" I started, but then Avery gasped. She had spilled her mug and the cocoa was running across the laminate tabletop.

I jumped up, grabbing a wad of napkins from the dispenser on the table to sop up the mess.

"You might ask your neighbor that question," he said.

Avery was crying now. Big, gulping sobs.

"It's okay, honey," I said. The cocoa was running down the front of her white sweater. Luckily, we had bleach now.

I patted futilely at the cocoa and, with a fresh napkin, at her tears.

I looked up again, wanting to ask the man what he was talking about, *whom* he was talking about, but he was already at the register paying his check. He tipped an imaginary hat at me on his way out the door.

I sighed and stared out the window at the waves pummeling the sand below us. I ordered another cocoa for Avery, even though this would ensure a sugar crash in about an hour. Sometimes, I took the easy way out. I always had.

* * *

That night, I dreamed of the pathway that led between our house and the mansion across the way. I was walking on the beach, gathering sea glass. Avery was with me. It was dusk in my dream, and the big house was bathed in a sort of orange light as the sun set behind it. I was so consumed by the beauty of this, the mystery of who lived there, I didn't see Avery disappear. But in a moment I was overcome by the truth that she was gone. That she had taken the stone steps without me. I ran to catch up, calling her name, following a path of blue and green sea grass to the top, where I stood at the entrance to the woods. Paralyzed, unable to go forward, though I knew Avery was in the woods.

I know you got a little girl.

Suddenly the sun plummeted, taking its sepia haze with it. The sky above me was black. And the house loomed before me, empty and ominous. And even when she began to scream, my legs remained fixed in that spot. My limbs like roots, my arms only branches reaching for the sky.

I woke bathed in sweat. At some point Avery had crawled into bed with me, but I had no recollection of her doing so. Her skin startled me. She was flat on her back, her arms splayed over her head in a surrender to sleep. I slowly climbed out of bed, pulled on a pair of yoga pants, wool socks, and my favorite ratty sweater before tiptoeing to the bathroom to pee, closing the lid rather than flushing and risking waking her up. I glanced at my watch. It was only 3 A.M. I thought about crawling back into bed, curling around Avery's little body. But I knew I wouldn't be able to sleep, and so I quietly descended that treacherous staircase, making a mental note to talk to Pilar about getting someone to come in to take care of it.

I made a pot of coffee in the dark kitchen, and as it brewed, I went to the dining room, where the birches stared at me, their thin white trunks looking like prison bars until I clicked the light on.

Because it was a dining room, the central light was a chandelier, which hung low. I had already whacked my head on it several times, sending it swinging, plaster from the ceiling crumbling down like snow. I was careful this time as I made my way to my easel. To the birches.

Furiously, automatically, I painted. And as the benevolent forest emerged on the canvas, I imagined it hanging in that ski lodge in Aspen. I imagined Ginger Hardy and her rich friends sipping hot toddies by the fire, my painting looking down at them. This painting, this shitty painting, neither imploring nor accusing. Only sitting obediently on the wall, demanding nothing.

By the time I heard Avery coming down the stairs, the sun had crested the horizon, and my hand and back ached. I had no idea how much time had passed. I had been so lost inside the margins of the canvas.

"Mama," she said.

"Yes, baby," I answered, as though she were calling me out of a dream, pulling me from a rare slumber.

"I wet my bed again."

Upset Down

Over the next two weeks, I avoided the birches in favor of readying the house for Pilar. I spent most days cleaning, making meals for Avery, and finding things for her to do to keep her occupied while I scrubbed and dusted and procrastinated.

Gus called Avery every night before bedtime, and like a tiny teenager, she'd take the phone and close herself off in her room, in the bathroom, in the downstairs closet. *For privacy,* she said. I tried not to eavesdrop, but I longed to hear their conversations. And when they were done, I took the phone from her and either translated what she'd told him or filled in the gaps for Gus.

"She said you painted her room upside down?" he asked.

"*Upset* down," I corrected, laughing, and explained.

He asked when we'd be able to come home for a visit, and with a sinking heart, I'd told him how much the car ferry cost (nearly eighty dollars round trip), never mind the cost of gas to get back down to the city, never mind the fact that the Honda needed new tires and there was a clunking sound somewhere deep in its bowels I hadn't noticed before.

"This isn't what we agreed on, Wynnie," he said.

"I know. I'm sorry. We can try to FaceTime again." The times we'd tried to FaceTime, the signal was so weak one of them invariably disappeared halfway through the conversation, sending Avery into a fit of gulping sobs.

"It's not fair to Av," he persisted.

I didn't tell him about her wetting the bed. I didn't tell him I'd starting having the dreams again, the ones that made me thrash in my sheets, lash out, cry out, awake drenched in sweat and breathless. I didn't tell him about the phone call, the e-mail.

"Maybe you could come for Thanksgiving," I tried. "It would be so nice for all of us to be together. Pilar will be here by then."

"I already told you I have to work that Wednesday and Friday."

"But where will you go for Thanksgiving?" I asked.

Gus and I had always hosted Thanksgiving at our house, no matter where we lived. When we were in school, we'd invite all of our friends who couldn't afford to go home, charge the food on our credit card, and feed everyone. The year in Colorado when we lived in the teepee, we'd had a friend bring a wild turkey over and cooked it over a spit in our "yard." And all the years in the duplex, we'd had our friends over, spent the day cooking and drinking and eating.

"I've got some plans," he offered vaguely, and I didn't persist, though I did wonder why he didn't just come out and tell me what those plans were.

We had plenty of friends in the city who would make sure he got fed. He was Gus. Sweet, adorable Gus. My heart throbbed in my chest. I was also sure there was no shortage of women ready to cook up a Thanksgiving feast for a poor guy whose wife had taken off with his kid. And if it wasn't a woman, why didn't he just come out and say who it was? It's not like anyone in his world was a stranger to me. He could have said, "Walter and Betsy are having me over," "Dennis and Pam are deep-frying a turkey," "I'm just going to get takeout with Topher and watch the games." But he hadn't offered up anyone's names. This nagged at me, like a scab that keeps snagging on a pair of tights. Stinging.

"I'm sorry," I said. "What about the weekend after, can you come then?"

"Maybe," he said, sounding defeated. "I'll check with Joe about getting a few extra days off. I really miss her, Wynnie." His words stabbed in me in the chest.

★ ★ ★

And so a week later, I felt awful dishing out the eighty bucks to take the car ferry to the mainland in order to go to the Walmart in Scarborough. But Pilar was coming, and we needed a turkey for Thanksgiving, paint to finish Avery's room, as well as some much needed supplies we'd been managing without but I had wanted to make sure Pilar had when she arrived: liquid hand soap, fresh towels, extra shampoo and toothpaste. I had planned to pick up another set of twin sheets too, to help keep the rotation going given Avery's potty relapse. There was no way we'd be able to carry everything on the pedestrian ferry.

Avery had never been in a Walmart before, and she was mesmerized. As we wandered the brightly lit aisles, her eyes widened at the toys and cookies and cheap clothes as I calculated the total cost of the items in my cart.

After I found the perfect shade of sky blue paint for her floor, we walked past the kids' clothing area.

"Oh look, Mama!" Avery said, holding out one sparkly thing then the next. It killed me that a seven-dollar shirt was an extravagance I had to deny her. I had left New York with roughly $1,000 in my checking account and a big fat zero in my savings. The balance had, somehow, dwindled down to $600. Gus would be sending a check, but not for another few weeks, and I wanted to give Pilar a proper Thanksgiving—with turkey and sweet potatoes and green bean casserole. Christmas was coming soon too. I needed to finish the commission so I could get paid, but I'd barely been able to look at the birches. I'd tried, of course, gone through the motions of gathering the colors I would need, the brushes. But whenever I got started I felt an inevitable sense of dread and a crushing sort of something I can only describe as guilt. Like I was betraying someone, something.

"*Please,* Mama, it's a kitty with glasses!" Avery said. She was holding the pink T-shirt up to herself, twirling around, looking at her reflection in the carefully placed mirror.

"Fine," I said, trying not to be angry with her for wanting

things. It wasn't her fault I was a financial disaster. What was another seven dollars in the grand scheme of my ominous debt?

We had made our way to the grocery aisles, which proved to be an even worse land mine. Cookies and candy, potato chips and a zillion other bad things screamed to her from their plastic packages. *Love me, buy me, eat me!* She was grabbing at the packages like a child possessed, and so I finally scooped her up and put her in the front basket of the cart.

I pushed the cart quickly into the freezer aisle, hoisting a generic frozen turkey from the freezer case, and then moved on into the canned goods and produce aisles, loading down the cart with all the other Thanksgiving essentials.

"You don't need to do anything special," Pilar had said. "And do they even do turkey in Maine? Don't they eat lobster three times a day?"

I'd been in Maine for three weeks and had yet to have a lobster. At ten dollars a pound, they were something to be observed in their tanks, not purchased and devoured. Avery and I had been living on PB&J and pasta. We'd made homemade pizza a couple of times, ate scrambled eggs for dinner more nights than not.

I pushed the cart to the checkout lane and loaded up the conveyer belt. As the clerk bagged the items, I felt distinctly nauseated, calculating my account balance had just been depleted by almost 20 percent.

In the parking lot, I loaded the trunk of the car and pushed the shopping cart back to its receptacle. If I had a shopping cart, I wouldn't need to take the car onto the ferry the next time. For a split second I wondered if I could somehow fit the shopping cart into my trunk.

Before Avery came along, Gus and I used to do crazy things like that. We'd go out carousing, steal things. Nothing that meant anything to anybody: glasses from bars, street signs, *shopping carts*. Once, he tore through a grumpy neighbor's garden and brought me a dozen red tulips, yanked up by the roots. We'd carefully planted them in a big pot we kept on the back porch of our apartment and watched in the morning as the crabby old lady, Mrs. D'Angelo, discovered she'd been robbed. My heart sank a little when she leaned out of her house as if the culprit might still be in sight, but then she started screaming her usual racist epithets, accusing the "motherfucking" *n*-words of taking her tulips, and we no longer felt so bad.

Thinking about that made my heart ache a little for Gus. Leaving him had left a mark, one that wasn't fading. A bruise that seemed to keep getting reinjured every time I let myself think about him. I was grateful Pilar would be there to keep my mind off of him. Still, this was better. I had to remind myself, every time I bumped into one of those sharp corners in my memory, we were better off apart.

After the shopping trip, when we drove off the ferry and back onto the island, Avery said, "Don't forget we need to mail the postcard to Daddy."

"That's right," I said, trying to smile even as tears threatened to fall. "Did you remember to bring it?"

She reached into the little purple vinyl purse she insisted on carrying everywhere. (Inside she kept her "credit card"—an old grocery store loyalty card—her "ID"—a photo I'd taken of her that Gus laminated at work—as well as a hairbrush, although she never brushed her own hair.) She pulled out one of the postcards we'd picked up in town, and I studied the stick-like letters scratched on the back of the card.

"I didn't know how to spell all the words," she said.

"Can you read it to me?" I asked, unable to decipher much beyond "Daddy."

I carefully translated her phonetic attempts below in my own careful handwriting, my heart aching with her plea: "Dear Daddy. I miss you. Maybe you can come live with us here. Our water smells like farts. But the beach has mermaid tears, and I am sad too. Love, Avery," she dictated, peering intently over my shoulder.

We parked at the post office, and I helped her drop the letter into the gaping mouth of the post box.

"Can we check our box?" she asked.

"Oh, sure," I said. We'd been in just once before, and it had been stuffed with circulars. The only people who had the address were Gus, Pilar, and my folks.

I had made the combination Avery's birthday so I wouldn't forget it. If anyone wanted to rob me blind (clear out my savings account, charge up my credit cards, steal my identity) they'd only need this set of digits. Of course, the bank account now had only $480, the cards were long ago maxed out, and frankly, my identity wasn't worth a whole hell of a lot these days either. *So have at it,* I thought as I ticked out the numbers.

I pulled out the wad of circulars, wondering if there was a way to get on a *do not send* list. I tossed the advertisements into the recycling bin and a blue cardboard card slipped out. It said there was a package, to pick it up at the counter. No return address listed.

My first thought was, *Pilar.* God, what had she sent? She was famous for packaging up just about anything and putting it in the mail. Once she sent me a hookah when she was backpacking across Turkey. I was relieved to find she hadn't sent any hashish to go with it. A few years ago she tried to send me some of her mother's chicken noodle soup when I was sick. From her hometown in Ohio. She froze it, thinking it would somehow survive the journey. Instead it spilled and soaked through the Styrofoam peanuts and newspaper she'd wrapped the Tupperware bowl in. I'd been summoned to the post office and scolded by a very pissed-off postmaster.

But when I handed the card to the woman behind the counter, my thoughts shifted away from Pilar.

No. He didn't have our address. He didn't know we were here. However, I felt sick with each passing moment she was gone.

When she finally came back out with two fat orange envelopes tethered together with a rubber band, I caught my breath.

The film! I'd almost forgotten.

I wanted to open them right away, but Avery was restless and wanted to be carried. She was much too big for this now, but I had a hard time saying no when she held her arms up to me, waiting.

"Come on, monkey," I said, hoisting her onto my hip. She gripped my neck and my waist with her arms and legs. "Let's go home."

When we pulled up to the house, it seemed familiar now. Even welcoming in all its catastrophic glory. The front lights glowed warmly onto the sagging porch, and the twinkle lights I'd strung up instead of curtains in all of the windows seemed to welcome us home.

Avery was hungry, so I heated up some leftover macaroni and cheese for her while I put away all of the groceries for Thanksgiving. It was already Monday, so I figured I'd better start defrosting the turkey in the fridge so it would be thawed out by Thursday morning. Pilar would be here on Tuesday. She had told us not to bother coming to get her, that she'd rent a car and drive onto the ferry. She said she'd be here just after lunch. And once she got here, everything would be just as we'd planned.

It wasn't until I started digging through my purse for the receipts to tack on the fridge, a monument to my shrinking bank account—and a visual reminder/nudge to get the commission finished—that I remembered the photos.

I got Avery situated with a giant bowl of macaroni and cheese, some sliced apples, and a sippy cup of milk and sat down with her at the table.

"What are those, Mama?" she asked.

"Pictures," I said.

"Can I see?" she asked. We had a few photo albums, of course, mostly from before she was born. She loved to look at the photos of

Gus and me when we were still in college. The ones taken at our wedding and throughout our early years together. My mother had also shown her the albums she had of me when I was little, the ones in which I looked almost exactly like her. But almost all of the photos we had of Avery were digital, conjured with the click of a mouse or trapped inside the screens on our phones, save for a few favorites I had printed and framed.

The first three photos from the first bundle were black. I felt my heart sink. I had spent twenty dollars getting the photos developed; I started to calculate all the things those twenty dollars could have bought me. Mac and cheese, even the organic kind, was only $1.50 a box. The cheap kind was three for a dollar. If necessary, I could have gotten sixty boxes of mac and cheese for what I'd spent on these photos.

I tossed the duds on the kitchen table.

The next picture was taken on some sort of boardwalk, which disappeared into a point at the center of the photograph. Nothing terribly interesting was happening on the boardwalk itself. The souvenir shops and fried dough stands were all closed. There were puddles suggesting a recent rain. In the distance, you could see the skeletal figure of a roller coaster and Ferris wheel against a cloudy sky.

I flipped through the next several shots. This roll appeared to be a study in light: a series of photos from various angles on this same abandoned boardwalk. I imagined it was early morning. Just after dawn. And indeed, one shot aimed at the beach below the boardwalk showed a white sun rising over the gray horizon.

Time skipped ahead in the next photo, though it was impossible to tell how much. But suddenly the boardwalk was no longer deserted. A hunched-over man pushing an Italian ice cart looked directly at the camera in this one. The lines of his face were deep, his eyes set on whoever had taken this photo. It was an expression not of anger, however, but of mild curiosity. It made me wonder about who might elicit this reaction. Who was the person behind the camera?

There were a few out-of-focus photos after this one. A couple of the vendors and people milling about on the boardwalk. A man wearing silky shorts and tube socks, a wild head of hair, and a parrot perched on his shoulder. Another of a woman in an American flag bikini and roller skates. The roll had said 1976, the bicentennial.

Then time accelerated again. I watched as dusk descended and the lights came on. The crowd on the boardwalk went from families to teenagers to seedier types. And the photos became much, much more alive. Here: a silky shirt unbuttoned, bell-bottom pants. His skinny chest pushed out, a violent clavicle and knobby Adam's apple. Behind him, a doorway, a pale leg exposed. The rest of the woman was out of the frame. I flipped to the next photo, hoping this time the photographer had captured her.

I held my breath. And there it was, the one photo the photographer had been aiming for all day, the single image—that happy accident of light and timing—the result of both serendipity and patience.

Here: the man, his dark skin catching the shining lights from the shops. The girl. She couldn't be any older than eighteen. Blond hair parted down the middle and hanging straight. A tube top, a tight skirt, platform shoes like a child playing dress-up. It was a black-and-white photo, but I swear I could see the blue eye shadow on her heavy eyelids. The sparkle and sheen of her drugstore blush.

The man was holding onto her arm, his long fingers tight around her luminescent limb, proprietary. Behind them the carnival rides were a beautiful blur of motion and light. And the old man from the earlier photos, the same man with the Italian ice cart, was pushing it past them, but looking right at the couple. The same look, that mild curiosity he'd offered the photographer earlier, now given to this man. *Pimp* or *john,* I wondered as his black fingers dug into the milky, freckled flesh of this girl.

But this time, it was the girl who looked at the camera, at the photographer. And her eyes were imploring.

Help me, she seemed to say to the camera. To the photographer. *To me.*

"Mama?" Avery said, startling me. I'd nearly forgotten she was here. "Will Pilar bring me my fuzzy slippers?"

Avery had realized not long after we arrived that she'd left her favorite slippers at home. She'd made a list for Pilar of all those important, forgotten things.

"I'll remind her," I said, leaning in close to the photo.

"I maybe would like to have my night-light too," she said. At Gus's she had a night-light shaped like a crescent moon. "Just in case I get scared in the nighttime."

"Okay." I nodded.

I restlessly searched through the stack of photos from the next packet. They were also taken during what I now gathered must have been a trip to some run-down beach resort. If it was Maine, then Old Orchard Beach maybe? Most of the photos in the second packet were of a seagull. The photographer had seemingly tracked this bird in its flight, as it scavenged the beach. As it soared and swooped along the coastline. One photo caught a little boy chasing the bird, arms flailing. None of the images was spectacular, memorable, though. None of them had that quality of the one of the prostitute. Had it been a fluke? A lucky snap of the shutter?

But then I got to the last photo and gasped. In it, the seagull had something in its mouth and the boy stood, mouth open in horror. It was another bird, a smaller bird, its neck broken, its wings dragging on the sand. The little boy's face was filled with anguish even as his mother, in a wide-brimmed hat, reached for him. He could not be touched.

Epitaphs and Prophecies. I had to Google *epitaph*—it was one of those words I thought I knew until I tried to remember the definition. Was it one of those phrases or quotes at the beginning of a book? No. That was *epigraph. Epigrams* were satirical statements. An *epithet* was a term of contempt. *Effigy? Elegy? Eulogy.* So many *e* words I thought I knew.

But an *epitaph* is an inscription, something written after some-one has died. In memorial. In remembrance. *In remembrance,* I thought as I studied the terror on the young hooker's face, the man's long, dirty nails pressing into her flesh. As the seagull snapped the neck of its young prey. And the world looked on.

When Avery fell asleep that night, I returned to the boxes of film and carefully lifted out each canister, lining them up on my counter in date order. I calculated what it would cost to get all of the photos developed, and sighed. There were forty-eight rolls of film left. That would cost almost five hundred dollars. Five hun-dred dollars for what, in all likelihood, was mostly washed-out, overexposed or underexposed prints never meant to be seen. But then why had the photographer bothered keeping the rolls of film at all? And were these photos *Epitaphs* or *Prophecies?* And what did that even mean? Five hundred dollars. I shook my head.

I had offered to pay Pilar rent, and she'd scoffed. The idea of living rent-free for four months had seemed like such a gift I hadn't thought about how quickly my savings would dwindle. Getting some random person's snapshots developed was not in the budget.

Still. I picked up the photo I had set aside, the one with the young woman, terror in her eyes, the man gripping her arm, and I felt my heart knock hard in my chest.

Using the counter for my laptop and a small printer/scanner I'd scored when Gus's work upgraded, I had set up a makeshift office in the kitchen. I grabbed the photo and put it on the scan-ner, scanned it in, and pulled it into Photoshop, zooming in so it filled the screen.

In art school, I had only taken a couple of units of photogra-phy, including a class on female photographers: Imogen Cun-ningham, Diane Arbus, Sally Mann. Cindy Sherman and Mary Ellen Mark. This photo could easily be a part of Mark's oeuvre. This quiet violence. It, like Mark's work, felt like the exposure of an open wound.

I clicked PRINT and watched as a larger version of the snap-shot in my hand emerged from the printer. I reached for the roll of blue painter's tape left over from painting Avery's room and brought the photo to my studio, where I taped it to the wall.

I felt an odd, yet familiar, urgency. Like a vague but undeni-able itch. An impulse. It had been so long since I'd felt this way, it scared me a little. I studied the prostitute's face, and she mine.

My father had found a bunch of my old canvases from high school in the garage and offered them to me before we left New Hampshire. They weren't in terrific shape, but they were all I had. I chose the largest one, pulled the birches painting off the easel, turning it to face the wall, and propped the blank canvas up. I got out my palette and dug through my stash of paints, trying to rec-ollect the colors. For years, this was how I had seen things: first the image and then the slow deconstruction, my mind breaking down the image not into shapes, but into hues. Some artists focus on the architecture, seeing their vision in shapes: a cylinder here, the smooth oval and rigid rectangle there. But my mind had al-ways perceived what it saw in individual colors. Leaves of green gray illuminated with a cadmium spray of sunlight. Dark woods, birches outlined in dioxazine mauve against an ultramarine sky. And the entrance to those woods, green umber leading to the in-evitable bone black. But when I reached for the right brush, the one to begin, I felt paralyzed. Unable, even, to sketch.

Bone Black

*B*lack *first.*
Then *a solitary source of light to illuminate the wreckage.*

The black should be easy, the darkness obvious. But there are too many options: carbon black, antimony black, bloodstone, manganese. Cobalt black, ivory black, galena, mars. There are a thousand shades of dark. An infinity of origins, an endlessness of hues.

The very first black pigment was made from charcoal. Oil, wood, vine clippings, the pits of fruit partially burned, carbonized, then ground with mortar and pestle. Carbon and ash.

I imagine what I might burn.

Bone black was made from the burning of bones. Ivory black from grinding of charred ivory, the tusks and teeth of hunted beasts preserved in Rembrandt's sitters' painted cloaks.

The blackest black known, however, is called Vantablack. The only blacker black is found in the colorless abyss of a black hole. "It's thinner than a coat of paint and rests on the liminal edge between an imagined thing and an actual one," artist Anish Kapoor says. It does not yet come in a tube, will not rest on palette or brush.

This blackest black is made of an arrangement of carbon nano tubes, each one, one ten-thousandth the width of a human hair. Kapoor compares this configuration to a forest of impossibly tall and impossibly thin trees, a forest so dense that when light enters it becomes trapped.

Here is the black I need, this ruthless forest, this light-sucking dusk.

Vigil

Avery watched out the window for Pilar all afternoon on the Tuesday before Thanksgiving. Perched on the sill in a ratty old nightgown she wouldn't let me throw away, she pressed her face against the glass. She wouldn't even come to the table for lunch, and so rather than fight it, I made her some cinnamon toast and brought it to her in a napkin. A sippy cup of orange juice. And she kept vigil.

Outside, the sky was dark, the clouds overhead ominous. And the waves seemed even more volatile than usual. I wondered if the following months would be as bleak as this, and at what point it would start to seem more *cruelty* than *novelty*.

"Does it snow here?" Avery asked.

"I think so," I said.

"Can we go sledding like at Poppy's?" she asked. "With the silver saucer?"

"If we can find a hill." The island was a whopping half mile in diameter. And while there were certainly cliffs, I had yet to see anything resembling a sledable hill.

Pilar showed up just as Avery finished her toast, the floor beneath her sprinkled with cinnamon and sugar. "She's here!" she screamed and jumped down off the back of the couch to run for the door.

"Put some shoes on," I hollered after her, but she ignored me and bounded through the door out into that dreary day, barefoot.

Pilar's rental car was loaded down with suitcases and a bunch of shopping bags she'd apparently gotten in town after arriving at the airport. She looked like a bag lady hobbling up the drive as Avery ran to greet her.

She looked different than the last time I'd seen her, in that way people do when you're used to seeing them every day then suddenly don't. Her mangled bangs had already grown out and been trimmed in a straighter line. All of her looked a bit more put together, as a matter of fact. The silver hoop she usually wore in her nose was replaced with a much more subdued diamond stud. Her glasses were new too, not of the thrift store caliber she'd been wearing. They looked *expensive*. Something about these minor changes was a bit disconcerting, disorienting even, but it was still Pilar. And I couldn't believe how happy I was to see another adult. She was *here*.

"Here," she said, off-loading three bags and her suitcase and running back to the car for more groceries and toiletries and one paper bag that seemed to be moving.

"Lobsters!" she said. "For dinner tonight."

I hugged her, smelling the same old stinky patchouli smell of her, and wanted to cry in relief. I smiled and helped her carry everything into the house.

"How long do you have the rental car?" I asked.

"Oh, as long as I need it," she said, shrugging. She squatted down next to Avery. "Show me your room?"

I followed behind them as they navigated the stairs.

"Crap," Pilar said. "I forgot how bad these were. You can't live with stairs like this. One of you will break your neck!"

"It's not a big deal," I said. "We're careful." I had taught Avery how to go down the stairs on her tush, the way she'd first learned to go down the stairs at my parents' house when she was a toddler.

"Well, I'm calling somebody today. There's got to be someone on the island who can shore these up, at least until I can get a contractor out here."

Pilar stood in the doorway to Avery's room and covered her mouth with her hand.

I had wanted her to do this. I had imagined her reaction. In a way, this room was as much for Pilar as it had been for Avery. I'd been buying this moment with every stroke of my brush.

I had painted the floors, as per Avery's request, a cerulean blue; cirrus clouds floated across the floor in delicate wisps. The violet walls and forest green crown molding and ceiling were like something out of a dream. I'd brought a plain white comforter from home, which, in this room, became the clean white puff of a cloud.

Pilar *oohed* and *ahhed* as Avery showed her every corner of the room.

"Here's the best part," I said, going to the window and pulling down the blackout roller shade I'd installed so Avery didn't get up at the crack of dawn every morning. "Close the door, Av."

The room was now in total darkness, except for the constellation of stars on the floor. I'd meticulously painted the Milky Way in glow-in-the-dark paint. It was wonderfully, deliciously disorienting to be in this room at night. Like being transported into space.

"It's like *The Little Prince*," Pilar said, just as I knew she would. "I love it. Avery, I want to live here with you. Can I come live here with you?"

That night we gorged ourselves on lobsters, went through two bottles of wine. Pilar had brought enough lobsters for us to each have three. But Avery was too afraid to try them, and it suddenly felt wasteful, six lobsters giving their lives for us.

"We can get the meat out, freeze it," Pilar said, reading my mind.

I nodded.

After dinner we lay on the two lumpy couches in the living room, our stomachs distended from the overindulgence. Avery fell asleep with her head on my lap while Pilar and I stayed up talking; she hadn't wanted to go upstairs and miss out on any of the conversation.

"So you don't know who owned the house before?" I asked.

"It was in probate for years. Why?" she asked, digging into the wheel of Brie she'd brought and a box of Ritz Crackers.

"I found something," I said.

"What's that?"

For just a moment I hesitated. The film, the girl in the photo. The boy staring in horror at the seagull. I hadn't told a soul about them. It was like some odd secret, and for some reason, it felt like I was breaking a promise. My stomach turned.

"In the basement," I continued.

"Like a *body* or something?" she said, eyes wide. "Spill."

"I found some film. A whole bunch of undeveloped rolls."

"That's strange," she said.

She was wearing the pajamas I had given her for Christmas the year before, the red flannel ones with the black Scottie dogs all over them. She looked ten instead of thirty-three.

"I actually sent a couple of rolls off to get developed."

"Cool," she said. "What are they pictures of?"

I knew words wouldn't do justice to that one photo.

"Are they *naked* pictures?" she asked, one perfectly plucked eyebrow rising upward.

And I thought of the woman, how exposed she was. His dark fingers pressing into her milky flesh.

"No," I said, forcing a laugh. "Just snapshots. Vacation pictures."

"Huh," she said. "They must have belonged to whoever owned the house."

"Maybe," I said, feeling strangely relieved she wasn't demanding to see the photos.

"Are you going to get the rest developed?"

I shrugged again. I knew financially it wasn't possible, but I never brought up money with Pilar anymore.

It used to be we shared our poverty. We lamented *together*. As students, we stood in line at the food bank on Saturday mornings and got the dusty castoffs from other people's cupboards, the stale generic Froot Loops and dented cans of wax beans and sweet corn. We used the one bank that offered five dollars if you had to wait longer than five minutes in line, telling the little old ladies in front of us to take their time. We maxed out our credit cards on cash advances to pay the rent. Got our furniture and clothes and books from thrift stores and Dumpsters. But things were different now, whether we wanted them to be or not.

"When is Gus coming?" Pilar asked.

"Next weekend, I hope."

"And when are you going to take him back?" she asked.

"When are *you* going to stop asking that question?"

"When you're back together. This is the stupidest breakup in the history of breakups. Just so you know."

I sighed. I looked toward the window, but instead of seeing the ocean, I only saw myself reflected back.

I shook my head. "I don't want to talk about Gus anymore."

Pilar reached out for my hand. I studied the familiar, ropey veins on the back of her hand, the collection of silver rings, a large lapis lazuli stone nestled into a new one.

"Let me see what you're working on," she said, leaping to her feet and brushing the Ritz Cracker crumbs off of her.

We went to the dining room, where I had set up shop. It was a primitive studio, but Pilar noticed the windows right away.

"This is the room I would have picked too," she said. She walked around the perimeter, her fingers grazing the rolling metal cart I'd found in the basement where I kept all of my paints, touched the tips of the brushes. She looked up and saw the photo I'd blown up.

"Whose is this? Diane Arbus?" she asked.

It both surprised me and didn't surprise me at all she thought a professional had taken it. I thought about the film, about all of those rolls, like tiny eggs in a nest waiting to be hatched.

"It's from one of the rolls I found," I said.

"Wow! It's incredible," she said. "There's this beautiful violence to it. It could be an Arbus. Wait, she was sixties not seventies, right? Maybe Mary Ellen Mark?" She nodded. "Wow."

I shrugged.

She reached into her pocket for her phone and held it up to the photo.

"What are you doing?" I asked, heat rising to my ears. The photo suddenly felt strangely private.

"Nothing," she said. "It's just so cool. Imagine what other photos there might be."

I felt queasy.

"Now show me what you're working on," she said, squeezing my hand.

I thought about that blank canvas, the one I'd stared at for hours the other night. Recalled that crippling hesitation, that fear, which followed the first rush of creative energy. And I wondered if that impulse would ever return.

I motioned toward the birches, shaking my head.

"This one is good, Wynnie. Really good," she lied.

"Yeah," I said. "I think Ginger will like it."

Giving Thanks

"So who lives next door?" I asked. "In the mansion?"
"I don't know," Pilar said.

It was Wednesday, and we were busy in the kitchen prepping everything for Thanksgiving dinner the next day. She and I had gone through this ritual dozens of times. While she rolled out dough for the pies at the kitchen table, I made the stuffing, Avery's favorite broccoli and cheese casserole, the sweet potatoes.

"Have you gone over there yet?" she asked.

"You mean and knocked or something?"

"Yeah."

She had a red bandana on her hair. We must look like Lucy and Ethel, I thought. Wasn't there an episode like this?

"Have you *seen* that place?" I asked, pulling the hot sweet potatoes from the oven, where they had been roasting for over an hour. The room smelled sweet. "I wouldn't be surprised if there were armed guards."

"Maybe it's a celebrity," she said, her eyes wide. "Or like a famous author or something. We should go. We should totally go."

Pilar has always been the brave one, the one with the balls. In college she was the one who initiated the more daring adventures. And Gus and I had always gone happily along for the ride. When she was experimenting with performance art, I was there for her when she needed a body. Someone to sit still as a stone in the middle of a quiet gallery, the one she could dress up or splatter with paint. An empty canvas. But she was the color, the vibrancy. Not much had changed over the years.

"Here," she said, pulling the apple pie that had been cooling on the counter into her flour-dusted arms. "We'll just bring this over. Introduce ourselves."

I rolled my eyes even as I knew I had no choice in the matter.

"What if it's some sort of recluse, somebody who just wants to be left alone?"

"Then he shouldn't come to the door."

"What if it's some crazy lunatic with a shotgun?" I said.

She shrugged again. "I suppose anything's possible."

And she was right. Anything *was* possible. I was the kind of person who stood looking at closed doors. Pilar was the one who would pick the lock, or just simply knock it down.

We hoped the sight of Avery, this doe-eyed child, might be enough to make us seem harmless. (As if two women in aprons and kerchiefs might somehow be threatening.)

"Is that a path?" she asked, motioning to the dark entrance to the woods separating the two properties.

"I don't know," I said, shaking my head.

Pilar didn't know the details of what happened to me, but she knew enough. She nodded at the realization and gestured to the rocky cliff. "Let's go this way instead?"

"Yeah," I said, grateful. "There's sea glass on the beach."

Avery led the way down the rocky cliff, more sure-footed now, knowing the best places to jump and climb and land. At the bottom, as if the sea had delivered them especially for us, were literally hundreds of bits of sea glass. We set the pie down and filled our pockets.

When we'd raked the enormous swath of sand for cobalt and emerald bits, Pilar grabbed the pie and made for the stairs that led up to the house.

The front yard was clearly taken care of, though I hadn't yet heard any evidence of this, no lawnmowers or leaf blowers. This was the kind of front yard upon which you'd expect handsome prep school boys to play football, little blond girls in white dresses to run barefoot. We slowly walked up the pathway. I looked at Pilar to see if she was nervous, but she was smiling like some sort of 1950s housewife with flour in her hair and a steaming pie in her arms. Avery skipped behind, and I wondered if I should have changed her into something less crazy. Since we'd gotten here, since she wasn't in school, I'd been letting her dress herself. Today she had on red, white, and blue striped tights and a tattered nightgown. White cowboy boots and a purple pair of mittens.

There were two giant pots of orange and yellow mums on either side of the door and a harvesty-looking wreath made of silk leaves hanging on the enormous front door.

I didn't see any cars, but I also didn't see any sort of driveway. I suppose it was around the back. Or, perhaps, underground. I'd read when Bill Gates designed his mansion in Washington, he'd planned an underground parking garage for ten cars.

Pilar took the broad porch steps a couple at a time and without hesitation rang the doorbell. When no one answered, she moved toward the closest window and pressed her face against the glass, trying to peer in. Avery followed, mimicking her, and my heart started to race.

"*Guys*," I reprimanded, just as the door swung open.

The man at the door looked to be about sixty. Tall and fit, wearing soft khaki pants and a crisp white button-down shirt rolled up at the sleeves. I noted his expensive leather boat shoes, worn without socks despite the chill. He had a full head of silver hair, which was long enough to touch that starched collar. Darkrimmed glasses.

Distinguished is the word most people would use. *Monied* would be my word of choice. As if money were something that could happen to you.

"Hi!" Pilar said, as effervescent as a shaken soda.

"Hi!" Avery echoed.

The man smiled dimly.

"We're your new neighbors," Pilar said. "I bought the house next door. My name is Pilar. This is Wyn. And *this,*" she said, as if she were presenting a gift, "is Avery."

"Oh," the man said. "Next door?"

"Yes," Pilar said. "The one on the other side of those trees."

The man nodded. *What an odd man,* I thought.

"We brought you a pie," I said dumbly. Silences like this always made me uncomfortable.

Pilar thrust the pie toward him, and he took it awkwardly.

"Who's there?" a voice said behind him, and he grimaced a little.

A woman came to his side. She too smelled of money. Of private school and legacies. Blond hair perfectly coiffed. A long, elegant neck that held the head upon it with confidence, arrogance. She wore an outfit not so different from the man's, a silky white button-down blouse and a knee-length khaki skirt. They looked like they belonged in a catalog.

"Who is it?" she said, but she wasn't asking him, rather us. Demanding for us to make ourselves known.

"They bought the house next door," he said, his voice all grit and grumble.

The woman's eyebrows raised almost imperceptibly, perhaps a Botox-induced restraint.

"Whatever for?" she asked.

"I'm an artist," Pilar said, her smile wide. "I plan to come here to work. Wyn is a painter too."

"We brought pie," I said dumbly. "For Thanksgiving tomorrow." I didn't know what was so disconcerting to me about this couple. I might have fared better facing a loaded shotgun.

"That place has been vacant for thirty years," the woman said, almost defensively.

"Thirty-*five,*" Pilar corrected. "Do you happen to know who lived there? Have you been here that long?"

"Thank you for the pie," the man said then. I'd almost forgotten he was there. "It looks delicious."

The woman uncrossed her thin arms, and her diamond tennis bracelet slipped down her arm to her bony wrist. "There are rats over there. I hope you plan to have an exterminator come in," the woman said, and, with that, shut the door in our faces.

"Happy Thanksgiving!" Pilar said to the closed door. And as we walked back down the steps, she muttered, "*Assholes.*"

"Assholes, assholes, assholes," Avery said, skipping down the stairs, and I didn't bother to correct her.

On Thanksgiving morning, I woke up in a cold sweat, trembling. Breathless. Every bone in my body felt rattled, but I couldn't hold onto the dream long enough to understand why. I disentangled myself from the twisted sheets and took several deep breaths, trying to regain my footing in this world, having been shaken to the core in my dream one.

But just as my nerves started to settle, Pilar's phone rang, the old-fashioned ringtone jangling me loose again.

Pilar's voice murmured softly downstairs.

I pulled on my robe and shoved my feet in my favorite, ratty pair of slippers and, after peering into Avery's room and seeing her curled up like a bug in her bed, headed down the stairs.

Pilar was in the kitchen, and the turkey sat naked and goose pimply in a roasting pan on the counter. She had the phone cradled between her ear and her shoulder as she opened one drawer after the next.

"Baster?" she mouthed.

I shook my head.

"Yes," she said. "But I need at least a few months. When would all of this happen?"

I made myself a cup of coffee, noting it was not the generic coffee I had bought in a giant tub at Walmart, but rather something in a tiny brown bag with a handmade label. Something Pilar must have brought with her.

"Okay. No, no. I am so excited. I just don't want to overcommit."

She hung up the phone and she stood, stunned, at the counter. "Who was that?" I asked.

"My manager. The National Gallery wants a piece."

"*What?*" I asked.

I remembered going to DC on a high school field trip, standing at the National Gallery looking at Van Gogh's sunflowers, at Botticelli's *Venus and Mars,* and feeling like I might burst into tears. The idea that Pilar's work would hang on these same walls, in this virtual cathedral of great works, seemed almost incomprehensible.

"It would be part of a traveling show, starting at the National Gallery. With three other contemporary portrait artists."

"Oh my God," I said.

Pilar's eyes were filled with tears. I went to her and grabbed her hands.

"Breathe," I said.

Pilar was prone to anxiety attacks. Even when news was good, *especially* when news was good, she sometimes got overwhelmed. It was as if a surge of any sort of energy would short-circuit her. I understood this feeling, although I never shared that with her. Instead, I just helped to talk her through it.

"Sit," I said, and put her in a chair.

I poured a glass of water from the filtered pitcher in the fridge. "Drink this. All of it."

My mind spun. *The National Gallery.*

I had watched Pilar grow as an artist like a mother watches her child develop from a fumbling toddler into a graceful dancer. When we met at art school, she was obsessed with watercolor pencils. It was the only medium she wanted anything to do with. She begrudgingly learned how to use oils and acrylics, how to manage the impulses she had. How to redirect them depending on the media. I, on the other hand, hungrily wanted to try everything. My high school had been ill-equipped to handle the handful of aspiring artists who walked the halls. My mother's art room was a makeshift classroom with poor light. There was no room in the budget for supplies, and so the supply closet was filled with donated items: half-used Cray-Pas, crusty jars of tempera, brushes that had seen better days. It's a wonder any of us persisted. Thankfully, my mother was an enthusiastic teacher who taught us how to make art out of nothing. We recycled magazines and turned trash into sculptures. My mom and dad supplemented my own personal stash as best they could, though I went through the boxes of pastels and sticks of charcoal and tubes of paint faster than they could afford to replenish them. When I got to art school it was as if I hadn't eaten, and somebody had brought me to an all you can eat buffet. I was gluttonous. My early paintings were almost three-dimensional with the gobs and gobs of paint I piled on. After school, I had gone back to leaner paintings. One could track my entire life in those paintings, not by the subject matter but by the materials used to create them, my poverty revealed in the thin colored pencil drawings, the years with Gus defined by the acrylics that could be purchased with a coupon at Michaels, the rare oil paintings usually following holidays (birthdays and Christmases) when those who loved me spoiled me with tubes of paint.

"You okay?" I asked.

Pilar nodded. "I'm pathetic."

I shook my head. I knew all too well how much a body could defy you.

"I think you're going to need to get used to this," I said. "Seriously."

She smiled at me and grabbed my hand.

"So listen," she said, her mouth twitching, "here's the crappy thing. I'm actually going to have to fly down to DC to meet with the people at the National Gallery."

"When?" I asked.

"Tomorrow."

"Tomorrow?" I said, disappointment like a lead sinker in my belly.

"I have a feeling I'm going to be down there for a while. I'm sorry," she said, sighing, squeezing my hand. "I know you really need a friend right now, and I feel like I am doing a really shitty job."

I shook my head even as tears stung my eyes. "No," I said, forcing myself to laugh, to brush her words away with the dismissive flick of my wrist. "This is amazing news. You have to go."

"I promise I'll make it as quick as I can."

We spent the next several hours in the kitchen quietly preparing a feast fit for a dozen people instead of just the three of us. I was grateful for the distraction, and by the time the turkey was in the oven, the disappointment of Pilar's impending departure had lost its sharp edges.

We drank the very good wine Pilar had been keeping in her trunk. Avery made us paper place mats with turkey drawings of her tiny hands, and we held hands at the dining room table as we did every year, reciting the list of things we were grateful for.

"I am grateful for my best friend, Wynnie," Pilar said, squeezing my hand. "Who loves me warts and all."

I smiled.

"And," she added, "I am grateful I get to spend Thanksgiving with my other best friend, Avery, who is the smartest, sweetest, and sassiest girl I know."

Avery giggled. Pilar looked at me to go next.

"I am grateful to this turkey for giving up his life so we can eat him for dinner," I said, nudging Avery, and she giggled some more. I took a deep breath. I needed Pilar to know it was okay, that I understood what an opportunity this was for her. "And I am grateful I have a best friend who is always there for me, even when she's far away."

"Thick or thin, baby," Pilar said, raising her glass and clinking it against mine.

"Your turn," I whispered to Avery.

Avery put her hands up in prayer. I have no idea where she learned this. She took on a somber tone. "I am grateful for this stupid turkey who got himself killed for our dinner. I am thankful for my best friend Pilar, who brings me lobsters and my fuzzy slippers. And I am thankful for Mommy for painting my room and for taking care of me."

I felt my chest swell.

"And I am thankful for my daddy, who carries me when my legs get tired walking home from school. The end."

"The end," Pilar and I said in unison.

We ate too much, drank too much, and left the dishes in the sink. After Avery went to bed, Pilar pulled out a joint and we smoked it quietly in the kitchen with the back door open to the cold November air.

"I'm glad you're here," I said.

"Me too," she said, stretching, vertebrae cracking like a handful of Pop Pop Snappers. "I can't believe I have to leave again tomorrow already."

"When do you think you'll be back?" I asked, feeling a bit panicky at the prospect of another week out here alone.

"I'm not sure," she said. "I have this DC trip, but my manager also wants me to meet a collector in the Netherlands. It could mean a really big sale. Realistically, I'm thinking New Year's? I can try to be back by New Year's Eve?"

The New Year was over a month away. By then we might already have heard from the court about a retrial. My stomach knotted.

"Have you heard anything from your lawyer?" Pilar asked again as if she were reading my mind.

"I've been trying not to think about it, Pill."

What happened with Robby Rousseau wasn't something I talked about with her, with anyone, ever. After the initial explanation for the scars I'd given her fifteen years ago, Robby Rousseau had not really come up as a topic of conversation again.

"I know you don't want to talk about this," Pilar started. "But if he goes back to trial, I can be there. I want to be there for you."

Really? She couldn't even be here now, when my world was

starting to fall down all around me. I shook my head. "Don't be stupid. I don't even think *I'd* go."

Her eyes widened, and she smiled sadly. "Well, could you at least write a letter or something? There's got to be something you can do without actually being in the same room with that asshole."

I winced.

And I recalled those weeks sitting in the courtroom as the lawyers sparred and parried while I sat, silently staring out the window at the snow falling. I hadn't spoken then except when I was forced to. Not a word. I was a keeper of promises. A curator of secrets.

Larry had already told my parents that in the unlikely event a retrial was granted I would have to testify. I was thirteen years old then, traumatized. But now I was a grown woman. There were twenty years between that day and me. This is what the jury would see.

But Larry and my parents didn't know the truth. And they would never, ever understand if I tried to explain.

"You're right. I really *don't* want to talk about it," I said, going to close the back door, shivering in the cold. "Let's talk about the National Gallery instead. Let's talk about how you are going to be an internationally famous painter." *Please, let's talk about anything but this.*

When my phone rang, I startled. Trembling, I glanced at the screen. Ginger Hardy. My client in Aspen, the one waiting on the commission.

"Happy Thanksgiving!" her familiar, nasally voice chirped. "I am so sorry to bother you on a holiday. But listen, Bob Chatham, my husband's friend, the art publisher? We've actually invited him and his wife out to the chalet for a ski weekend in January. And I was thinking, if you were able to get the painting to me by then, if they saw your work in person, there's no way they wouldn't go for it. We're talking *Ikea*."

I was kind of stoned. I wasn't sure I was hearing her right.

"Ikea?"

"*Ikea,*" she said. "I told him all about you, and he's excited to see the painting. I have a good feeling about this, Wyn."

Ikea. I tried to imagine my birches mass-produced, hanging in the staged rooms of Ikea. Price tags hanging from the modular furniture, drapes pulled across imaginary windows. Faucets that drew no water.

"Of course, the compensation would be significant," she said.

I thought about what I would do if suddenly I had a windfall of money. What would it be like to not worry, for once, every time I opened my wallet? To release that albatross that clung to my neck? The burden of it was as familiar as the weight of my own arms. What would it be like to be able to give Avery everything she wanted, needed? For Gus not to have to break his back at the sign shop?

Gus. What would he think of this?

I knew exactly what he'd think of this. That I was selling my soul. To some Swedish corporation. That by doing this, my work became no better than a $4.95 plate of Swedish meatballs served up on a conveyor belt.

"Do you think you'd be able to get it done by then?"

"Sure," I said. "I mean, of course."

Later that night, still buzzing from too much wine and contemplative from the weed, I crawled out of bed, tiptoed past Pilar and Avery's rooms to work on the tree painting with a bowl of heated-up mashed potatoes and gravy to fuel me.

The painting was huge. Normally, I kept the commissions to a manageable size, 11 x 14, 16 x 20. But this one needed to be made for a room Ginger had described as *cavernous,* with cathedral ceilings, I imagined. It had barely fit in the trunk of my car. The canvas alone cost me nearly half of the deposit she gave me. And the other half was long, long gone.

I laid out the swatches next to my palette and began to mix the colors, feeling increasingly pissed off with every brush stroke.

Umber, sage. I imagined her bragging about it to her friends: "Yes, this is an original piece. I told the artist, *It needs to match the Chesterfield sofa, the Bandhini throw pillows.*"

Still, I painted. If I didn't paint, I wouldn't be able to buy groceries. To eat. I couldn't even think about Ikea; I needed to think about getting this done. If I could just finish, then I could get my check. I could send this off to Ginger to show the Ikea people. It could change everything.

But as I worked, I felt the eyes of the woman in the photograph staring at me. Of course, she wasn't really looking at me. She was looking at the photographer, whoever had captured this private moment.

Still, they seemed to implore me. And I felt queasy as I painted the happy birches, the legion of stiff soldiers standing guard in their tiny rows. I blamed the wine. The weed. The mashed potatoes. The trees themselves. I blamed Pilar getting a show at the National Gallery. I blamed Gus for carrying Avery when I made her walk. I blamed Robby Rousseau. And I blamed myself.

Inquiry

" So you don't remember if Robby was at the school still or if he had already left with his brother?"

"Miss Davies. I know this is difficult. But we are trying to establish at what point he began to follow you. And when you became aware you were not alone."

"Can we get you some water? Are you thirsty?"

"Okay. So you were late leaving school, and you decided to take the shortcut across the lower playing fields and through the woods to your parents' home. You were unaware you were being followed at this point."

"A simple yes or no will suffice, Miss Davies."

"Miss Davies?"

In Remembrance

Avery held onto Pilar's legs as she tried to make her way out to the rental car the next morning. Inside the house, the repairmen were already working away on the list of items Pilar had noted needed fixing: the downstairs toilet, the broken, dripping faucet in the kitchen.

"I'm sorry, the carpenter guy I want to do the stairs is on vacation," she said. "When I get back, we'll tackle the rest."

"Are you coming for Christmas?" Avery asked as Pilar picked her up and squeezed her. "Will you bring me something from your trip?"

"Av," I said. "Don't be rude."

"I won't be back until New Year's Eve, but I promise I will bring you lots and lots of presents."

"Something smells spoiled," I said, pinching my nose with my fingers.

I didn't remind Avery she'd be with Gus then. He would have her from Christmas until the second week of January. I was trying not to think about it myself.

"Love you, honey," Pilar said, setting Avery down and hugging me. She was wearing a vintage coat I remembered her finding on one of our thrifting trips. It was made for a man, a massive shearling coat in perfect condition. But peeking out from underneath the thrift store find was a new pair of boots. Burberry riding boots. Ones we'd ogled over in a *Vogue* magazine in the Planned Parenthood waiting room earlier in the fall when she came with me for my annual exam.

"Have a safe trip," I said, hugging her and kissing her cheek.

"Good luck with Gus next weekend," she said.

I nodded. God, Gus would be here in just a week. I missed him. A lot. But I also worried having him here would likely tear the delicate scab starting to form on that wound.

After we said our lengthy, tearful good-byes, we went back inside and I made potato pancakes for Avery from the leftover mashed potatoes. Pilar had gotten up before the rest of us and cleaned the kitchen so the workers could get to the sink. I was grateful now, as my hangover set in, not to have to deal with the dishes. I was searching the counter for the spatula when I noticed an envelope sitting on top of the new iPad she'd brought. Inside was a note: "Thank you for such a lovely visit. Love you both so much. Let Hank know what needs to be fixed. Here's his number. He'll just bill me later. And this is for anything else that pops up." Five crisp one-hundred-dollar bills fell on the table. I felt guilty, but with this, I wouldn't have to touch my checking account for at least a couple of weeks.

"What are we doing today, Mama?" Avery asked, shoveling the pancakes into her mouth.

Normally on the day after Thanksgiving we'd go into the city to look at the lights. To see the tree at Rockefeller Center. To gaze in the windows at all of the beautiful Christmas displays.

Upstairs, I heard the banging and clanging of pipes, the scratchy music of the workers' radio. Not good for my headache.

"Why don't we go into town," I said.

"Can I send a letter to Daddy?"

"Sure."

I found the stack of photo envelopes the guy at the drugstore had given me, and while I was tempted to send them all off, I filled out only two more of them with our address and my debit card info. We drove into town, and at the post office, I mailed two rolls of film (these both dated 8/15/76) and taught Avery how to open the mailbox. I watched her as she concentrated on the little dial like a thief cracking a safe.

"Look!" she said, reaching her tiny arm into the deep recesses of the box. "It's from Daddy!"

There were two envelopes inside, both of them from Gus. One was for me and one was for Avery. Mine had a child support check with a sticky note. "A little extra here for the holidays." Avery's was filled with My Little Pony sticker sheets. A photo of him standing with his arms outstretched. On the back in Sharpie, it said, "This is a hug."

It made me angry for some reason. All of it. He was making this so difficult. I used to scoff at the idea of couples staying together for their children, living out their miserable lives together simply to appease their bratty kids. But every time he did something like this, I felt like I was betraying Avery. Depriving Avery. Gus was a great dad. Probably one of the best. And because I was selfish and bitter, I had taken this away from my daughter. He made me hate myself without even trying.

"When is Daddy coming?" Avery asked when I tucked her into bed later that night.

"Soon, baby." Avery's concept of time was still so nebulous. Days of the week meant almost nothing to her. The passage of weeks could be years as far as she was concerned. I wondered sometimes at what point children began to live within the realm of time. She seemed to exist above it, beyond it. *Tomorrow* was the only thing she could understand. Even *yesterday* was sometimes too hard to grasp.

"I haven't seen him forever," she said.

And so I didn't correct her, tell her it had only been a few weeks. That it felt like forever to me too.

The next batch of photos came the day before Gus was set to arrive. Avery and I had taken the walking ferry into the city to pick up a few things for his visit and stopped by the post office on our way home. I waited to look at the photos until we got back to the house, savoring the anticipation. I knew it would be a while before I could dish out any more money to get additional rolls of film developed. This was an extravagance. A luxury. And if the last batch was any indication, a good number of these would be either under or overexposed. And so I delayed looking at them for as long as I could stand.

Avery and I ate grilled cheese sandwiches made with the thick, delicious bread Pilar had picked up at the health food store in Portland, with creamy Havarti cheese and sweet pears inside like some sort of decadent treat. Pilar had spoiled us. I'd held onto Gus's check rather than cashing it, though. It was safer in my wallet than in the bank. I'd need to save it for Christmas presents.

While Avery played quietly upstairs, I made a cup of tea, still enjoying the suspense. When the tea had finally steeped, I opened the envelope and shook the stack of photos out into my hand.

Both rolls appeared to have been taken in a parking lot somewhere, outside of a Shaw's grocery store. A 1970s Plymouth was at the forefront of the first photo, and leaning against the hood of the car was a teenage couple. The boy was sitting on the car and had his hands wrapped around the waist of the girl, who wore a striped tube top. She teetered on a pair of platform heels, and his knees seemed to trap her on either side of her skinny legs.

With only a cursory glance, it would look like a couple of teenagers maybe playing hooky to make out. But as I leaned closer, I could see that while you couldn't discern the details of her face, you *could* see she was pulling away. Resisting. But his hands were big, encircling her waist. And she couldn't leave. I held my breath as I looked at the next photos in the stack. Each photo was of the same couple, in each one her resistance becoming more and more clear until the struggle was both obvious and futile. But while those photos were raw, scary, that first one was the most heartbreaking. Because in it, you could see the beginnings of her body's defiance. The impulse, the urge. She was on the precipice of flight, but seemed to know as soon as she moved, he would squeeze tighter; that she was trapped.

I scanned and blew this one up as well, hanging it next to the photo of the prostitute.

And after I checked to make sure Avery was sleeping, I returned to my makeshift studio and pulled out the painting of the birches. *Ikea,* I thought. But my eyes were drawn to the two photographs hanging on the wall.

"What?" I said to the prostitute whose imploring gaze haunted me, to the teenager with panic in her eyes. "What do you *want?*"

Inquiry

"I don't know what you want from me."

I knew exactly what they wanted from me. They wanted to travel with me across the playing fields, they wanted to hold my beating heart in their hands. They wanted to feel the terror that made me fear my bowels might release as I peered at the woods before me, and at the car still idling at the road. To be trapped with me. They wanted to be me. In order to believe me.

"Why don't we talk about what happened after. Maybe that would be easier?"

"Okay."

"How did you get out of the woods? After?"

"I walked."

"But you had been hurt."

"I didn't feel anything."

I felt everything. I felt the cold, damp grass against my bare ankles. I felt the stinging, throbbing, wetness, bleeding. I felt the moon on my shoulders; even moonglow hurt when it touched me. I felt alone.

"And you were naked?"

"Yes."

There was so much blood, I kept slipping on it. It felt like the first time I went ice-skating. On this same field, which they flooded in the winter and turned to ice.

"And you went to your parents' house?"

"Yes."

I remember standing in the backyard, looking at the lights inside the house. How warm and inviting it seemed. I could see the silhouette of my mother, talking on the phone. Home. But I couldn't make my legs move. I knew the second I climbed up the back steps . . .

"I crawled. Up the steps."

. . . it would change everything. I remember thinking, This is your family. You are safe. You are a girl. Your name is Wyn Elizabeth Davies. You are thirteen years old. This is your family.

"What did she say when she saw you? Your mother? She's the one who found you?"

My mother came to the door. Thought there was an animal in the backyard. A skunk. A raccoon. She'd been on the phone calling Hanna to see if I'd gone to her house. She wasn't worried yet. When she heard the scratching at the screen door, she thought it was the neighbor's cat.

"I don't want to talk anymore."

She didn't recognize me. I am a girl. My name is Wyn Elizabeth Davies. I am thirteen years old. Her eyes were so scared. "What happened, oh my God, what happened?" Her hands touching my face, wiping the blood out of my eyes.

"Do you need to take a break?"

"No. I'm finished."

Snow Family

I didn't sleep for more than a couple of hours each night the week before Gus arrived. Instead, I'd get out of bed and work on the commission. I'd paint for hours, manic, holding my breath as the brush moved across the textured canvas, though it seemed like my progress was slow, each stroke a sort of Sisyphean task. No matter how hard I worked, I couldn't seem to finish. When I finally fell asleep again, my dreams were dark, frantic. In the morning, I was delirious and exhausted.

I didn't know what to expect from Gus's stay. Unlike Pilar's visit, Gus's made me anxious. Instead of being excited to see him, to show him this beautiful place, to watch what was certain to be a joyful reunion between him and Avery, I felt a prevailing sort of dread. At first I thought it was simply that I'd been living such a solitary life out here, and an invasion of this sort might disrupt the small amount of peace I'd located. But that wasn't the case. Having Pilar here had been a *relief,* an encounter with civilization, with grown-up conversation.

Finally, as I was making a bed for him in one of the empty bedrooms, leaving the bottom untucked (he always untucked the ends of the sheets before he got into bed, feeling trapped otherwise), I realized what it was. Since that argument, the one that shattered fifteen years of history with a single, careless blow, I'd been unable to control my bitterness. As if this, *all of this,* were his fault. I hated myself around Gus. I deplored who I had become. And isn't that why we split up in the first place? It was like he'd turned a mirror and made me look at exactly who I was now.

There was no hiding from myself when Gus was around. There *was* no running away.

That night as we waited for him to arrive, a storm front came down from Canada, and with it a terrible, bone-chilling cold. The waves were high and hard and loud. The sky was completely opaque.

I made chowder in the Crock-Pot with the leftover lobster, and Avery helped me bake biscuits. Earlier, we had unrolled a long sheet of paper from the roll I'd taken from her easel when we left New York, and spread it out across the dining room floor. She had wanted to write *Welcome Home, Daddy!* But I couldn't bring myself to help her. This wasn't our home. And he wasn't returning. He was just here for a long weekend. And so instead, when I spelled out the words for her on a scratch piece of paper, I wrote *Welcome to Bluffs Island, Daddy!*

She had carefully, meticulously copied the letters onto the banner, used my acrylic paints to fill the letters in, and painted a rainbow across the background, weaving it expertly through the words. It was pretty impressive for a four-year-old. God forbid, we had an artist on our hands, but truthfully, how could it be avoided?

Outside it wasn't really snowing, but rather teasing us with the promise of snow, a few solitary snowflakes fluttering down from the sky. Avery insisted on bundling up in her snowsuit (the one my mother had found at a consignment shop in Haven). I wrapped her up in a scarf, made her wear mittens and boots, and watched as she paced up and down the front yard, skipping on an imaginary hopscotch board. After about a half hour of this, she got bored and sat down on the front steps. I made her a cup of cocoa in the microwave, added extra marshmallows, and took it out to her.

"When is he *coming?*" she asked, sighing, the weight of the world on her two small shoulders.

One amber curl had dipped into the cocoa. I plucked it out, sucked it.

"Gross, Mama!"

"Yummy," I said, smirking. "He'll be here soon. The ferry might be running late because of the storm. I'll call him."

"I'm on the ferry," he said. "Is Avery waiting?"

I peered out the window at her sitting on the steps.

"Yuh," I said.

"You're starting to sound like a real Mainer."

"Ha."

"I brought everything you said you needed," he said. "I hope I remembered everything."

"It's fine," I said. "If you forgot anything, I mean." I had asked for him to bring me my robe, the gorgeous post-breakup cashmere one Pilar had gifted me. The long thermal underwear I had, somehow, neglected to pack. The portable speaker to plug my iPhone into to play music while I was working.

"If there's anything else you need, I can always send it."

"Cool," I said. I hated the small talk that composed most of our conversations now. Gus and I were talkers. As a couple, we had never, ever been at a loss for words. Our sentences tumbled over each other's like kids rolling down a grassy hill. Words and syllables tangled up, apologizing for the collisions. But now, there were vast pauses between our syllables. It was as if the further apart we grew, the longer these pauses and the shorter and terser our sentences became.

"See you in a bit," he said.

He hung up, thankfully, before I blurted out those old, familiar parting words. A verbal habit, a tic: *Love you.*

Gus pulled into the driveway just a half hour later.

Avery was still waiting on the steps for him while I lingered inside. I took a cursory look around the kitchen, lifted the lid of the Crock-Pot and stirred the thick chowder so I'd have something to do with my hands.

The door opened, and Avery led Gus into the house.

"Daddy's here, Mama! Look!"

"Hey," he said, setting down his duffle bag.

"Hey." I smiled and hugged him awkwardly. He smelled good, like clean laundry.

"It smells good in here," he said.

I gestured stupidly at the Crock-Pot. "Thanks. It's chowder."

Avery was like a child possessed. Manic, wild, dragging Gus by the hand up the still-precarious staircase to her room. Likely standing on tiptoes to yank the blackout shades down, shutting the door to watch the constellations appear on her upside-down sky. Their voices were muffled from where I stood in the kitchen. I tried not to eavesdrop, but couldn't help but feel excluded. Avery and Gus in their own private universe. They were in the same house with me, but it felt like they were on another planet entirely.

Within an hour, Gus was poking around in the shed, looking for a decent board to make the swing he'd promised her. He crawled up into the attic and located the beams to which he could safely install the hooks to suspend the ropes. In the kitchen I watched them through the window in the yard as he sawed and sanded and Avery watched on.

It grew dark early, and they came in when I called them both to supper.

We sat around the small table in the kitchen. Avery chattered away and our spoons clinked and clanked against the bowls' sides.

"There's plenty of lumber in the shed. I might be able to fix the stairs for you," he said.

"That's okay." I shook my head. The chowder was too hot, and I'd burned the roof of my mouth. "Pilar's hired a carpenter to come by as soon as the right balusters come in. They had to special order them."

"They're kind of dangerous," Gus said. "I want to at least put up a barricade until you can get a railing up there."

"Okay, if you want. We're careful though," I said. "How's the shop?"

The talk was growing smaller and smaller with each passing moment. I wondered when we'd revert to the weather.

He shrugged. "Good. We got a big job for a new hotel going up in the city," he said. "I've been getting a lot of overtime. I worked almost sixty hours this week. To make up for taking Monday off."

Gus would stay with us through Monday and then take the late ferry home on Monday night.

"Are you drawing?" I asked, handing him a beer.

"Yeah, actually, a lot. With you guys gone, I've got a lot of time on my hands."

Gus's art was a contradiction. Instead of using canvas, he salvaged tin sheets (corrugated roofing and siding). Oxidized and rusted out. They were all metal and grit at first glance, but then, as you looked closer, you could see the most tender, meticulous drawings (usually done in a white grease pencil). Realistic images inspired by the photos of him and his brothers salvaged by his father when his family's house burned down. He grew up in Queens in the '80s and '90s, with a single father and two brothers. The drawings depicted the boys, each one nearly identical to the next, doing boy things: playing marbles in the street, leaning up against parked cars, hunching over a card game (one boy looking back over his shoulder, standing watch). The boys in these images were restless boys. Innocent boys at the precipice of something, at the edge. For one of them, Gary, this buzzing disquietude would eventually lead him to drugs, to jail. For Sam, the second, suicide. And for Gus, the third, the boy looking over his shoulder, it led to art.

In every piece, that boy, that young version of Gus, stood guard over the others. Even though he was the youngest. Even though they should have been the ones taking care of him. My favorite, the only one I could bear to look at without feeling like my heart was being ripped out, was one of them playing with a hose, unraveled from the side of a house. In this one, a six-year-old Gus holds the hose and aims it at the backs of the two older brothers, who are, for one oblivious moment, unaware of what is about to happen.

Avery was shoveling the lobster chowder in her mouth. I thought it was too rich, too buttery, too sweet, but she couldn't seem to get enough of it.

"How about you?" he asked softly. "Are you painting?"

This was such a sore spot. Like a bruise that wouldn't heal. I imagined my heart a mottled green and blue.

"I've started something." I thought of the empty, pristine canvas.

"Another commission?" he asked, and I heard just a hint of disappointment. Of disgust.

And this pissed me off.

"*No*," I took a deep breath so I wouldn't explode. "Something else."

Gus nodded. Silent.

"So what did you do for Thanksgiving?" I asked, taking a long swig of my beer.

He shrugged. "Nothing much. Went over to Ned's for dinner. Out for drinks afterward. There's a new place near his house."

Even as my stomach turned and my body cautioned me to stop, I persisted. "Who all went?" I asked.

He shrugged again, his mouth twitching a bit. "Ned, Wes, Mia. You know."

Mia? I didn't know who Mia was.

"Who's Mia?"

"Just some chick Wes knows."

"Huh," I said.

"Yeah, she's cool. You'd like her. She works part-time at a new gallery in SoHo."

Mia. And suddenly, I felt overwhelmed by something, a sort of need to be fascinating, interesting, pretty. I hadn't felt like this with Gus since we started dating. It was as if I needed him to *want* me. It was illogical, stupid even. But I'd had two beers, and my heart was broken. I felt this need like something hot and alive in my blood.

"Actually, I showed her some of my work, and she said she'd talk to the gallery owner. But who knows."

Mia. She materialized in my imagination: long legs, bobbed blond hair, cool glasses.

I became achingly aware of my body, what he must see sitting across the table. The extra pounds I'd put on since we'd gotten here. The blemish on my chin. My hair, which was frizzy and unwieldy in this salty humidity. I suddenly, regretfully, wished I'd worn something sexier than the jeans and sweatshirt I'd mistakenly thrown on thinking it might send the message that I didn't care. That I wasn't trying to impress him. That he wasn't worthy of my putting on anything pretty. What the hell was I doing?

I watched my hand reach across the table, touch the wedding band that still circled his ring finger.

But even as I leaned in, I felt him pulling away.

"Let's get that swing strung up, baby girl," he said to Avery, pushing his chair away from the table. The legs made an awful squeaking sound on the floor.

"Yay!" she said, leaping from the table and bounding up the stairs.

"Slow down," Gus warned her. "And I am fixing those stairs," he said to me.

I watched Gus climb the stairs and felt the loss of him more acutely than I had in months. Here he was, stuck with me on an island, and he'd never felt farther away.

Later, I did the dishes alone in the kitchen, listening to the sound of Avery literally swinging from the rafters above me, her gleeful squeals and Gus's husky voice cooing at her. They must have been up there for an hour before Gus came down alone.

"Where's Av?" I asked.

"She crashed out. Too much excitement for one day, I guess," he said, and smiled. "Can I get another beer?"

"Oh, yeah, of course," I said, motioning to the fridge.

He grabbed two beers and handed me one. I was sort of buzzed already, but I didn't know what to do with my hands, and so I accepted it. We stood awkwardly in the kitchen, in a strange sort of impasse. Outside, the sun was gone, and the sky was dark. Moonless. The air felt electrified. Swollen.

"So what have you been doing besides painting?" he asked.

"Hanging out with Av," I said, shrugging. "We're working on her reading. She likes to help me cook too. Oh," I added. "I found something."

"Huh?" he asked.

"In the basement," I said. "I was down there to light the pilot on the furnace when we first got here."

He raised his eyebrow at me in disbelief. And I had to smile. I didn't even like lighting the pilot on the gas stove at the duplex. He'd had to come over at least a half dozen times to do it for me while I cowered in the doorway hoping the house didn't blow up.

"It was hidden in a weird hole in the wall. A box filled with undeveloped film."

"Wow. Who took them?" he asked, his face alight with the soft glow of the table lamp.

"I think it was whoever lived here before."

"You mean the person who sold Pilar the house?"

"No, the house was in probate. The house has been empty since the early '80s." I couldn't take it anymore. I'd been holding on to this secret too long. "Let me show you," I said, then felt a sudden, distinct ache. Guilt. Like I was somehow betraying the women in the photos.

I thought about Pilar snapping pictures of the one on the boardwalk with her phone. And so instead of showing him the photo on the wall, I went to the dining room and grabbed the boxes from where I'd left them on the floor.

"Jesus, Wyn. There must be fifty rolls in here."

"I know," I said. "It would cost me a fortune to get them all printed."

"I could have Wes do it," he said. Wes was our friend from school who had a darkroom in his apartment.

"Oh, no," I said. "That's okay."

Regret fell heavily across my shoulders. I felt the same way I felt sometimes after a party where I drank too much, said too much. The remembered conversations (gossip or mean-spirited sentiments set loose by the liquor) like tiny, sharp pebbles in my shoes for days afterward.

"I mean, I got a couple rolls developed, and it's nothing exciting. Just some vacation pictures."

"Still," he said. "Aren't you curious? I mean about what's on the rest? The fact that whoever took them went so far as to hide them? And what do you think it means, *Epitaphs and Prophecies?*"

I shrugged. "I don't know. But it's expensive, paper's expensive." I was backpedaling now, wondering what selfish impulse had led me here. Why had I shared this? Again I was furious with myself.

"Seriously. He wouldn't have to make prints. But he could at least develop the film, get you negatives. Contact sheets if you wanted."

I thought about my dwindling account. About the remaining rolls of film. I thought about the trek I had to make just to get to the post office to send off the film. It could take me years before I was able to get them all developed. I also thought of those photos I had already seen. The feeling I had when I found them. The sense of discovery.

I started to nod. "Okay, okay. That would be cool. But he doesn't need to make prints. Just the negatives would be great."

Gus nodded.

"God, I really wonder who took them," he said.

I suddenly flashed on the old guy I'd met at the restaurant in town. I wondered if the woman he was talking about was the same one who'd taken the pictures. I also thought about the way the next-door neighbor responded when I'd asked who had lived here. The man's bewildered face, the woman exclaiming about rats and slamming the door in our faces. The old guy had said something about asking my neighbor.

"I think the people next door must know something," I said.

"Next door?"

"Yeah. That huge mansion on the other side of the trees."

"Let's go check it out," he said, grinning impishly.

"Oh, I don't think they're home," I said, shaking my head. "I think it's just a vacation house."

"So, it's empty?" he said, his eyes sparkling. I knew this look; I'd seen the same wonderful, mischievous sense of adventure in his eyes a thousand times. "Come on. Let's go take a peek."

"What about Av?" I said.

"We'll bring the monitor."

Back at home we'd hang out on the neighbor's porch after Avery went to sleep at night, chatting with our neighbors, the monitor perched on the railing. We'd hear her if she woke up. Still, she was never more than a few quick steps away.

"She'll be fine. I promise. We'll be quick," Gus implored.

I hesitated, but when he reached for my hand, I felt my heart quicken. This was the way things were supposed to be with Gus. This is who we were supposed to be, who we *were* together.

I made sure the baby monitor was on in Avery's room, and that she was still fast asleep, and grabbed the receiver. We put on boots and mittens and hats, wrapped scarves around our faces. Gus shoved a couple of beers in his pockets, and we headed out into the cold night.

"Lock the door," I told him. "Just in case she wakes up. And seriously, we'll have to be quick."

I led him down the rocky cliff to the beach, and we stood looking out at the water. The moon was obscured by the thick clouds overhead but illuminated the sky from behind. The sand was unyielding, hard. Frozen. I imagined all of the pieces of sea glass that lurked beneath the surface waiting to be unearthed later.

The monitor crackled in my hand. I listened carefully. Heard her sigh.

"She's *fine,*" Gus said. The sounds of her sleep were familiar to both of us.

At the foot of the stone steps, I motioned for him to follow me.

When we reached the top, the mansion sat before us, just a silhouette against that wild sky. There wasn't a single light on.

"Holy shit," Gus said.

He walked toward the dark house, and I felt like I should reach out and stop him. Gus was always more bold than I was, always the first one to step through a doorway, me always at his heels.

"Have you met them yet?" he asked.

"Pilar and I brought them a pie."

Gus turned to me. "A pie?"

"For Thanksgiving." I shrugged. "A couple answered the door. Older. Like sixty or something. They looked like they were from a J. Crew catalog. The lady was weird. Totally slammed the door in my face."

"Have they always lived there?" Gus asked.

"I don't know," I said. "I suppose."

"Do you think they knew the owner of your house?"

Something about the way he said this felt strange. It was Pilar's house, not mine. My house was that duplex back in Queens. *Our* house.

"Do you think anybody's home?" he asked, creeping across the lawn.

"I don't think so," I said. "It's totally dark."

"Let's go see," he said, and the boyish smirk, the one I was powerless to resist, beckoned me.

We made our way across the massive expanse of the front yard. The ground was crisp, hard beneath our feet. I kept checking the monitor. Still, just the quiet sound of Avery sleeping on the other end.

Gus ducked deep into the shadows and slipped around the side of the house. I had to run to keep up with him. The house was even more enormous than it appeared from the front. Easily five or six thousand square feet. The only fence, however, was the natural one made by the woods that separated the mansion from Pilar's property.

When we got to the backyard, Gus stopped.

"Wow," he said.

"What?" I asked, breathing heavily, bent over to catch my breath.

"*Look.*"

The backyard was like something out of *Gatsby*. A swimming pool made to look like a natural body of water, circled by a labyrinth of foliage. The pool was empty now, drained for the winter, I supposed. Surrounding it were rocks and hedges. Weeping willows hanging overhead like something from a dream.

"Come on," Gus said. It was a phrase he'd said a thousand times to me over the years. Words filled with the possibility of adventure. Of excitement. At the end of that single, beckoning directive was, inevitably, the promise of fun.

"What about Av?" I said.

"She's right over there," he said. "We can be at the house in thirty seconds if we go through those trees."

I peered at the trees, and my heart pounded hard.

Gus went to the edge, climbed down the ladder into the depths of the empty pool, and motioned for me to join him. I could feel his hands on my hips guiding me down into the dark hole. Grateful for the certainty of them. The steadiness of him.

When we reached the bottom, he pulled one beer out of his pocket, unscrewed the cap and handed it to me. It was nearly frozen. I was nearly frozen. We were in the deep end. Over our heads.

We sat down on the cold bottom of the pool and drank our beers in silence. The monitor crackled, but she remained asleep.

It was so dark, I could barely see the outline of him. I could have been alone here, at the bottom of this pit.

When he finally spoke, his voice echoed.

"This is awesome. Look up!"

When I looked up at the sky, my eyes were confused at first. It looked like constellations, but it couldn't be. The sky had been filled with clouds. I thought of Avery's room, of that upside-down night sky.

"It's snowing!" I said, when the first few snowflakes fell on my open face. Cold, then melting on my cheeks.

"It's snowing!!" Gus said. "Woohoo!" His howl echoed against the concrete sides of the pool.

He reached for my hand and pulled me up to my feet. And we ran up and down the bottom of the pool, faces peering up into the sky. Finally, breathless, I stopped. He held me. It took me by surprise. I was buzzed and freezing cold and exhilarated and vertiginous from the darkness, from the dizzying sky. The snow, the snow, the snow.

And then we were kissing. The heat of our mouths in such contrast to the bitter cold around us. His beard scratched my face. And the tears that fell down my cheeks were also hot, salty as they fell into our open, hungry mouths.

His hands reached underneath my parka, wrapped around my waist. And I didn't care my middle was soft; I only cared about his hot skin on my hot skin. I was shaking, trembling, quaking.

I squeezed my eyes shut and let him kiss the tears off my cheeks, let his lips find my ears, my neck.

"Mama!!!!" The sound was tremendous. The crackle and hiss, the echo of her cries.

He touched his forehead to mine.

"Shit," he said. "I'm sorry." But I didn't know whether he was sorry we'd been interrupted, or sorry it had happened in the first place.

"Hurry!" I said, regretting leaving her alone. Feeling like a crappy mom.

We ran back around to the front of the mansion. He was still holding my hand. On the monitor, Avery's wails grew and grew.

"Let's cut through here," he said, motioning to the trees.

"Mama!!!" Avery cried. "Mama!!!"

And so I nodded, and I let him lead me into those dark woods. The trembling I had felt earlier took over my body as we made our way along the path between the two houses. I held my breath the whole time, closed my eyes, and trusted (because I had no choice) he would get me to the other side.

She'd wet her bed again. She'd been wearing footie pajamas, which were soaked through. There had to have been a gallon of piss pooling inside her PJs.

"I'm going to give her a bath," I said to Gus. "Would you mind stripping the sheets?"

I took Avery into the bathroom, wrapped her in a dry towel while I ran the water. The room filled with the smell of rotten eggs.

She was shivering, her skin cold and clammy.

"Come here," I said, reaching for her. I helped her into the tub and she curled her knees to her chest.

"I was crying and crying. Where were you, Mommy?"

"I'm sorry, baby. Daddy and I were just outside looking at the snow."

"It's snowing?" she said.

I grabbed the washcloth draped over the faucet, dried stiff. I dipped it into the water and squirted a dollop of liquid body soap on it. I ran the washcloth down her back, noting the little ladder of her spine, and how long her legs were getting. How many more years would she need me to bathe her, to make swirls across her back?

"Can I make a snowman?"

"Tomorrow," I promised. Her body relaxed. By the time I lifted her out of the tub and slipped a clean nightie over her head, she was half asleep again. I carried her to my own room and laid her down. The windows rattled in the wind. I noticed there was a small crack in one pane of glass. I would need to call Pilar's guy, Hank, to repair it before it got much colder.

I made my way down the stairs. Gus had brought the wet sheets down to the washing machine in the basement. I could hear the pipes groaning as the water came on. The teakettle was whistling on the stove. I poured us each a cup of tea as I heard Gus's footsteps coming up from the basement.

Gus sat down at the little kitchen table. I handed him the mug of tea and sat down across from him with my own cup.

"So, is this the first time she's done this?" he asked.

"No, it's happened a couple of times."

"She's *four*," he said in disbelief. "She's been totally potty trained for over a year."

"She's fine. It was just an accident. We can't make a big deal out of it. You need milk?" I got up and went to the fridge.

"Well, it wasn't happening back at home," he persisted.

I poured the milk in my tea, left the carton on the table between us in case he changed his mind.

"She's in a strange place," I offered. "There have been a lot of changes for her lately."

"*Exactly*," he said, setting the mug down hard on the little kitchen table. "It's messing her up. She's regressing. She's wetting the bed, because of us."

I suddenly felt like he was attacking me. Blaming me.

"She's wetting the bed because you let her drink a huge cup of chocolate milk right before bedtime," I said, trying hard to lighten the mood.

But Gus clenched his jaw. "Kids regress when they're upset. When their worlds are turned upside down."

I shook my head, tears filling my eyes. I thought of her upside-down room. *Upset down.*

"She's confused," he said.

"*I'm* confused," I countered.

"Can't you see this is messing her up?"

"What?"

"Taking her away from me."

"I didn't take her *away* from you," I said. "She's not a toy I took out of your goddamned toy box."

"Then what do you call it? You're on a fucking island. It took me twelve hours to get here. You haven't come home to visit. It feels *away* to me."

"So, it's better to have her think everything is fine and freaking dandy at home? Pretending like it's totally normal for her parents to live next door to each other like neighbors?"

"*Yes,*" he said, throwing his hands up.

"Well, it's a lie," I said. "Because nothing about that is *normal*."

"And since when have you been concerned with normalcy?"

"What is that supposed to mean?" I said.

"Just what I said. You've never cared about *normal* before. About the status quo."

I felt that familiar, awful burn of his words.

"That's funny, because that's pretty much what you've been accusing me of for the last year, right? *Pandering to the status quo?*" I mocked and gestured toward the stupid commission painting in the other room.

Gus closed his eyes and leaned his head back, rolled his neck. "Can't we just talk this through?"

"I don't want to talk," I said, standing up.

"Great," he said. "Then let's just *not talk* about it."

"I'm going to bed," I said.

"Because that *always* works, right?"

I slept curled around Avery that night, her small body enclosed in a cave made of blankets and arms and legs. When she struggled to break free in the morning, it was as if she were being born again, emerging from the hot womb I'd made to keep her safe.

"Daddy's up!" she whispered. "I'm going to go see Daddy."

And for one disorienting moment, we could have been in the big, lumpy bed at our house in Queens. The bluegrass music Gus loved, jangly and light. The smell of coffee and bacon and something sweet beckoning us. But we weren't at home. We were in a freezing cold room in a crumbling house at the edge of the world. Wind rattled the windows, and cold air sliced through that crack in the glass. Outside, the sky was bright, and the snow, at least a foot of it, was blinding. Everything was obscured. Suffocating.

I pulled on the long johns Gus had brought me from home, my slipper socks, and my robe. I glanced at myself in the mirror only quickly, piled my hair into a ponytail, and tried to pat down my bangs, which stood up, willful and defiant against gravity.

Downstairs, the kitchen was a disaster. Gus had brought a waffle iron from home as well, and I could see there was a red velvet cake mix sitting next to the counter. Red batter oozed out of the edges of the machine.

"Cake waffles!" Avery said.

This was a Gus invention, one he'd come up with back when we were still students. The food bank often got donations of cake and muffin mixes, and Gus had discovered if you poured them into a waffle iron, they made delicious waffles. We didn't always have a functioning stove, but we always had a waffle maker, and so we always had waffles: German chocolate, blueberry, confetti waffles for my birthday one year.

Gus and I didn't speak. He took a shower. I did the dishes. Without a word.

"Daddy and I are going to make a snowman," Avery said later. "Come on, Mommy. You come too."

I shook my head. "I have some work to do, sweets," I said. "You and Daddy have fun."

★ ★ ★

After they both got bundled up and headed outside, I went to the dining room and looked at the commission painting propped up on the easel and tried to see it through Gus's eyes. Only two trees completed, the others sketched, ghostlike on the canvas. Beside the easel was a rolling cart that held my paints and turpentine and rags. The brushes fanned like a bouquet of thin flowers in a coffee can vase. I plucked the smallest brush, ran its tip across my palm. Made of the smallest cluster of hog bristles, it was the one I used for the detail work. For the meticulous, compulsive even, rendering of these goddamned trees.

Outside, Gus and Avery made a family. A mother, a father, and a baby.

When they came in, each red-cheeked and breathless, I was grateful for the interruption. I hadn't made even one stroke on the canvas.

"I wanted to make a snow mermaid," Gus said, as if in apology, as we looked out the window at the snowmen below. "But Avery said there's no such thing."

"Of course there is," I said to Avery. "Remember, we found her tears?"

"It's make believe, Mama," she said, and I felt my heart sink.

I didn't know how to tell her there was no such thing as this family she'd made either. That *Mother, Father, Daughter* was just as much a fantasy as a woman with shimmery fins instead of legs.

I willed it to snow again that night. When we each went to our respective rooms, I said a childlike prayer the sky would fill with clouds again, that the snow would come down in cold, hard slivers. That it would enclose us, making it impossible for Gus to go home. For as angry and guilty as he made me feel, I didn't want him to leave.

I listened to the sound of him reading to Avery on the baby monitor, which crackled and hissed on the nightstand.

He was reading *Where the Wild Things Are,* her book of choice because he was so good at making the grumbly voices of the wild things. "We'll eat you up, we love you so . . ." And she giggled. And she whispered.

I strained to hear what she was saying, turning the volume up on the monitor. Desperate to hear the secrets she was sharing with him. And more than that, wanting to *be* with them.

"I miss you, Daddy," I made out.

"I'm right here," Gus said, his voice sad and soft.

"I miss you even though," she said.

"I miss you even though too," he said.

I clicked off the monitor, my head pounding, my heart pounding. And I wished I hadn't been so curious, so needy. That I hadn't eavesdropped on this private, quiet moment.

Despite my prayers, it didn't snow again. And the snow that had accumulated the night before melted in the new, bright sun. When we walked Gus out to the car the next morning, the snow family had begun to melt; the mother was listing to one side. She'd lost an arm. The father looked resigned to his fate too. Only the child remained upright. Optimistic.

Gus hugged me quickly, but he already felt so far away.

"I'll let you know what Wes says, hopefully he has time to process the film for you." He wouldn't look at me, not even when he was talking to me. "You sure you don't want prints?"

"No. That's cool. Maybe just contact sheets? And if he could do them in date order, that would help. All of the canisters are dated."

"And the plan is still to meet at your folks' for Christmas?" he said.

I nodded again. We were going to spend Christmas Eve with my parents in New Hampshire, and then Gus would take Avery back to New York with him for two weeks. He'd arranged to have the week between Christmas and New Year's off, as well as the first week of January, so he could spend time with her. And I would go back to the island alone until Pilar came back from her trip.

"Let me know if you need me to send anything at all," Gus said.

I shook my head. "We've got the waffle iron, what more could we need?" I offered a small smile, but he didn't return it.

December

The knock on the door startled me. I was engaged in what was turning out to be an ongoing battle with the plumbing in the downstairs bathroom, Avery's chosen place to conduct all number two business. She liked to sit on the toilet with the door open so she could talk to me as she waited for her bowels to move. Sometimes, she'd sit there waiting for ten or twenty minutes. No matter what I fed her—vegetables snuck into her pancakes, sweet, plump prunes on top of her morning oatmeal, dried apricots, which I promised tasted like candy—whatever was happening inside that tiny belly was wreaking havoc on the pipes.

I'd already had Hank come by twice. Both times he'd snaked the toilet and found nothing of significance. He suggested perhaps the roots from the trees out in the front of the house were somehow encroaching. He'd stood and shaken his head, mystified.

"Usually it's a toy," he said, in his thick Maine accent. "Barbies, Legos. You name it. Kids like to flush things."

"Avery's not a flusher," I'd offered. And it was true. To a fault. Once, before Gus and I split up, we'd been showing the other side of the duplex to a prospective tenant, and when we opened the door to the bathroom, we'd found one of Avery's happy little turds floating blissfully in the bowl.

After the second visit to Pilar's house, Hank had offered to go down there with a camera, sort of a colonoscopy of the house's innards, but I'd declined. Who knew how much something like that would cost her? Especially when the problem could most often be remedied with a plunger and some patience.

Today's battle had been going on for nearly an hour, though, and I was exasperated. Sweating. A headache creeping in.

The pounding on the door was so disorienting, it took me a moment to remember what that sound even was.

"There's a man at the door!" Avery said.

"What kind of man?" I asked, feeling my heart quicken as I set the plunger down.

"A regular kind," she said.

And so I washed and dried my hands quickly, hoping it was just the guy to fix the stairs, and went to the front door. It took a moment before I recognized him.

It was the man from next door. From the mansion. He looked different standing in my doorway than he had in his own massive one. It was probably only about twenty-five degrees outside. He was wearing what looked like a Lands' End wool jacket, seemingly fresh out of the package. Jeans and L.L. Bean boots, soft leather uppers and forest green rubber bottoms.

"Hi," he said. "I'm from next door."

I nodded. Then I thought, *Shit. Gus and I are totally busted.* Had we left something behind at the pool? Could they tell we'd been traipsing through their backyard? I started to formulate my defense, my apology, when he said, "May I come in? It's cold out here, and I forgot my gloves."

"Oh, yes, please. So sorry." I gestured for him to come inside. Avery clung to the back of my legs.

We stood awkwardly in the foyer for a moment, before I remembered the etiquette.

"Would you like to come in? Can I take your coat?"

He seemed grateful for the niceties.

I handed the coat to Avery and said, "Av, can you hang up Mr . . ."

"Ferguson. Seamus Ferguson," he said, and awkwardly extended his hand to shake mine. "I'm sorry our last encounter was so . . .

rushed. Fiona, my wife, is going through a difficult time. There's no excuse. I'm sorry. The pie was lovely."

He was so *genteel*. Even in the soft plaid shirt and perfectly faded jeans.

He didn't mention the pool.

Avery took the coat from me and hung it up on the wooden rack by the door. She stood there, curious.

"Why don't you go for a swing in your room," I said.

She frowned but then obeyed, tiptoeing carefully up the stairs. I was so grateful to Gus for the temporary fix he'd made, but still eager for the stair guy to finally get here.

"Would you like a cup of coffee or something?" I asked the man, who was slipping off his wet boots.

"That would be wonderful," he said.

I offered him a seat at the kitchen table, which was covered with the detritus of Avery's latest artistic endeavor, the wooden surface sparkly and sticky with glitter and glue. "Sorry," I said, pushing aside the stacks of construction paper and Popsicle sticks and pom-poms to make room.

I filled the coffee pot with water and started to pull out the industrial sized can of generic coffee from the cupboard when I suddenly remembered the fancy coffee Pilar had brought. I dug through the freezer, found the little bag, and filled the filter.

"So, are you and your wife here for Christmas?" I asked. Christmas was just a week away now.

"No," he said, shaking his head. "We spend Christmas in Colorado with Fiona's sister."

I thought of my client in Aspen, waiting on the birches painting, and felt a little shock of anxiety.

"I'm just here to check on the house. Make sure the pipes don't freeze."

I would have thought people like this would have an entire staff to take care of their homes, their *pipes,* while they were away.

"Are you enjoying the island?" he asked suddenly. And then, awkwardly, "You and your . . . wife?"

I smiled. He wasn't the first person to assume Pilar was my lover.

"Pilar is just my friend. She's actually the one who bought this place."

"And the little girl? She's your daughter?"

I nodded. "Yes, Avery."

He took a sip of coffee. "Your friend, she said you're both artists."

"Yes," I said. "In fact, she's going to be profiled on *CBS Sunday Morning* just after Christmas. She's an incredible painter."

"And you," he said, seemingly unfazed by Pilar's fame. "You're a painter too?"

I sighed and shrugged. "I paint."

The man, Seamus, looked around the room suddenly, as if he had just woken up and realized where he was. "The house is the same," he said.

"Yeah, I'm pretty sure nothing has been done to it in the last thirty-five years," I said, laughing. Then it struck me. He'd been in the house before. What on earth would he have been in this house for? "Have you been here before?" I asked.

He nodded, slowly. His mind was elsewhere. "A long time ago."

"Your wife didn't seem very happy about us moving in," I said.

He looked at me, his eyes peering intently into mine.

"You haven't happened to find anything . . . any photographs?" he asked.

I thought of the box of film now in Wes's darkroom. I thought about the pictures blown up and hanging in the dining room. I felt *caught*.

Upstairs, I could hear Avery swinging. The *squeak, squeak* of the swing.

Suddenly, I felt panicked. Uncomfortable. What on earth would this man, in his expensive socks and hand-knit fisherman's sweater, want with the photos I'd found?

"No," I said. Not a lie exactly. Negatives weren't *photographs.*

"Oh," he said. "Of course, they were probably disposed of."

"What?" I asked, confused. "Did a photographer live here?"

"Listen, I'm so sorry to take up your time. I just wanted to apologize for not being more welcoming before. And to thank you for the pie."

I nodded. He stood up abruptly and walked out of the kitchen and down the hallway to the foyer like someone who knew the floor plan of the house. Like someone who had been here *many* times before.

He sat down on the bench by the door and quickly put on his boots, grabbed the coat from the rack, and thrust his arms into the sleeves. It was suddenly as if he couldn't get out of here fast enough.

I heard Avery jump down off the swing. Of course she'd want to see where he was going.

"We'll have you over some time," he offered.

"Sure," I said, shrugging.

The moment I closed the door behind him, I grabbed my phone and dialed Gus.

Straight to voice mail.

"Hey Gus, it's me. I was just checking to see if Wes had had a chance to develop that film yet. Maybe, if he's able to get it done before Christmas, you could bring the negatives with you when you pick up Avery?"

And I went to the dining room, studied the photos. The insistent gaze of both female subjects. I wondered, when the photographer captured these photos, if he or she had known what they'd caught. But then it dawned on me, ridiculously, that whoever took these pictures had never gotten them developed. For all the photographer knew, every photo taken could have been out of focus, overexposed, underexposed. They had no idea what they had captured, and yet they'd clearly spent a whole day at the beach studying, preparing, shooting. Watching the young couple, waiting for what might happen between them. To what end then? It baffled me. Why would someone work so hard only to let these images sit undiscovered in a box for thirty-five years? How could the *act* of taking the photos be enough? It would be like painting a picture in the darkness of night and then destroying it before the sun came up. Why bother to put film in the camera at all? It made me think of the sand castles Gus and Avery had made one summer when we drove out to Coney Island. All afternoon they spent building an elaborate castle replete with moats and turrets and drawbridges. Then the tide came in and took it all away. It had made my throat grow thick to watch their hard work decimated by the crashing waves, but neither one of them had seemed even remotely disappointed. Avery, as a matter of fact, had laughed and laughed, thrown herself down onto the sand where the castle used to be. Such unadulterated joy, such bliss.

It seemed like a contradiction. Photography was meant to *seize* a moment, to hold onto it. These moments, these *thousands* of moments had been captured, only to be stored away in tiny little time capsules in the basement of this house.

Art Brut

*T*hey weren't in my art history textbooks, not as anything other than
footnotes anyway. They call them outsider artists. Artists who ex-
isted only in the margins of those pages. In the margins of society.

Helen Martins was a South African woman who meticulously, almost religiously, transformed her parents' home using crushed glass to decorate the walls, which were reflected by mirrors, illuminated by tinted
windows and candles. Outside she built a private garden of sculptures
made of concrete and glass. When her eyesight began to fail due to years of
exposure to the crushed glass, she killed herself by drinking caustic soda.
Her home, The Owl House, once derided by the locals in her village, became a museum after her death.

Adolf Wölfli, a Swiss man who was physically and sexually abused
then orphaned, spent almost his entire life within the walls of an asylum
after he himself was convicted of child molestation. Psychosis, hallucina-
tions. He was driven by madness to create a forty-five-volume epic com-
prised of 25,000 pages and 1,600 meticulous illustrations.

Felipe Jesus Consalvos, a Cuban-American cigar roller, created an
800-piece body of work (a collection of collages made of cigar rings),
which was discovered at a yard sale.

Miroslav Tichý, a Czech photographer, fashioned his cameras out of
cardboard tubes, empty spools, and tin cans, using road asphalt to seal out
the light. He created lenses from Plexiglas, sanded and polished with
toothpaste and ash. He was a voyeur, using his homemade cameras to
covertly take photos of women in his village, about ninety images per day.
He printed the photos using a homemade enlarger, but as soon as they

were printed, he discarded them like the waste from which they were made.

Henry Darger was a Chicago custodian who wrote and illustrated an obsessive 15,000-page, fifteen-volume work, In the Realms of the Unreal, *which remained undiscovered until just before his death when his landlord found the treasure trove.*

Most of these artists are self-taught, naïve, insane. Compulsive, prolific, and secret. Poor. Many outsider artists' work isn't discovered until after their deaths. Sometimes it's referred to as "visionary art," as though these people are not only artists but seers. I always preferred the term the French use: "art brut"—raw art. Art like an open wound.

Christmas

A very and I crafted homemade Christmas gifts for everyone. She made drawings, which I covered in thin sheets of Plexiglas before framing them in her homemade Popsicle stick frames, hand-painted and covered in glitter glue. I drew single-line portraits of each of my parents, of Gus and Avery together. I made frames for my drawings out of some reclaimed wood I found in the shed behind the house.

Two days before Christmas, we loaded up the car with our creations, locked up the house, and drove to the ferry. It had been nearly a month since we'd left the island. I couldn't remember the last time I'd read a newspaper. I occasionally checked CNN online to make sure we hadn't gone to war or the plague wasn't sweeping the country, but there was something liberating about becoming completely and absolutely *untouched*.

While I loved going to my parents' house for Christmas, part of me was dreading what I knew was going to be an inevitable conversation about the case, about what would happen once the DNA results came back, if the court granted the motion for a new trial. I knew there would be a visit from Larry. In the guise of holiday cheer, he might stop by with a tin of fudge before beginning his entreaty.

I tried not to think about this as we drove over the river and through the woods. I tried instead to think only of being in my childhood home. Of Avery being the one to hang the angel I'd made in the sixth grade at the top of the tree (my parents had insisted on waiting to put up and decorate the tree until we got there). I tried to think only of my mother's kitchen: the coconut cherry bars, the gingerbread men. I tried to focus on the smell of pine. A fire in the fireplace. Plumbing that worked. *Gus.*

I missed him. While I had hoped being separated (truly separated) from him would help me to get the distance I needed, instead it just made me ache for him. For us. For me and him and Avery together. The longer I was away, the more uncertain I became. The *less* assured that I was doing the right thing.

I held my breath as we flew down Route 9 and sped past the Rousseaus' yellow farmhouse. I flinched but did not slow down as the same dog chased us again, and I glanced only once at the rearview mirror, to see it standing in the middle of the road behind us, barking.

And by the time we pulled into my parents' driveway, my heart and hands had steadied again. I could do this.

My father was at the woodpile, grabbing an armload of wood. He set it down and came to the car, opened the back door and lifted Avery out and into his arms.

No circle of long-lost friends and distant relatives looking at me with sad eyes. Just my dad with the smell of trees on his coat and cold candy canes at the ready in his pocket.

In the kitchen, my mother was cussing at the piecrust. My mother had never, ever been able to make a decent piecrust. Yet she persevered.

"Gahhh," she hollered as the dough stuck to the rolling pin. "Goddamn. Goddamn."

"Gawd. Language, Mom," I said as Avery climbed up onto the counter next to her.

"You need to put tights on the rolling pin, Grammy."

"That so, Muffin?"

"That's what Pilar does. You put tights on and it doesn't stick."

"Well, good thing you're here then!" she exclaimed. "Can I have these?"

Avery, despite the subzero temperatures outside, had insisted on wearing a dress and tights. Cowboy boots with no treads whatsoever. And a hat that looked like a moose, the stuffed antlers jutting out from her head. She looked like she'd been swallowed by Bullwinkle.

Avery giggled as my mother tickled her knees, the tights with the snowflakes threadbare where her skinny bones poked out.

"When does Mark get here?" I asked.

"You mean Maronica?" my father said, coming into the kitchen, followed by Husky, their terrier.

"Maronica?" I asked.

"Mark and Veronica," he said. "It's their ship name." My father spent too much time around teenagers.

"Eww."

"I know," my mother said, reaching out and squeezing my arm. "Wasn't she just such a B-I-T-C-H when he was in high school?"

"You two are terrible," my father said. "She's a nice girl now. Very sweet. A good mom."

Something was burning.

"Crap on a cracker," my mother said. And she opened the oven to a cookie sheet filled with charred gingerbread. "This is not my day."

My father had chopped down a tree from the woods behind the house; the tree had been leaning against the garage for days now waiting for our arrival. When he dragged it in through the front door, I was so overwhelmed with nostalgia, it felt like an almost physical thing, sentimentality an illness. Waves of it, like seasickness, rippled through my body.

And I remembered the trips with my father to pick out the perfect tree. He and I would set out, me carrying the thermos of cocoa, him swinging the ax. We only traveled across the backyard, but in the winter, when the world was made of snow, it felt like we were in the wilderness. I liked to pretend I was Laura Ingalls Wilder out with Pa on the prairie. We'd spend the next hour or more in the woods, examining the prospects, narrowing our choices down to one or two. Then he'd let me pick. My mother preferred the spruces for their lovely branches. But I liked the smell of the Scotch pines. My father would swing his ax, hacking away at the trunk, hollering, *Timber!* into those quiet woods. And I loved the soft hush as it fell. This was a moment of grace, though I didn't know to call it that then. And together, we'd grab the trunk and drag the tree back across the field. The sun sometimes readying itself for bed by the time we made our way out of the woods and home again.

But after what happened with Robby, I never went into the woods with my father again. It was unspoken, this decision. I remember watching him from my window, as he disappeared into the forest. And later when he returned. Watching him drag the tree across the field made my heart ache.

When I was little, Christmas Eve at our house was never the stuff of storybooks. Quiet all through the house, nothing stirring, all that. Instead, it was loud. With all *sorts* of creatures stirring. My parents loved to throw parties, and our house was the obvious place to have them. On Christmas Eve, they made a vat of spiked eggnog and invited anyone (and everyone) in their various social circles who wasn't leaving town for the holidays to come join us: the faculty at the high school, my mother's artist friends. Neighbors, my parents' many, many childhood friends who, like them, had grown up here and never left. Everyone drank too much, including my parents, and danced hard. I distinctly remember the headmaster of the high school getting so drunk he climbed up on the second story roof and sang "O Holy Night" at the top of his lungs. One year, Mrs. Wharton (my pre-K teacher) wouldn't stop kissing people under the mistletoe my mother had hung, including our neighbor, Mrs. Babcock, who smacked her in the face with her beaded handbag. I remember seeing *Breakfast at Tiffany's* when I was in college and telling my friend that was what my house was like at Christmas, pagan, hedonistic. I loved it.

But after that summer when I was thirteen, they stopped having parties. My father's colleagues didn't know what to say or do, and celebrations of any sort seemed inappropriate. I remember that first Christmas feeling lonelier and sadder than I had ever felt before.

Of course, over the years, they returned to a new normalcy, inviting a few friends over to help trim the tree on Christmas Eve, for my father's famous lasagna for dinner. But those wild, wonderful parties were a thing of the past.

This Christmas Eve, the only guests were Maronica (funny, how easily that rolled off the tongue), Mark's best friend, Joey Fannan, his wife, and their new baby, and my parents' friends, the Dickinsons. The Dickinsons had known my parents since college. They were mainstays at our Christmas parties, as well as just about every other holiday celebration at our house.

Avery put on her sparkly red dress, the one I'd bought for her to wear when Pilar took us to see *The Nutcracker* at the Met last year. It was too small and wouldn't button up the back, but she insisted, so I'd jerry-rigged it together with safety pins. She also had, somehow, talked my mother into buying her a pair of se-quined silver boots that looked like miniature disco balls on her feet as she ran through the house.

"Here," my mother said, handing me a board with a giant cheese ball balancing precariously on it. My mother was notorious for her cheese balls. One year, she'd made one as big as a basketball and so filled with rum I'd gotten drunk for the first time after spreading it across a handful of Wheat Thins.

"What a modest cheese ball this year," I said, chuckling at the softball-sized ball.

"Well, I figured since it's just us." She winked.

Mark and Veronica arrived with Joey and Christina in tow. Veronica's towheaded daughter clung to her leg shyly before Avery grabbed her hand and said, "Let's go play upstairs. I have Legos."

Veronica didn't look anything like I remembered her, but what did I expect—for her to show up in her Haven High cheerleading outfit? She was still pretty but had rounded out, softened. Aged.

My father said her husband was shot down over Kabul four years ago; she'd given birth to her daughter while he was deployed. He never even met the baby.

My mother swooped in on Joey and Christina's baby like some great bird of prey, leaving Christina wide-eyed with disbelief as my mother plucked the new baby out of her arms.

"I just want to put you in my mouth and carry you around in my cheek all day," my mother cooed to the baby. "Oh my *God*, I want to eat this baby," she said to Joey.

"I read an article about that," Christina offered. "That feeling of wanting to nibble on their legs. It has something to do with the way babies smell. It activates some chemical in a woman's brain. Like certain foods."

"Well, whatever it is, I am going to start with the toes," my mother said.

"Hi," Mark said, leaning into me for a bear hug. He was ten years younger than me, and it was really only in the last few years he had grown from a pudgy teenager into a man. A big man. With huge shoulders.

"Nom, nom, nom," my mother said.

"Hi," I said to Mark. "Want a drink?"

"God, yes," Mark said, taking off his coat.

While everyone settled into the living room with my mother's cheese ball and all the other relics from her Betty Crocker cookbook (fruitcake and tangy Swedish meatballs, pineapple upside-down cakes and a pile of salvaged gingerbread cookies), Mark and I hung back in the kitchen for a shot of Irish whiskey.

"So, how's Maine?" His cheeks were already red. We were one-quarter Irish on my father's side. That Irish blush came out whenever he had even a bit of alcohol. He could never get away with drinking in high school because his cheeks gave him away. I think that's why he started smoking weed.

"Maine is strange. It's beautiful and quiet. And cold," I said, feeling the whiskey warm my chest in the way only whiskey can.

"Gus came to see you?"

"He came to see Avery," I said. I knew my family was holding out hope Gus and I would somehow make amends. They loved Gus. They might have been as much in love with Gus as I was.

When Gus and I started dating, Mark was only nine or ten. He was like a brother to Mark. Like the older brother he'd always wished he'd had. When Gus and I split up, Mark actually cried. Like a little boy. It had broken my heart.

"And he's coming tomorrow?"

I nodded.

Mark grabbed the bottle and poured another two shots into the empty glasses. We clinked our glasses together and threw our heads back. This one went down like fire.

"I've got a ring in my pocket," he said, raising his eyebrows.

"Like a diamond?" I said, in disbelief.

"Not *like* a diamond. An actual diamond. And shhhh . . ." He leaned toward the doorway to make sure nobody was eavesdropping on our conversation.

"Is she pregnant?" I asked.

"*No*," he said. "Just because you got knocked up and had to get married doesn't mean that's the only reason *everyone* gets married."

"Ouch," I said. "And you know that's not why Gus and I got married."

"Whatever," he said.

"When are you going to give it to her?" I asked. "Not in front of us, I hope. That's just cruel."

"Why?" he said, his face falling.

"Oh my God, Mom will try to eat her or something. And Dad will cry. You can't do that to her. She actually seems nice."

"You think so?" he asked, hopefully. And I realized, in a weird way, he was asking my permission.

"Yeah," I said. "And you seem happy."

"I am happy."

"And kind of drunk," I said.

Nobody climbed up on the roof to sing "O Holy Night," and

there were no lesbian forays under the mistletoe, but everyone laughed and my father got out his trumpet and played some long-forgotten jazz tune. The Dickinsons won a pretty hardcore game of charades, and my mother's cheese ball got eaten in its glorious entirety. And Avery and Veronica's little girl, Amber, fell asleep watching a DVD of *Rudolph* on my parents' bed.

After everyone was gone, I told my parents I'd clean up, and they climbed up the stairs to bed. I hung Avery's stocking on the mantle and stuffed it with all the things I'd picked up for Christmas. Through the window, I watched Mark carry Amber to the car. And after Veronica buckled her into her car seat, Mark, cheeks as red as Saint Nicholas in the porch light, dropped to one knee as he reached into his pocket for the ring. Veronica's hands flew to her face, and she nodded, pulling off her mittens so Mark could put the ring on her finger. I felt my throat swell, my eyes well.

Gus and I had gotten engaged one night when we'd been out adventuring. There had been a party held in a water tower, at the end of a wild scavenger hunt facilitated by one of our artist friends. We'd been told to dress up in 1920s costumes, that we'd be going to some sort of speakeasy. We'd followed the clues all over the city, finally locating a password that would gain us entrance to this crazy party. I'd found a vintage flapper dress at Goodwill, and had worn a headband with a feather in my hair. Gus had a borrowed zoot suit and a fake mustache. All night we talked to each other in affected twenties speak. *How 'bout some cash?* he said in that Bugsy Malone voice, and I kissed him. *Thanks, dollface.*

The party wasn't nearly as amazing as the rest of the adventure had been, but it was fun anyway. There actually had been the very real danger of the cops busting us, just like in a true speakeasy, and so it was with a sort of happy dismay that we descended the dangerous ladder from the water tower at the end of the night.

We'd stood on the rooftop of a building that seemed like it

could quite conceivably crumble into a pile of rubble at any moment, and Gus had grabbed my hand.

"Looks like you've had a little too much giggle water," I said as he tripped over an exposed pipe. "You're zozzled."

I kissed him again. When he dropped to his knee, I thought he'd just stumbled. I reached out my hand to help him up. But he shook his head.

"What are you doing?" I asked.

"I got something for ya, see?" Gus said, never breaking character.

I remember my body suddenly flushing with heat. I had been shivering, freezing cold in that strapless dress, a phony fox stole doing little to keep me warm. But now I was hot.

We'd never talked about marriage. Not even when I'd found out I was pregnant about a month before. Somehow getting married seemed like a bigger deal than having a baby.

"What is that?" I asked, stupidly, when he pulled the tiny diamond out of his pocket.

"It's a manacle, see?" he said.

"Gus?"

"*Well? Will you?*" His gangster voice gone. Just Gus. Just my favorite person in the whole world, Gus.

The ring was now sitting inside my jewelry box next to the birthstone ring my grandparents gave me when I was ten and my National Honor Society pin.

Outside my parents' house, Veronica grabbed the keys from my drunk brother and tried to hold him up even as his feet windmilled across the slippery walk.

After they pulled away, I turned out all of the lights, unplugged the Christmas tree, and loaded the dishwasher. And as it began to hum and whir, I sat down at the kitchen table and cried.

Gus arrived midmorning on Christmas Day as my father was lighting up the barbeque in the snow-filled backyard. He'd bought some frozen meat online and insisted on grilling it despite the subzero temperatures outside.

I was busy packing Avery's things, though she still had enough stuff at Gus's house to last her for the next week. I hadn't been away from Avery for even one night since she was born. As I rolled her tiny socks and tights, folded her skirts and little jeans, I wondered what I had been thinking agreeing to this. And the idea of being back on the island alone for a whole week until Pilar came home was daunting.

When Gus pulled up in a silver Prius, I thought it was just one of my parents' friends coming to wish them a happy holiday. They'd already had three or four people stop by with gifts and cookies.

Avery must have sensed him coming though, because she was tearing down the stairs, her pinwheeling legs a blur. She didn't even have shoes on, but that didn't stop her from opening the heavy wooden door and running outside to greet her dad.

Gus picked her up, brushed the snow off her stocking feet, and rushed her inside.

"Crazy girl," he said. "You don't want to be sick when we go home!"

Home. That word was like an icicle in my heart.

"Hey, Wynnie," he said, kissing me on the cheek. His skin was cold. He'd carried the weather inside with him. "Merry Christmas."

"Come in. Dad's making steaks out back."

"Listen," he said. "I'm so sorry, but I can't stay long today. I've got Mia's car, and I promised I'd have it back to her before six."

Mia? My ears burned, and my chest hurt. He just met this woman and she was already loaning him her car?

"You were supposed to spend the day here. It's *Christmas.*" I didn't mention Mia, but I couldn't, *didn't,* disguise my disappointment. "We haven't even opened presents yet."

"I can stay until noon, but then we have to go. I'm so sorry. I was going to rent a car. But because of the holidays, the prices are all jacked up. Mia is staying in the city today but needs the car to drive to her folks' house in Greenwich tonight."

Greenwich, Connecticut? Nothing said WASPy rich girl like Greenwich. No wonder she was able to work only part-time at a gallery and still manage to live in the city. I took a deep breath to keep from saying something I might regret.

"Fine. Then we better open gifts now."

None of this was what I had imagined. None of this was what that small part of me had hoped for. It wasn't until Gus was loading Avery's presents, which she'd unwrapped in a haste made not from eagerness but from necessity (my parents' generous offerings and the few things I'd managed to procure online and have sent to my parents' house), that I acknowledged I'd been hoping this Christmas would be like the other Christmases. That we'd leisurely open gifts, that we'd eat so much our stomachs hurt and lounge around watching *A Christmas Story*. That when the sun went down, maybe Gus and I would take Avery on a walk around the neighborhood to look at the Christmas lights.

Instead, at noon, Avery clung to my legs for a moment then let go, running after Gus and leaping into the car seat, which I'd transferred from the Honda to *Mia*'s car.

She rolled down the window, and I pressed my palm against her cheek, kissed her forehead, and said, "I'll see you in two weeks, baby girl. You and your daddy stay out of trouble."

"We won't get in any trouble. Daddy's a good boy, Mama."

I swallowed hard and kissed her again.

Gus finished loading the trunk with her presents and came around to the side of the car with a small box in his arms.

"Here you go," he said, and for a split second I thought he was handing me a Christmas gift. Unwrapped, but boxed.

I cocked my head, confused but slightly delighted he'd thought to do something. I had considered getting him a gift but decided against it.

"It's the negatives," he said. "Wes spent a whole weekend developing them."

"Oh," I said, taking the box from him. "Oh my God. That's awesome. I almost forgot."

"Me too. Glad I had to get into the trunk!" he said.

"Thanks, Gus. And please tell Wes I owe him one."

He nodded. "Sure thing. He said there's some crazy shit in there."

"What?" I started, but he was already ducking into the car. The engine was running, and the exhaust blew like dragon's breath into the cold air.

"Roll your window up, Av!" I hollered as the car rolled down the driveway.

Then they were gone. And I was at home alone with my parents. Mark was spending the day with Veronica's family, who also still lived in town. No neighborly visits were planned. And so there was no buffer. Nothing to keep my parents from asking the question they'd been waiting to ask ever since I got home.

They barely waited until I came back through the door, shivering and sad after Gus and Avery pulled away. I peeled off my coat, shoved my scarf and hat and mittens inside the sleeves, and hung the coat on the rack by the door. I kicked off my boots and slid my slippers back on. I wanted nothing more than to trudge up the stairs, look at the contact sheets, and maybe go back to bed for two weeks until Gus brought Avery back to me.

The house, the same one that had seemed so festive and alive with Avery here, now felt like it did when I was in high school. Like everyone was trying too hard to make happy. The Christmas lights, blinking stupidly, seemed to mock me. The Christmas music playing on the radio felt almost accusatory.

I started toward the stairs.

"Wyn?" my mother called. "Come here for a minute?"

Here we go.

She was in the kitchen, doing the breakfast dishes. My father, I presumed, had charged her with this task. Not the dishes, but the plea I knew was coming. He always left her in charge when the questions were hard.

I grabbed a dishrag with a gleeful-looking Christmas tree appliqued on it, and stood next to her, bracing myself.

"Listen," she said, knowing I was liable to start in on my defense before she even opened her mouth.

I sighed.

"You probably know we've been talking with Larry about what will happen if the court grants the motion."

I nodded even as tears began to sting my eyes.

"I know you don't want to hear this, but he says this time you'd need to testify. It would be a new jury. They might even take it to the next county over. Where people don't know you. Where people don't remember."

I shook my head.

"He says even if the so-called new evidence isn't that compelling, the defense would get a second chance. To spin this thing differently. Larry says he's been a model prisoner, he's been taking mental health classes at the prison. He's become religious. He was a boy when it happened. A child. They're going to look at that."

"*I* was a child, Mama."

"Nobody is arguing that. Nobody," she said, setting down the glass she was washing. "But if you don't testify, if they can't see what he did to you. How he . . ." She paused. "How he damaged you . . ."

"You think I'm damaged?" I asked. The word felt like a blade.

My mother rubbed her eyes. "Of course not, that's not what I meant."

"Because I think I bounced back pretty well given what happened," I said, feeling defensive and angry. The idea that I was damaged goods, somehow permanently flawed, and this was how my family saw me, was unbearable. "I finished school, early even. I went to college; I have a career. I got married. I'm a good *mom*," I said. And even as I ticked off my "accomplishments," I felt my argument unraveling. Sure, I'd finished high school in three years.

Not because I was some sort of genius, but because I just wanted out of this town. Out of this house. And art school, my *career*, what had that become? I was painting on command, nothing more than a trained monkey. My marriage had fallen apart. Being a mom was the only thing I hadn't royally screwed up. But Avery was only four. I still had plenty of time for that.

"You're missing my point here, Wynnie," my mother said softly, reaching for my hand. "Your father and I are just hoping to God you'll change your mind. It could mean the difference between him staying in prison and being set free. I get that you don't want to be there. That it would be difficult."

"Difficult?" I almost choked, laughing. "Changing a tire is difficult. Climbing a mountain is difficult."

"Please," my mother said, her face a question. A plea.

When I refused to meet her gaze, to answer her, her tone turned cold. She picked up the glass she had set down and started scrubbing it. I worried the glass might just break in her hand.

"If not for yourself," she said solemnly, "then for the other women he might hurt. If he were to be let out. You have to think beyond yourself, Wynnie. Sometimes, not everything is about you. You have a daughter of your own now. I'd have thought this would make you understand."

And just like that, she'd taken that one last thing I was holding onto, the idea I was a good mom, and shattered it. I thought about Gus and me leaving Avery at the house. About her wetting the bed. About the sadness in her eyes when she talked about missing Gus.

"I'm going for a walk," I said, feeling suddenly as if I might crawl out of my skin.

"Please don't," my mother said softly, her hesitation the same one I knew so well now. Every time I left the house after that day, I felt this tug. My parents not wanting me to go out the door, the irrational fear that this time I might not make it home.

But I couldn't breathe in this house, and so I grabbed my coat from the hook by the door. "At least bring your phone then," she said.

And so I grabbed my phone from the console table by the door and shoved it into my coat pocket. I slammed the door shut behind me. And then I walked.

It was cold outside, the kind of bone-chilling, wet cold you can feel in your marrow. I shoved my hands in my pockets and, head down, trudged forward.

My parents' neighborhood was not far from town. I walked everywhere when I was a kid. Rode my bike in the summer. Haven was the kind of town you only see in the movies. Tree-lined streets, picket fences. The downtown village without a single chain store or restaurant. The town had fought long and hard to keep McDonald's out. When a Starbucks was slated to open in the village, protesters filled the streets, and the Starbucks folks backed out. This was a community that fiercely protected itself. That rallied. Generally, when it came to things like raising money for a new public pool or keeping chains out, it was a good thing. But it was a mob mentality nevertheless. I shuddered to think what would happen if Robby Rousseau were set free. A public lynching would not surprise me.

I made my way downtown. When I was little, I loved this street: the trees laced with white lights, like winter fireflies captured in their branches. Antique shops and coffee shops, and quaint bed and breakfasts. My favorite bookstore, a pet store, and a comic book shop.

But it was Christmas, and everything was closed. It was almost as desolate as Bluffs Island. The lights in every shop were out except for the neon sign at the one little Irish pub on the corner. They couldn't possibly be open, I thought. But as I approached the door and peered into the window, I could see a couple of men sitting at the bar. A bartender moved slowly behind the bar.

I opened the door, the sleigh bells strung on the back of the door jingling. A collective turning of heads as I entered. I made my way to the bar and sat down, smiling at the bartender, who was wiping his hands on his apron. I didn't recognize him.

"What can I get for you?" he asked.

It wasn't until now that I was sitting that I realized how cold I was. I shivered. "Brrr . . ." I said, completely involuntarily. "God, it's cold out."

He nodded.

"Can I get an Irish coffee?" I asked.

"Sure thing."

I looked down the bar at the two men who were sitting there and wondered how it was they were spending Christmas here. I smiled and they returned my smile with a couple of nods.

The bartender brought me the coffee and I put five dollars on the counter. I blew across the top and sipped, letting the hot coffee and whiskey warm me from the inside out. My toes were starting to itch and tingle. They were wet and cold.

"You Ned Davies's kid?" he asked suddenly.

"Yeah," I said, mystified as to how he knew that. Then I realized he was looking, though trying not to, at my neck. I pulled my scarf tighter.

"I remember when you were just a little thing. Ned used to bring you in here. You loved my onion rings."

I had an odd, fleeting memory of sitting at a bar, dipping onion rings into ketchup. God, if he could remember this, I'm sure he could remember a lot of other things about me too.

And sure enough: "I heard that boy might get another trial."

I bristled.

"Seems to me he should be rotting in prison for what he done."

"Yep," I said. What else could I say?

I finished the coffee and the bartender came to me with the coffeepot and a shot. "Top it off?" he asked.

"Sure."

"On the house. Merry Christmas."

"Thanks."

"You here for the protest?" one of the men down the bar chimed in.

"What?" I asked.

"Here," he said, pushing the newspaper he'd been reading down the bar at me. There on the front page was the headline:

LOCAL RESIDENTS TO PROTEST POSSIBLE
RETRIAL OF CONVICTED RAPIST

I set down the second cup of coffee and was both suddenly jittery from the caffeine and buzzed from the booze.

> A man convicted in the brutal 1996 rape and attempted murder of a thirteen-year-old classmate, Wyn Davies, is hoping for a retrial after serving twenty years in state prison. Robert Rousseau's case has been reopened due to the efforts of his defense team and the New Hampshire Innocence Project, who insist new DNA evidence is substantial enough to exonerate Rousseau of the crime. However, many community members in Haven are outraged a convicted felon, one who confessed to the crime, might be afforded this second chance. Demonstrators have set up a makeshift tent city in front of City Hall, demanding the motion be denied.

Why hadn't anyone mentioned this to me? Neither my parents nor my brother had said a word.

> Community activists have organized a protest for December 26, followed by a candlelight vigil in

the lower playing fields at the school where both
Rousseau and Davies attended the eighth grade.
It is unknown whether or not Miss Davies, whose
parents still live in Haven, will speak at the event.

I stood up, knees quaking, and yanked on my coat before
heading back out into the cold. I walked briskly to the end of the
street. There, as promised by the *Haven Gazette,* in front of the
brick City Hall building, were a half dozen brightly colored
tents, some strung with Christmas lights. I swooned with nausea.
Several people, outfitted in parkas and other arctic gear, sat in
lawn chairs outside the tents. I thought about going to them,
telling them to go home to their families. That it was freaking
Christmas, so *for Christ's sake,* go home.

Instead I briskly walked toward them and their shiny red
cheeks. Moving quickly past their odd commune, I held my
breath, shoved my hands in my pockets, and lowered my head.
Would they know me? Would they have any idea this was about
me? Or maybe it wasn't at all.

The community had rallied immediately after the attack as
well. But I was a child then. A little girl. Now I was just another
woman. Anonymous.

"Merry Christmas," a man sitting in a camping chair said,
raising his steaming metal thermos at me as if in cheers.

I stopped and looked at him. Propped up next to his chair
was a sign. On it, enlarged to pixelation, was my seventh grade
photo. This was the photo that was printed in the papers. The
one I had fussed over when it first came back from the photographer. My hair too frizzy. My smile too crooked. My eyes wide.
The cops had chosen this photograph rather than my eighth
grade picture, in which I looked older, was wearing lip gloss and
a sort of half smile on my face. Larry had warned them a photo
should be chosen that showed me looking "innocent." I was thirteen. I was a virgin. I still slept with stuffed animals in my bed. I

was innocent. But my parents had complied. They didn't want to take any chances I might be blamed for what happened to me.

A woman approached me, holding onto a clipboard.

"Would you like to sign this petition to deny a retrial for Robert Rousseau?"

She smiled as if she were a Greenpeace activist outside a grocery store, as if she were trying to save the planet.

"No," I said, the word bursting her bubble, cracking her plastered smile.

"Aren't you concerned a convicted rapist may be released into our community?" She was angry with me now. "Do you have children?" she demanded. As I walked away from her, she insisted, "He violated a *child*. What if she were your daughter?"

I know you got a little girl.

I pressed my mittened hands against my ears and my legs began to run. And when I closed my eyes, I was running across that field again, legs spinning. And I didn't stop until I'd reached my old school.

I stood, breathless and buzzing, in front of the brick K-8 school, closed for the holidays. The windows were filled with construction paper Christmas trees, paper snowflakes. I remember sitting inside those stuffy rooms, cutting and pasting. Learning how to read and do long division. The hours I spent inside those walls almost unfathomable now. I was a little girl then. I thought of Avery, and my chest ached.

Still trying to catch my breath, I walked around the back of the school to the playground and sat down on one of the swings. I could feel the cold metal chains through my mittens. I pushed off and swung. From the highest point, I could see the tops of the trees in the forest that separated the playing fields from my parents' neighborhood. From here the woods appeared to be exactly what they actually were: just a small patch of trees.

I jumped off the swing the way I used to as a kid, and the impact nearly brought me to my knees. And then I ran again, across the blacktop where we used to play dodgeball and foursquare and down the street and to the lower playing fields where I played soccer and the boys played flag football. I ran, the icy snow dampening my pant legs, burning my skin. I ran and ran, the cold air sharp like knives in my chest. I sank down to my knees when I reached the tree line. And I let out a wail I barely recognized. The last time I'd made this sound was almost twenty years ago.

Inquiry

"I know this is difficult, but we need to back up. We need to talk about what happened after you started to make your way across the field. Just so I understand, you knew you were being followed, yet you still went into the woods?"

"Yes. I mean yes, I went into the woods. No, I didn't know I was being followed. I don't remember."

"Were you afraid?"

"Afraid?"

I felt the bass in my heart before the car pulled up next to me on the road. And when I realized who it was, I did feel fear. But I was also thirteen. Nothing bad had ever happened to me; I'd been assured again and again the bogeyman wasn't real. That here, I was safe. And so the beating of my heart, the sweat on my neck, the loose tingle that crawled up my back like my mother's tickling fingers did not register right away as warnings. I'd not yet learned to trust my instincts, my gut. And so instead of turning around, instead of confronting him, instead of yelling at him to stop following me, I shook my head and started down the grassy slope toward the playing fields, toward the woods that would lead me home.

"Again, Ms. Davies, when did you realize you were not alone?"

As if time mattered. As if my knowing anything mattered.

"Can you to tell us what happened when you realized you were being followed?"

His ragged breath behind me, following me.

"Why did you go into the woods, if Robert Rousseau was behind you?"

"I don't remember."

They were in the car, and the car was idling at the edge of the road. But I started into the woods anyway. I was just trying to get home as quickly as possible. This was the shortcut, and I knew on the other side of this path was home. I was thirteen years old. I didn't know then that people could sometimes be monsters. That someone I knew could be capable of hurting me.

And so, while I was afraid of Robby Rousseau, those fears were of him shoving me on the playground, of him saying weird things to me during silent reading that awful time the teacher had moved him next to me. My fears were of his words. His pushing hands. Of his brother in his idling Camaro who seemed to me like a bad guy in a movie. Robby, to me, was more of a nuisance. A jerk. Someone I might actually roll my eyes about to my friends.

The sound of the bass, thrumming like a heartbeat. Pounding in time with my feet, with my heart, as I ran across that green expanse. I was a fast runner, the fastest girl in my class. This is what I thought as I ran toward the woods. I can get away. If he follows me. If they follow me.

"When did you realize you were being followed?"

When the music stopped. When I slipped into the woods and his hands were on my back.

"I don't remember."

"Miss Davies, I'm sorry, but you really need to tell us."

Protest

"Why didn't you tell me?" I said breathlessly as I entered my parents' kitchen.

My father was bent over the open oven, checking on his homemade mac-'n-'cheese. My mother stood at the counter, cutting shallots. The room smelled like Christmas, like the memory of Christmas. The shallots made my eyes burn.

"I was trying to, before you left . . ." my mother started.

"Who are those lunatics down at City Hall?"

My father closed the oven door and turned to me. His shoulders seemed narrower than they once had. "They're not lunatics, sweetheart. They're people who care deeply about you."

"They don't even *know* me," I said, thinking of that seventh grade photo. About how mortified I'd been when it was delivered in its windowed envelope to me at school. How I hadn't shared the wallet sized versions with any of my friends and instead put them in my father's shredder and watched as the blades sliced the images of me into strips. I thought about how I had saved my babysitting money for almost six months to go to the salon and have my hair straightened. How I'd scoured thrift store clothes and the clearance racks at The Limited at the mall. I thought about how I'd practiced a new smile in the mirror, but had wound up feeling silly. Stupid. No breasts, no hips. Just a little girl playing dress-up.

"We were going to talk to you about it."

"When?" I said, feeling my face flush with heat. "It's tomorrow!"

"Larry actually thought it might be a good thing for you to attend. To maybe even say a few words?" my father said.

"She doesn't have to speak," my mother said, as if I were still that thirteen-year-old girl. I didn't need their permission then for my silence, and I didn't need it now.

"I'm going back to Maine," I said. "This is insane. Those people are insane."

"They're saying if he's released he'll probably live here with his brother. Rick still lives here, you know, out on Route 9 . . ." my father said. "People are afraid, Wynnie."

My stomach turned. Again, I pictured Robby walking home, his brother long gone, when the police pulled up next to him and saw the blood, *my* blood, all over him. I imagined him, head down, shoulders sloping forward. *Son,* they might have said. *Son, are you okay?*

I shook my head, tried to rid my imagination of what happened after they realized he wasn't just some kid who'd fallen off his bike. When they took him away and came back with a warrant and discovered what had been going on inside that house. When they found the photos. When they talked to his sister, Roxanne.

"I can't stay here," I said, feeling vertiginous again. Venomous. Poison spiraling through me. I pressed my hands against the wooden kitchen table to ground myself.

"Please don't go back to Maine yet," my mother pleaded. "It's Christmas. Let's forget about all of this. Please."

My laughter was like a bark. "Sure, let's forget all about it." And suddenly I was channeling my thirteen-year-old self. I felt peevish. Ready for a teenage tantrum. "You think I haven't spent the last twenty years trying to do just that?"

My mother looked like I had slapped her, and I felt the horrible crush of guilt that inevitably followed one of these outbursts.

"I'm sorry, Mom," I said, but it was too late. The damage was done. Even though she nodded, I could see the cracks, the fissures

I'd made. I was starting to recognize them; I was destroying everything I loved.

Her eyes were glossy with tears. "Honey, we wanted to wait until after Christmas to tell you, but . . ."

"What?"

She sighed, looked at me with sorrowful eyes. "The DNA results came back."

I felt my legs starting to give beneath me. I gripped the kitchen chair and sat down.

"What did they say?" I asked, feeling light-headed. Like I might pass out.

"I have no idea, sweetheart," my father said. "Larry doesn't even know. It's just my understanding the defense has petitioned the motion for a retrial. That they're going ahead with this."

The Devil and the Deep Blue Sea

I left early the next morning, before my parents woke up. Before the protesters could gather at the courthouse. No matter how benevolent their intentions, it still felt like a violation. Like a betrayal. I imagined them gathering with their candles and their goodwill and it made me want to vomit.

I stopped for gas and, inside the brightly lit mini-mart, grabbed a coffee and a newspaper. On the front page was that old photo of Robby Rousseau, his pocked face and sad eyes. Next to the photo was the image of a bearded man. At first I thought it was a current photo of Robby, but it didn't look anything like him. And the man was not wearing a prison jumpsuit but rather a collared shirt, a sweater. And he was smiling.

DOCUMENTARY FILMMAKER INSPIRED BY LOCAL CRIME

For Christ's sake.

Oscar-nominated documentary filmmaker Michael Ash was also a thirteen-year-old when eighth-grader Robby Rousseau was convicted of the rape and attempted murder of his classmate. But it wasn't until recently Ash became aware of the crime or the controversy surrounding the conviction. When the case was reopened last fall, Ash was inspired to pursue the story of the family behind one of New England's notorious juvenile criminals. "Here he was, a kid my age, who has spent two decades in prison for a crime he might not have committed. On one level, I identified with him. And I just felt like it was my responsibility to tell his side of the story through my art."

I rolled my eyes. *What the hell?*

I threw my money on the counter and tucked the paper under my arm as though I were just another customer coming in for coffee and the paper. As though Robby's eyes hadn't been staring right into mine.

It was still dark, the sun simply a suggestion, as I drove out on Route 9. I took a sip of coffee, realizing I'd forgotten sugar, and it flooded my mouth with bitterness. As I drove by the Rousseau house, I almost missed it. There was no porch light on. No evidence of life, the dog thankfully nowhere in sight. Then the Honda clunked loudly as I drove past the driveway, and I felt my heart drop. *Please, do not break down here,* I prayed. It clunked again, and the engine shuddered. *God, no.*

I pressed my foot hard on the accelerator, and the car lurched forward and, thankfully, kept on moving. I didn't realize for almost a mile I had been holding my breath. I didn't look back even once.

The drive back to the island was lonely. Even though Avery always fell asleep after a few moments under the spell of the lulling engine, it still felt comforting to have her with me, sleeping peacefully in her car seat, her cherub cheeks reflected in my rearview mirror. More than a dozen times I glanced up, looking for her face, only to see a reflection of the empty seat behind me. The empty road.

In four years, I had not been without her for this long. Even when I moved to the other side of the duplex, only a wall separated us. She would knock against it at night, and I would knock back. Gus didn't know about this routine; it was our secret. We'd never been separated by nearly this much time or space. And the implications of this did not hit me until I was driving up onto the ferry. Until there was a body of water between us. It felt scary and sad, while oddly electrifying, a strange freedom.

I wondered if this was what he would feel if he got out. He was thirteen years old when he was arrested, handcuffed at the side of that road. He went peacefully, it was said, though this may simply be a part of the legend. The fable that grew out of what happened to me. The day the rules of the universe were broken, when I went from being a scrawny little girl with an overbite and a blurting sort of enthusiasm about the world to a cautionary tale. I wondered how many hundreds of parents had sent their children off to school, saying, "Remember that little girl, Wyn Davies? *Remember?* Never walk home alone."

He was a man now. Gus's age. Yet, he had spent the bulk of his life in a state penitentiary. Twenty years. Twenty years of concrete walls and cafeteria food and God knows what else. Because of the nature of the crime, he was tried as an adult, although he was not an adult until afternoon. He was just a kid. Like me. Just like Michael Ash, *Oscar-nominated documentary filmmaker.* Goddamn it.

My mother had known not to bring the retrial or the protest up again before I left. Instead, we pretended, as we had so much practice doing, that her words hadn't sliced into me as if I were an overripe peach. And that I hadn't bitten back, an angry dog.

She didn't know, would never know, the reason for my stubborn refusal. The only comfort I took, even as I sensed the anguish I was causing her, was that the truth would cause her more. The lesser of two evils, I thought. Between the devil and the deep blue sea.

This was what I thought as I stared out at the water later on my way back to the island house, the lights of Portland disappearing: *between the devil and the deep blue sea.*

That night I fell asleep alone in the quiet, cold house. And I dreamed of Avery. She slipped in and out of my dreams like a ghost. After a particularly troubling dream about her having a raging tantrum (something she almost never did—she was a placid, easy kid) and my own fury, I got out of bed and went downstairs to the dining room.

I thought I might paint, but then I remembered the box of negatives and contact sheets I'd brought in.

The wood floors were freezing, and as I dug through Avery's closet for her toy magnifying glass (amazed by how quickly this house had begun to fill with our stuff, with the accoutrements of our lives), I swore I could see my breath.

The magnifying glass was, of course, buried in the depths of a makeshift dress-up box, hiding under a knight costume Pilar had bought for her, thrilled Avery had eschewed the princess in favor of the armor and shield and sword.

I set everything up at the kitchen table. I got a piece of paper to create a log so I could keep track of which images seemed to merit enlargement. Thankfully, Wes had put all of the contact sheets in date order with their corresponding negatives in an envelope stapled to each sheet.

The first batch was primarily made up of duds, and I was grateful I hadn't spent the money getting them developed. I quickly moved to the second contact sheet and peered through the magnifying glass.

It looked like these had been taken at some sort of rural county fair. We used to go to the Lancaster fair when I was a kid. I had a hazy memory of being on a Ferris wheel with my father, peering over the edge at my mother holding my baby brother in her arms, waving up at me. But the images in these photos were not of the Ferris wheels and 4-H animals, of cotton candy and rows of shiny candy apples. Instead, these were images of the grizzled-looking carnies and their beaten-up trailers. The freak show tents, and the people lined up to pay a dollar to see The Amazing Lobster Boy or The Headless Lady. Carnival barkers and teenage boys, maybe twelve years old, smoking cigarettes, posturing like men in front of the girlie show stages.

There were three whole rolls of film of the girlie shows.

I vaguely remembered someone telling me about this, about these carnival strippers. In the Depression era, they were traveling burlesque shows. Burlesque had made a comeback in the city in the last few years. Wes actually dated a girl who danced for a burlesque review on the Lower East Side. She'd trained as a dancer at Juilliard, but now she looked like a forties pinup girl, and, according to Wes, could twirl tassels on her boobs in opposite directions. Apparently, this was a highly coveted skill in the burlesque world.

But the images in the negatives were not old-timey burlesque with boas and garter belts. These were strippers. Seedy, raunchy strippers. And the photographer seemed obsessed with them. There were photos of the stages, the backs of the men's heads as the men peered up at the torn fishnets, and the blank, glazed stares of the women. There were also photos taken from the stage; the photographer must have somehow gotten behind them, in order to peer out at the sea of hungry faces, at the leering, jeering men with their greasy, slicked-back hair and their rotten teeth.

The strippers smiled. Teased. Flirted. Behind them, hand-painted banners read: *Exotics from World Famous Show Places, Oriental Dancing Girls, Girl World.* And the most straightforward: *Girls. Nude.*

There were also photos of the tent behind the stage, the place where the men could line up and pay three dollars to see and *do* a whole hell of a lot more than they could on the midway. One entire strip of negatives was of this striped canvas tent, as if the photographer had circled around to the back. And finally, a hole, probably something cut out by one of those teenage boys to peep through.

In the first photo, the depth of field was shallow, focusing on the tent, the torn canvas; whatever was on the other side of that hole was a blur. But the photographer corrected the aperture in the next one, and so the tent, the foreground, blurred, and the image inside came into focus.

A completely nude woman squatted at the edge of a stage. A man wearing a baseball cap high on his head shoved his face in her crotch while the other men cheered him on. And the woman gazed intently, straight at the camera. Locking eyes with the photographer. And it was a look neither pleading nor accusatory, but rather one of defiance.

Go ahead, she seemed to say. *Look at me and what I am allowing this man to do.*

Inquiry

"When did you realize he intended to hurt you?"

At first I didn't resist. Funny, how a woman's inclination is always to placate rather than to fight. When his hands touched me, reached out and grabbed the back of my shirt, instead of pushing him away or kicking at him like a wild animal caught in a trap, instead I tried to talk to him. "I have to go home," I said. "I have a lot of homework."

I have no idea why I thought this logic would appeal to him. Robby Rousseau was notorious for not doing his homework. Every day, the teacher wrote his name on the board in the detention box when he failed to turn in his work. It was clearly not something that concerned him.

When he didn't let go, but instead pulled harder, and my shirt started to pull off my shoulder, I kept trying. "My mom's waiting for me. She's going to wonder where I am."

Again, nonsense to a boy whose own mother was a mystery, a gaping hole.

It wasn't until he had not only my shirt but my body in his grip that I started to fight back. I couldn't help but wonder what would have happened had I not been trained my entire life to try to reason with people. If I hadn't learned to appease rather than argue, to engage rather than enrage.

Even as he shoved me down onto the wet green leaves—God, the whole world smelled like rain—I tried to think of the words that would save me. The syllables, if strung together in the right order, that might sway him. The last time he'd pushed me, the teacher had found him. Had made him apologize. "Please," I said.

"Miss Davies?"

Depression Glass

I pored over the contact sheets for hours. There was one sheet for each roll of film, and it took me forever to examine the tiny frames with my primitive magnifying glass. There were almost two thousand images. And while there were many rolls that held nothing but missed opportunities—shots taken the moment *after* something had happened, a missed glance, a turned head, the blur of something just out of the frame—there were other strips of images which were nearly perfect in their composition. I found myself at a loss as to how I would select which ones to print. It was exhausting, culling through these pictures, and as I discovered each incredible, ephemeral moment that had been captured inside these little shells, I felt a strange sense of responsibility. I had somehow become the unofficial curator of this photographer's work. It was daunting.

By the time I looked up again, my neck was stiff from being hunched over and the sun was coming up. I stood up, stretched my back, listened to the *rat-a-tat-tat* of my bones cracking.

Normally, Avery would be getting up hungry and talkative, wanting to relay her incomprehensible dreams to me. She would climb up into the kitchen chair, babbling about waterfalls and slides and fairies and giant blocks of chocolate and cats that could talk and all the other fantasies of her four-year-old mind while I made pancakes or waffles or oatmeal. She liked her oatmeal with apples but no raisins, extra cinnamon. And when it was cooked, I used a spoon to make a little pool in the center where I'd pour the fake maple syrup I practically had to buy in bulk. I didn't eat breakfast until later. And even then, it was never a sit-down affair: a slice of toast with honey, a hard-boiled egg peeled and popped into my mouth almost as an afterthought.

The world felt off-kilter without Avery here. And I still had two weeks to go.

I peered out the window down at the rocky shore below the house, at the sun rising over the watery horizon. And I thought of the person who took the photos. Had they lived here? What might have brought them here? Seamus seemed to know something about the photos. I wished I'd asked him more questions. Maybe even told him about the photos; I wasn't sure why I'd lied. I guess I wasn't ready to share them yet. Pilar's response to the one photo she'd seen was enough to convince me I wasn't crazy. These were amazing photographs. Moving. Raw. Visceral.

I set the contact sheets aside, feeling weak with hunger. Standing with the refrigerator door open, I stuffed a fistful of sandwich meat into my mouth, then decided to go on a walk.

I climbed down to the beach, my instinct (that habitual, maternal impulse to caution Avery to go slowly, to not get too close to the frigid water crashing against the sand) now connected to nothing. I walked the length of the beach looking for sea glass, but I didn't find even a single piece. It was as if these little treasures weren't here without Avery present. Illogical, I know, but the beach seemed more barren, less yielding than it had when she was here with me.

"Hello down there!"

I pressed my hand against my chest, startled. I peered up the cliffs ready to run, my legs poised to flee. But it was only Seamus Ferguson standing at the top of the rocky stairwell, waving.

I lifted my hand away from my chest and waved back.

"Mind if I join you?" he hollered down.

I shook my head.

He climbed down the stairs toward the beach. He was wearing the same outdoor catalog getup he'd had on the other day, and now, with the wind in his hair, he looked every bit the part of the J. Crew "distinguished older guy."

When he reached me, his face broke into a smile.

"Merry Christmas," he said. "Did you have a nice holiday?"

I shrugged. "I suppose."

"Where's your little one?" he asked, peering down the beach as if I'd just let her wander off.

"With her father."

"Oh," he said. But he didn't ask why he wasn't here with me. It was amazing to me how everyone so quickly jumped to the conclusion we were simply divorced. As if there were anything simple about what was going on between Gus and me.

I suddenly thought about the swimming pool. The fact that Gus and I had been pressed up against the cold blue tiles of this guy's pool. How far we might have gone if the baby monitor hadn't gone off. I was grateful for the bracing wind, which would hopefully explain my bright red cheeks.

"How long are you staying?" I asked.

"I'm just here for the weekend, but we'll be back for New Year's Eve. We always have a party at the house," he said. "We've got people flying in from all over the country."

I knew there was a small private airport on the island. I'd both heard and seen some private jets, biplanes, and helicopters.

"Wow," I said.

"Would you like to join us?" he asked. Then his face fell. It was barely perceptible, but I noticed. He was thinking about his wife. This was confirmed when he peered back up toward the house, which loomed in the distance like some grand sand castle at the edge of the sea.

"Oh, that's okay. Pilar's coming back that day too. We'll probably just celebrate at home. Get some champagne, watch the ball drop online."

Back in New York, before Avery was born, New Year's Eve was one of my favorite holidays. Pilar, Gus, and I would get dressed to the nines, finding gowns at the thrift store around the corner, wearing impossible heels. We didn't bother with Times Square. We didn't have to, because somebody somewhere was always throwing a huge party. We'd drink ourselves silly and wait until the clock struck midnight. Then we'd hold onto each other, falling over, kissing. There was such promise in those moments. It's hokey, but I always loved being at the edge of the New Year. The metaphorical implications of it. The freshness. Like being handed a blank canvas upon which to paint my life. I secretly wrote down my resolutions, curled them up into tiny scrolls, and popped them into the empty champagne bottle. All year long, they'd live there. Most of them, of course, were abandoned. But many were kept. Little promises to myself.

"Pilar is your friend, the one with the pie?" he asked.

"Yes," I said.

"Well, of course you're both invited," he said. "And we won't take no for an answer."

I was pretty sure his wife would, indeed, *happily* take no for an answer, but the truth was, I was curious about what was inside that massive house. How does one even furnish such a place? When Gus and I moved from our studio apartment into the duplex, there were huge empty spaces, like missing teeth in a child's mouth.

"If she's not too tired when she gets in, maybe we'll come by," I said.

"That would be great! It's always quite an affair," he said, and started back across the beach. "Well, look at this!" he said suddenly, bending over to pick something up from the beach.

"What is it?" I hollered after him as a cold gust of wind blew across the beach.

He came over to me and handed me the bright red stone.

"Wow, I've never seen a piece this color before," I said.

It was sea glass, scarlet red, blood red.

"I read somewhere they had to use real gold to make red glass. It was so expensive, it was never mass-produced," he said.

Mass-produced. I thought about Ikea. About the birches. *Bjorkar,* the tag might say. Forty-nine dollars.

"Wow." I studied the perfectly tumbled glass in my palm. "What was the red glass used for?" Certainly not beer and soda bottles.

"Oh, lots of different things: car brake lights, Depression glass. Around here though, it's most likely from a warning lantern on a boat."

"Cool," I said. I started to hand it back to him, but he shook his head.

"Give it to your daughter. She collects them, no?"

How did he know that? Had he watched us on the beach?

"Thanks," I said. "I will. Most of the pieces she has are blue and green."

He nodded awkwardly.

"See you on New Year's Eve then," he said, and headed back up the stairs.

Inside I put the piece of glass on the shelf by the kitchen sink. And I wondered whose boat had to wreck in order for it to survive. If a mermaid's tears could be made of blood.

Self-Portrait

Back inside, I returned to the contact sheets. Curious. Looking for clues, though I had no idea what mystery I was trying to solve. The first canister had been dated July 1976, and there were approximately twelve contact sheets for each year, twelve rolls of film, one for each month. But then there was a big gap: 1976, then 1978. Not a single roll from 1977. That was strange. I wondered if it was possible Wes had lost a year. But then I counted the sheets again, and they coincided exactly with the number of rolls I had counted before I sent them off with Gus.

I shuffled to the next contact sheet in the pile. The date marked in grease pencil at the top said 5/1/78. I grabbed the magnifying glass and peered at the first strip of images. It was a house. *This* house. Taken from a distance, and possibly through the windshield of a car, but it was definitely this house. I could tell from the peak of the roof, from the gray clapboards and paned windows. The next photo was similar, only closer up, and this time I could clearly see the dash of a car in the foreground. Whoever took the picture must have been driving toward the house. At first it was unclear what the next photo was of, the frame filled with what could be a series of brushstrokes. I realized it must be the trees that lined the road on both sides.

And then there was the house again. It reminded me of the photos I had seen of my mother when she was in her twenties, the images both her and not her. The architecture of her face the same, the slant of her grin, the expression of mild amusement in her eyes identical to the same woman who was now approaching seventy. But at the same time, so young. It was impossible to identify what was different except for the vague certainty of youth. A tightness, a tautness, an enthusiasm and curiosity and hopefulness. So too was it with the house in the photo. While it bore a striking *resemblance* to this house, it also possessed a freshness, an optimism it no longer did. It looked *hopeful*, this black and white imposter. It was obviously shot before the house began its slow and inevitable decline.

The next sheet was dated 5/14/78. The images in the top strip were completely out of focus, but the shape of a woman standing in a mirror was clear. I peered through the magnifying glass, moving from one frame to the next, finally settling on one image. Also a bit out of focus, it was still this woman, a towel wrapped around her body, leaning forward toward what I assumed was the camera on the counter before her. I felt my throat thicken.

This was *her*. The photographer. That was her camera.

The next image was the same woman, but this time, the photo was sharp and clear. Now naked from the waist up, she was holding an infant, also naked, in the crook of her left arm. The woman's nipples were like dark, flat saucers, her breasts swollen and beaded with breast milk. The baby couldn't be more than a couple weeks old. It still had the black nub of its umbilicus, peeling skin on its feet, and fine, downy hair covering its body. I looked at the woman's face, which was half in shadows, her long, dark hair like a curtain. The ends of it reaching her waist, which was soft and swollen. The camera was sitting on the counter, obscuring her pubic area.

I strained my eyes; even with the magnifying glass it was hard to see the details, but it seemed this was the upstairs bathroom, the one off the bedroom where I'd been sleeping. The door was open behind her, and while the background of the photo was out of focus, I could see the soft blur of a bed, rumpled sheets.

The next strip was of the same woman, the same bathroom, perhaps only seconds later. In the first image, the baby had woken, and its eyes were struggling to focus. Its mouth was open and its small chest was constricted and shoulders hunched. I could almost hear the beginnings of a familiar wail, the small sorrows of a newborn. In this photo, the woman was staring at her own reflection. She had captured the exact moment before she was needed, that split second before she was called away, pulled out of herself, removed from this moment of peace. And indeed, in the next picture in the stack she was now attending to the infant, awkwardly cupping her breast into the child's mouth, her nipple raw and bruised. She was wincing. In this photo, her hair now completely concealed whatever was happening in her eyes.

There were several rows of overexposed photos on the sheet below this. A few shots of the doorway, of the empty bed. Ten photos of the crumpled sheets, of sheer curtains blowing through the open window, *my* window, which looked out at the turbulent sea.

I went to the scanner and scanned the contact sheet, using Photoshop to zoom in on that one photo. On the infant. I studied the way the light caught each individual rib as her chest contracted prior to the scream. The baby was a girl, the swollen genitals further indication she was very, very newly born. I scrolled up to the woman's face, the only element of the photo that lacked perfect clarity. Though her hair obscured part of her face, the one eye that was exposed stared back at me, almost as if imploring. Challenging. Like the other women she'd photographed: *accusing.*

This is my story, she seemed to say. *Here is my truth.*

Inquiry

"Miss Davies, when you take the stand you are going to be sworn to tell the truth. Do you understand that?"

"Yes, sir."

"And so it's important you tell us everything that happened, exactly as it happened."

Sometimes I dream the smell of the air that afternoon. The green, muddy, spring smell. The blossoms and bloom. Sometimes I only dream this: not his face, not his hands, not the knife. Just the scent. And for some reason, those dreams are nearly as terrifying as anything else my mind could conjure.

There are several weeks in the spring in New Hampshire when the ground is still cold, frozen in places, while the leaves and trees assert themselves. Defiant. It is purgatorial, this place between the chill of winter and the promise of spring. This is where I lived: between winter and spring, between childhood and adolescence. Between that grassy field full of sunshine and the terrifying depths of those woods. At the precipice. At the sharp, thin edge.

A shove. That is how it began. Two hands pressed against my back so hard it took the wind out of me, and then I was facedown in the mucky leaves. They were cold, almost frozen. My eyes blurred, and the musky scent of the leaves filled my nose. I tried to stand up, but he pushed me down again.

"So he followed you into the woods. Once you were there, did he push you down? What did he say to you?"

He said nothing. There were no words for what was happening. Maybe he knew this too.

I remember he wore sneakers, filthy, his toes pushing through the ends. And for just a moment, I felt sorry for him. That his shoes were falling apart, and that the ground was so wet. For one, bizarre moment, it was pity I felt for him.

And I still believed then in the possibility I could somehow get out of this. That this was all just a cruel joke or some sort of misunderstanding. I racked my brain for something that would explain why Robby Rousseau in his ratty sneakers and Wrangler jeans would be angry enough to knock the wind out of me and drag me into the forest. Had he heard me say he was creepy to someone during lunch? Had I accidentally done something to offend him? I struggled to understand what I could possibly have done or said or even thought, because in this moment I believed—I had to believe—I still had the power to undo it.

His hands were on my shoulders then, pinning them to the ground. I felt the cold, damp earth soaking through my T-shirt. And he was above me. I remember the sun made a sort of golden aura around him. His features were obscured by my own blindness.

"I'm sorry," I said. But I knew even as the words left my mouth it was ridiculous, a blanket apology for anything I could possibly have done to him.

There was terror in his eyes. I do remember this. And for just a moment I thought he was going to let me go. His grip on my shoulder lessened. He was scared. But then I looked up and saw his brother standing there, leaning against a tree, smacking gum between those vicious jaws.

"Miss Davies, are you okay?"

Auld Lang Syne

That first week alone at the house without Avery, waiting for Pilar, crawled. I became obsessed with the photos. With this woman, this photographer, who had lived here all those years ago. Was she the woman whom the man in the restaurant was talking about? If so, what happened to her? Where did she go? And why did she leave her photos behind? Seamus had to know something, but I wasn't sure how to ask him. Especially not with Fiona around. Maybe at the New Year's Eve party I'd get a chance to speak to him again.

In the mornings I dragged myself to the dining room to work on the birches, avoiding Ginger, who checked in at least every other day on my progress. Avoiding those other, empty, canvases too. In the afternoons (often into the evenings), I'd go through the contact sheets. By the time New Year's Eve arrived, I had at least fifty negatives I wanted to have printed. I cataloged them chronologically. It seemed important to me to get it right. To what end, I still didn't know. With every image, I felt like a voyeur.

All of the sheets from 1978 featured the woman (the woman from the mirror, though her hair had been chopped away now). In one whole roll, she was reclined on a chintz sofa, in a dress too small for her body. The thin straps dug into her shoulders and her breasts pushed uncomfortably against the tight bodice. The images on the contact sheet were small, and it was difficult to see the details, but when I peered closely, I could see something lying on the floor, half of it outside the frame. I squinted to make out what it was. Then I realized: it was the baby. Its fat arm reaching toward the woman. But her gaze was at the camera, again somehow both accusation and plea.

There were more pictures of the infant, but she always appeared at the periphery, screaming in a playpen in the background of a self-portrait of the woman smoking on the couch, a pile of ash collecting on the chintz sofa. In a high chair at the table, head resting on the tray, while her mother stood as still as stone in front of the camera, her head out of the frame, just her ravaged, nude body in the forefront.

I thought of my own body after Avery was born, how I could barely bring myself to look in the mirror. How I'd refused to undress with the lights on. How I couldn't bear for Gus to see what pregnancy, what *birth* had done to me. Her audacity made me feel ashamed. Made me feel vain. The images offered such raw and unapologetic honesty.

A few of the rolls confused me, however. They weren't taken in this house. Not as far as I could tell anyway. Instead they seemed to be photos of the insides of someone's drawers. Careful rows of stockings and socks. The hint of lace from a folded pair of panties. There were also photos of objects: watches, earrings. A hairbrush. The bottom edge of a mirror, which reflected a massive, ornately carved wooden footboard. There seemed to be someone in the bed. The shape of a man? There were also ten photos taken from inside a bathtub. But it wasn't the tub I sat in each night. This one seemed to be a claw-foot tub with chrome fixtures, her naked body reflected, distorted in the elaborate faucet. There wasn't much of interest in these photos other than piquing my curiosity. I x'ed out most of those negatives, except the ones I wanted to blow up in order to see more clearly.

I was starting to think of the photos as being of two groups: those taken before she moved to the island, and those taken after. But which ones were the *Epitaphs,* and which were the *Prophecies*? I looked up *epitaphs* again online, and most of what I found were engravings on tombstones. John Keats's: ". . . Here lies One

Whose name was writ in Water." I Googled the phrase, and found it originated from a line in a seventeenth-century play: "All your better deeds Shall be in water writ, but this in Marble." Could the older photos somehow be that marble? The only permanent thing evidencing her life?

But what, then, of the other photos, the domestic ones? Were these *Prophecies*? And if so, what did they predict? What sort of divination did these sad photos offer? While the *Epitaphs* photos captured something vibrant, raw and dirty and terrifying, but *alive*, the *Prophecies* photos seemed a study in domesticity: a haggard mother, the trappings of a woman's life. There was one negative strip of just the wallpaper in the upstairs hallway, its tangled vines and cabbage roses like plump fists. She focused in on the roses until it was impossible to discern what they even were anymore. As I cataloged the *Prophecies* photos, I felt suffocated. The walls of this house closing in around her. Around me.

It had only been a week since Christmas, but I was so hungry for company. I was driving myself crazy trying to make sense of the photos. What did any of it matter? Was I just using them as an excuse to avoid the birches? Or maybe just a distraction from the looming court decision. I knew the phone could ring at any moment with the news Robby would be granted another trial. I really just needed Pilar to get here. To have someone to talk to besides myself.

I cleaned the house, changed the linens, made lasagna and three dozen of her favorite cookies. I woke up three or four times during the night before she was set to arrive. The anticipation was almost childlike.

On New Year's Eve day, the sky was bright, as if the sun knew Pilar was coming and was making a special effort to shine. But as I was gathering my things together to meet her at the ferry, my phone rang, and before I even picked up, I knew.

"Wynnie?" she said.

"Yep?"

"I'm stuck in Philly. It's snowing like crazy, and my flight is canceled."

I looked out the window at the bright blue sky and felt betrayed. How could it be snowing in Philadelphia when it looked like spring here?

"When's the next flight?" I asked.

"I don't know. There are only a handful into Portland each day. I'm thinking I could maybe fly into Manchester if I have to and rent a car to drive up. But it would probably be late."

Disappointment felt like a brick in my chest.

"But what about the party?" I asked. I had told her about the New Year's Eve party and she'd been just as intrigued as I had been.

"The last ferry is at six o'clock," I said, "because of the holiday."

"I know. I'm sorry. Do you think I might be able to stay at your folks' house tonight? On my way?" she asked.

"Of course," I said. "Do you have their number?"

"I think so. And I'll leave their place at the crack of dawn. I should be there by midmorning. We'll drink champagne then."

Now that Pilar wouldn't be here for New Year's Eve, I thought about skipping the party, just putting on my long johns, heating up the lasagna, and watching Ryan Seacrest. I'd asked Gus what he and Avery were doing, and he said he was taking her to see the fireworks in Prospect Park in Brooklyn with some friends.

"She'll never be able to stay up until midnight," I'd said, feeling a little jealous. I had sort of thought I'd be with Avery when she did the countdown for the first time.

"I'm bringing the wagon, with lots of blankets and pillows. She can snooze if she wants."

"Just make sure she wears a hat," I'd said, sounding more bitter and bossy than I intended. I wondered if Mia would be there. Pictured her tagging along. Would people mistake them for a family?

I needed to get out of the house, out of my head. If even for one night.

I dug through my clothes, looking for something, anything at all appropriate, to wear to a fancy schmancy mansion party. Finally, when my own closet yielded nothing more than jeans and cords and wool sweaters, I went to Avery's room and dug through her dress-up box, which she'd insisted we bring with us to Maine. I vaguely recalled putting the dress I'd worn to that speakeasy water tower party in here, thinking there would never again be an occasion for me to wear such a thing. And sure enough, beneath the superhero capes and the princess gowns was my dress. That shimmery, 1920s beaded affair with fringe at the knees.

I wondered if it even fit me anymore. Before Avery was born, I'd been built like a boy. Narrow hips, small breasts. Pregnancy had given me curves for the first time in my life. But now, I felt like a deflated balloon. Swollen up to capacity and then popped. Stretched out. I thought about the photo in the *Prophecies* pile I'd seen that was a close-up of something unidentifiable at first. It had taken me several minutes to figure out it was the woman's stomach. A network of stretch marks like a spider's web, the hollow black hole of her belly button like a fat spider at the center.

I stripped out of my clothes and pulled the dress over my head, yanking at it until I remembered the hidden side zipper, which, thankfully, made the job a bit easier, and as the fringy bottom tickled my bare legs, I looked in the mirror. And I realized I hadn't looked in the mirror, not more than a cursory glance to make sure I didn't have anything stuck in my teeth, in weeks. I barely recognized myself.

My hair was frizzy. I'd stopped wearing makeup, unless you counted Burt's Bees lip balm, and so my face was colorless. Gone. I looked like a ghost of myself. And I was horrified. Was this the way I had looked when Gus was here? I tried but couldn't remember if I'd bothered to check my reflection before his visit.

In high school, I'd worn a lot of makeup. Too much makeup. I studied *Seventeen* magazine to learn how to apply liquid eyeliner and eye shadow and lipstick. I spent the little bit of allowance my parents gave me on drugstore mascara and blush. I knew it made my parents uncomfortable. Why I'd want to call attention to myself was beyond both my mother and father's understanding. After everything that happened, most girls would likely want to disappear. What I couldn't explain was that my face was my first canvas, that cheap makeup my paint. And what I was doing was painting the face of someone normal. A regular girl. A girl who went on dates and sat in the bleachers at football games hoping one of those boys on the field would notice her. I painted the face of a girl who went to dances and ran for president of the class. I painted the face of a girl who volunteered after school at an arts center for underprivileged kids, who won art contests and public speaking contests and got a nearly perfect score on her SATs. I painted the face of a girl who wasn't completely broken inside. A girl who hadn't taken a shortcut home one spring afternoon in the eighth grade.

Maybe they knew. And maybe they understood that painting this new girl meant erasing the old one.

I dug through my drawer looking for a pair of stockings, finding mostly pilly wool leggings. Finally, I found a pair of soft pink ballet tights I'd worn exactly once, when Pilar convinced me to take an adult ballet class with her. Now the only thing I needed to conjure from thin air was a pair of shoes. The shoes I'd actually worn with this dress were long gone; the heel had snapped off that night as Gus and I descended the ladder from the water tower.

I rummaged through my closet: clogs, Uggs, sneakers, a pair of vintage motorcycle boots. Finally, near the back, I found a pair of ballet flats. They'd have to do.

I had nothing to wear to keep warm besides my big, lumpy down parka. I shrugged. Whatever. It was freaking Maine after all.

All afternoon, I had heard the whirring sound of helicopters overhead, delivering guests to the island, I supposed. I could also hear the party from my house. It was so strange for the still air outside to suddenly be filled with the distant sounds of music. I could also see the lights from the living room windows. The whole house was so illuminated that the lights glowed through the trees separating the two properties. Still, I didn't want to be the first to arrive, so I waited until nearly ten thirty before I made my way (down the rocky ledge, across the beach, and up the steps) to the Fergusons' house.

I was greeted at the door by a gentleman who looked like he was dressed up as a butler before I realized he probably *was* a butler. He ushered me into the house, taking my lumpy parka.

I was shivering, and my body trembled when the air hit my bare arms.

"Come in, please," he said. And he motioned for me to follow him across the cold marble floors of the great room, toward the sound of the music.

He left me at the ring of the doorbell.

I stood at the threshold of a formal living room, staring at a sea of people who seemed not to have noticed my entrance at all. And I wondered for a minute if I was really here. If this was a dream.

There was a string quartet set up around a grand piano to the left, the musicians sawing away at their cellos and violas. To the right was what I assumed to be an open bar, where a man in a tuxedo was pouring drinks. The bottles of liquor and wine reflected the lights of the enormous chandeliers hanging overhead. Most of the people seemed to be contemporaries of the Fergusons, elegant older ladies and gentlemen. Powdery skin, coiffed silver hair. Every person here was white. There were a few people who looked closer to my age, women in expensive dresses and impossible heels. Men in tuxedos, laughing loudly. There was more money in this room than in all of Maine, I suspected.

I almost turned around and went back the way I had come. Seriously, I did not belong here, but suddenly Seamus material-

ized at my side. "Wyn," he said. "I'm so delighted you were able
to come. Where is your friend? Pilar, is it?"

"There's snow in Philadelphia," I said. "She won't be here
until the morning."

"Oh, no," he said. "We're missing a few of our guests from the
West Coast because of that storm. The party's usually much bigger."

I looked around at the room full of guests. There had to be
two hundred people here.

"Can I get you something to drink?" he asked.

"Whiskey?" I shrugged. I knew wine wasn't going to cut it
tonight.

"Sure thing," he said, not taken aback at all by my request.
"How about a nice single-malt Scotch?"

"Perfect," I said.

"Come," he said and we walked toward the bar, where he
leaned into the bartender's ear. Within moments, I had a cold
glass in my hand. And Seamus had one too. "Chin chin," he said.

We clinked glasses and I took a good, long swallow. A couple
more, and I might lose both the chill I'd brought in from outside
and the weird chill in the room.

"I want you to meet some people," he said.

I really, really wished Pilar were here. She'd gotten good at
hobnobbing in the last year. It was part of her job now. And despite the fact that she looked like an eccentric artist, she would
have been completely comfortable in this room. I, on the other
hand, felt like someone wearing something from her four-year-
old's dress-up box.

I wondered where Fiona was.

"Harry," Seamus said to an older gentleman with one wandering eye. "This is our neighbor, Wyn Davies." I could not recall
ever giving Seamus my last name.

"Wyn, this is Harry Johansen. He's one of my oldest, dearest
friends."

I extended my hand, which he bent down and kissed. I'm

pretty sure this was the first time anyone had ever kissed my hand.

"Hi," I said.

"Wyn and her friend, Pilar, are artists," he said.

"Pilar Santiago?" Harry said, his eyes widening.

Again with the last names. Maybe this was some sort of psychic convention.

"Yes," I said. "How did you know?"

"I just read the profile the *Times* did on her. I am dying to get my hands on one of her early pieces."

Her "early pieces." This made me almost laugh out loud.

And I recalled being in the studio at school, smoking weed and squeezing out tubes of paint onto the canvases. Those paintings, to me, represented a time of false prosperity. Because as soon as we graduated, it was gone.

"Do you know if she's interested in selling?" the little weasel of a man asked me.

"I don't think so," I said. Though who knew? It seemed like Pilar was selling almost everything she was making lately. But somehow it didn't seem nearly as icky as my commissions. She simply painted whatever she wanted to paint, and people emptied their pockets for whatever was at the other end of the paintbrush. That felt inspired to me, while my own commissions (especially during the times when my trees were in the highest demand) made me think of the line curling around the HoneyBaked Ham shop at Easter. People lined up like robots, buying the thing they were supposed to love.

"Well, when she returns, I would love to talk to her. I'm sure I could make a tempting offer."

I'm sure.

I really, really wished Pilar were here. These were the types of phonies we poked fun at. But then again, this was her world now. Perhaps she wouldn't poke fun at all. It was people like these who were funding her entire life (and, peripherally, my own, if I were

being honest with myself). Maybe it was good she wasn't here. I
didn't think I could bear to see her suck up.

Seamus introduced me to several more people, most of whom
were primarily interested in Pilar. Then finally, we were alone for a
moment.

"Listen," I said. "I was wondering if I could pick your brain a
little bit about the house next door, Pilar's house?"

His mouth twitched. "Oh, sure," he said.

"Did you know the woman who lived in the house? I think
she was a photographer? You mentioned something about photos?"

"Yes, yes. Of course, but she didn't live there very long. I
think she moved back to the mainland after a couple of years."

"With her baby," I nodded.

"No," he said, shaking his head. "I don't recall she had any
children."

"Yes," I said, confused. "She had a daughter."

"I'm sorry," he said, clearing his throat. "As I mentioned,
we're only here a few times a year. I really didn't know her."

Suddenly, Fiona approached us. Or rather *floated* toward us.
She was wearing a pale yellow evening gown. It looked like
melted butter, pooling on the floor behind her.

"Ms. Davies," she said so formally it made me straighten my
posture. She caused what I thought of as *the principal effect,* that
hot, liquid feeling of being a kid and having been caught doing
something bad. She'd only said my name, and I already felt scolded.
She may have been wearing melted butter, but she was cold. Practically congealed.

"Hi!" I said, as cheerfully as I could.

"So pleased you could make it. Your dress is stunning."

I looked down, having practically forgotten what I was wearing. I noticed some of the fringes had knotted. I felt like Avery
playing dress-up.

"Yours too," I said, nodding. She, on the other hand, clearly remembered *exactly* what she was wearing, as her gaze never left my eyes.

"How is the house coming along?" she asked, as if I'd been sent in to renovate rather than caretake. "I told Seamus they should have burned it down years ago."

Wow, this lady was ballsy. What on earth did she have against Pilar's house?

"Actually, it's been really nice staying there," I said, feeling defensive. "The light in the dining room is gorgeous. Even now that winter's come."

She threw her head back in laughter. "This, my dear, is not *winter*. Come talk to me in February."

Again, I felt like I was being accused of some sort of wrongdoing.

She continued, "The only reason why I agree to come here is because Seamus has an attachment to this place. It's practically umbilical."

Seamus bristled just a bit, and I couldn't help but wonder what it was she was trying to get at. Everything she said seemed to have an undercurrent. She was a walking riptide, this woman.

"Well, do let us know if you need anything over . . . there," she said, and then she slipped away.

Seamus smiled apologetically.

"What did she mean?" I asked softly, leaning in and speaking almost conspiratorially. "About your attachment to the island."

He looked at me intently, like he was trying to figure out if he could trust me. I gave him no reason not to. I had this effect on people. People opened up around me.

"I was born here," he said.

"You were *born* here?" I said in disbelief. I thought I'd sensed something faintly European in his accent. How could I have possibly mistaken *New* England for England?

"Yes," he said. "My father was a fisherman."

"Where did you go to school?" As far as I could tell there wasn't even a one-room schoolhouse on the island.

"My mother homeschooled me until I was thirteen, then I got a scholarship to a boarding school in New Hampshire. I wound up at college in Cambridge, and that's where I met Fiona. She was an undergrad and I was at law school."

Cambridge must be code for Harvard.

"We got married, and I started my career. But I missed it here. Clearly, we could never live here because of my work, but I didn't want to lose my connection to this place. I thought when we had children . . ." He trailed off here.

"Oh, do you have children?" I asked, imagining his *children* would likely be my age.

He looked at me as if forgetting what I'd asked. He shook his head and said, "No. No children."

"Well, it must be nice to have such a beautiful home on the island where you grew up," I offered, feeling like he too had slipped away, though he was still standing here.

"Fiona despises Bluffs Island," he said.

"Why?"

He shook his head again. It was his turn now to lean in conspiratorially. When he did, I could smell the booze on his breath. Now I wasn't sure if it was me or the liquor that was having the truth serum effect.

"Fiona despises anything that makes me happy."

"Oh," I said, feeling suddenly uncomfortable.

People have always told me their secrets, since I was a kid. I should have become a chaplain or a therapist. Once, a little boy told me he'd accidentally killed his new kitten when it had slipped under the rocking chair where he was sitting, but he'd told his mother the dog snapped its neck. In high school, a girl I barely knew took me into the bathroom at a school dance and showed me the cuts she'd made with a key, like hash marks across her skin. In art school, a guy in my art history class told me he was gay, but he hadn't told anyone yet. That he might never. Even Gus seemed incapable of keeping secrets from me, at least until now.

It's a strange burden to carry, this weight of trust. Maybe people simply sensed my mastery at concealment.

"But never mind. We're here to send off the year and welcome in the next one," Seamus said, clapping his hands together as if he were snapping himself out of some sort of hypnotic haze. "Only five minutes to go."

I grabbed a glass of champagne from a tray that floated past me like a lily pad in water. A plump, drunken raspberry sat at the bottom of the glass.

I stood surrounded by these strangers, smelling the scents of their aftershave and perfume, feeling dizzy from the alcohol and lights and glittery glow of the gowns.

Fiona appeared at the top of the stairs, seemed to hover there, and began the countdown.

Three . . . two . . . one. And then it was snowing. At least it appeared to be snow, though as it landed on my bare arms, I realized it was only confetti, a million miniature snowflakes. They landed in my hair, in my champagne. The string quartet broke into "Auld Lang Syne" and the same wonky-eyed guy I'd met earlier, Harry, goosed me before leaning in and giving me a sloppy kiss on my cheek.

What a way to start the year.

I wanted to go home, but I had to pee really badly, and I wasn't sure I could hold it for the trek back home. I had no idea where the restroom was, but I suspected it was at the beginning of the long line of people near the stairwell in the great room. There was no way I was going to be able to wait that long. I spotted Seamus and walked over to him, divulging my own little secret in exchange for his. "I need to pee. And I don't think I can hold it," I said quietly, gesturing to the line.

"Come with me," he said, and led me toward the front of the house again. The double stairwells looked like something out of *Gone With the Wind*. "Upstairs, to the right. Third door. Or fifth, if that one's taken."

"Thanks," I said and sped up the stairs. I would have taken two at a time if I weren't so worried about peeing myself.

I got to the top of the stairs, found the door, and shut it behind me, locking it, yanking my dress up, and peeling my tights down as quickly as I possibly could. The toilet seat was cold, and I must have peed for a full minute.

I sighed. *Phew.*

The bathroom was immaculate. Pale gray walls and white fixtures. The counter seemed to be made of marble, and the sink was just a glass bowl hovering above the counter. There was a bathtub in here as well, freestanding, a claw-foot tub with fancy chrome fixtures.

My heart stopped.

I walked over to the tub, and, glancing at the door to make sure I had locked it, hiked my dress up and climbed in. I sat in the cold depths of the tub and stared at the faucet. At the wall behind it.

This was the tub in the photo. I was sure of it.

But what would she have been doing here? In Seamus and Fiona's tub?

Oh, shit. No wonder Fiona had her panties in such a twist about me and Pilar and the house!

I reached for my clutch and grabbed my phone, snapping a quick picture.

Someone knocked on the door. "Hello?" the woman's voice said.

"Just a minute," I said, my voice echoing off the porcelain. *Damn it.*

I had a hard time getting out of the tub, and even after I'd managed to get myself out, I realized I'd left a half dozen paper snowflakes behind.

I bent over at the waist to pluck them out of the tub, and realized quickly this was a futile task. I thought about running the water and letting them slip down the drain, but I didn't want anyone to wonder what I was doing in here.

Knock, knock.

"Coming!" I said, and scurried to the door, leaving a trail of paper snow behind me.

Fiona stood in the doorway. In this light, she looked older somehow, as if the chandeliers had had some sort of magical effect on her. A trick of the eye.

"The guest powder room is downstairs," she said coldly.

But rather than stick around to defend myself or explain, I simply nodded, muttering my apologies and slipping past her, down the stairs, and out into the night. I was in such a hurry to get home, I didn't even realize until I was walking down the stone steps to the beach that I'd left my coat with the butler. And by then, all I wanted to do was get back to the house to find the negative to see if it matched the photo I'd taken on my phone.

Beautiful Fools

The next morning, my head was aching from the champagne and the effort of straining my eyes to see the tiny images on the contact sheets. I was convinced now the woman who owned the house not only knew Seamus, but knew him *well*.

It was a holiday, but I called the drugstore in town, and they said they'd be open and their photo kiosk did, indeed, make enlargements from the negatives. Pilar also left a message during the party that she'd made it to my parents' house and would leave at the crack of dawn to drive to Portland. I told her I'd meet her at the dock on the island; we could get lunch then drive back to the house.

I wanted to tell her about the photos. Show her what I'd discovered. I couldn't explain it, but I felt afraid for the woman in the pictures. And I couldn't understand why on earth Seamus would deny there was a baby.

"I have some super exciting news for you," Pilar said in the message.

This was becoming a refrain lately with Pilar. And while I was certainly happy for her, I admit I sometimes wondered if this would be the trajectory of the rest of her career, just one bit of super exciting news after the next.

I had no idea how much the prints would cost, but I figured I could afford to at least do some of them. The important ones now were probably the ones taken inside Seamus and Fiona's house. But I figured while I was at it, I could also enlarge some of the girlie show pictures, and the one of her holding the baby.

I gathered the negatives into an envelope and tried to think if there was anything else I needed in town. I couldn't imagine anything was open, certainly not the post office. We might not even be able to find a place to have lunch.

As I went to the hallway closet to get my coat, I suddenly remembered in my hurry to escape Fiona the night before, I'd completely forgotten to grab my parka. I went to the kitchen and checked the thermometer hanging just outside the window. Twenty-two degrees. Yeah, the thin polar fleece or my denim jacket wasn't going to cut it.

I glanced at my watch and figured somebody would be up next door. I wondered if the butler actually lived there or if he had a house somewhere else on the island. Or maybe he traveled with them back and forth between houses. Some sort of traveling butler? Was there such a thing? I knew nannies sometimes traveled with the families whose children they cared for. I'd had a friend in college who spent every summer on Cape Cod caring for a pair of bratty twins while the parents drank and sailed and sunbathed.

I threw on one of Gus's fisherman's sweaters I'd adopted as my own, a pair of boots, and a hat and mittens and made my way as quickly as possible. To call it *cold* outside would be the grandest of all understatements. It was bitter, in every sense of the word, the air itself feeling hostile. There was violence to this type of cold. Fury.

I rang the doorbell and waited.

Shivering.

The house was massive. Cavernous. I had no idea how long it would take someone to get from one end of it to the next. I'd never lived anywhere where two people couldn't hold a conversation from opposite ends of the house. Even in the duplex, if we'd wanted to, we could have had a conversation with the wall between us.

I gave it about a minute then tried again. Nothing. Shit. Was it possible they'd already left? I thought about the parties Gus and

I threw, the ones we had gone to over the years. There's a certain amount of time it takes for a house to recover after something like that, though I suspected the Fergusons had *people* for that.

I gave it three more minutes and realized I could no longer feel my own face. "Shit, shit, shit," I cussed and grumbled, looking around as if there were some way I could just break into the house and grab my coat from whatever massive coatroom it was hiding in.

Finally, I gave up and started back down the steps, thinking I'd have to just layer my clothes. At least the heater in the Honda still worked. For now. I just needed to get from the car to the drugstore, which I assumed also had heat. It would be okay.

I was heading back across the frosty lawn when I heard Seamus call out.

"Wyn! Wait!"

I turned around. Seamus was standing in the doorway, motioning for me to come back. And fast. He was barefoot, wearing pajamas and a robe.

I ran back to the house, the air slicing at my lungs.

"Come in," he said. "What are you doing out there without a coat on?"

"My coat is *here*," I said. "I left it last night. By accident."

"Oh," he said. "You forgot your *coat?*"

"I had an . . . encounter," I said, still feeling the chill of Fiona's gaze, "with your wife. I don't think she was very happy to have me here."

Seamus took a deep breath.

"Come in," he said, and when I hesitated, he said, "She's not here. She flew out this morning. She had a charity event in Atlanta."

He must have been referring to the small plane I'd heard about an hour ago.

I followed him into the immaculate foyer, through the room that just last night had been filled with guests, and back to the

kitchen. There wasn't a shred of evidence anything out of the ordinary had happened here.

The kitchen was spotless. Cold. But it smelled of coffee, and
when he offered me a cup, I knew I'd need it if I had any plans of
thawing out. He motioned for me to sit down on a barstool at the
marble-topped island. I could practically see my reflection in it.

"I can only stay a minute," I said. "I'm picking up Pilar in
town when the ferry comes in."

"Of course," he said, and grabbed his own mug, standing on
the other side of the island from me.

"Thank you for inviting me last night," I said. "It was a really
nice party. I wish Pilar could have been here."

"I apologize for Fiona," he said. "She tends to be a bit, um,
abrasive?"

Yes, that was exactly it. Like sandpaper. There was a grit to
her, her words leaving a raw burn.

"She hates it here," he said. "She only humors me because
that's what we do, no?"

"What's that?" I asked.

"Marriage. So much of it is about tolerance. Over time, you
stop complaining and simply put up with things because it's easier than the alternative."

"What's the alternative?"

"I suppose it depends on what it is that's being tolerated. For
some, it's little nuisances: socks on the floor, the way somebody
chews or sips or interrupts. Then, there are the bigger things: the
way your husband or wife treats other people, or the way they
handle money, or if they are unfaithful. If you choose not to tolerate the small things, you bicker. You nag. You complain and
gripe. Every moment becomes a little struggle. But if you choose
not to tolerate the larger things, then you *argue*."

I thought of the grievances I had with Gus, all those small,
petty nuisances: he left empty cereal boxes in the cupboard, he
never hung up his towels, he often thought for too long before he

said what he was thinking. But I could enumerate the bigger issues with one finger. Or maybe my thumb. He didn't respect me. He thought I was selling out. It was one big, fat complaint, but it sort of trumped everything else. How do you stay with someone who thinks you have sold your soul?

"If you're not careful," he said softly, "after a while, all grievances start to have the same weight. Infidelity becomes no different than leaving the toilet seat up. Just another annoyance to contend with."

I had no idea where he was going with this.

"And the island?"

"It used to be a big grievance," he said, and he seemed to almost wince. As if the thought caused him physical pain.

"And now?" I asked, feeling the coffee starting to defrost me.

"And now, it's just another wet towel on the floor."

"That's sad," I said. And it was. The idea that whatever, or more likely *whoever*, caused Fiona to feel so strongly about this island had become something she merely put up with seemed somehow pathetic to me. For a moment, I even felt a bit sorry for her.

"What's wrong with the island?" I asked. "Besides the wind chill, I mean?"

"It's not really the island," he said. He didn't elaborate, but he didn't have to. I knew this was about the woman in my house.

"And what about you? What do you tolerate?" I asked. "There must be something you put up with?"

Seamus smiled a bit sadly.

"She is an intelligent woman," he said. "Smarter than I ever was. But her intelligence is a bit of a curse."

"Would she be better off a *beautiful fool?*" I asked, thinking of Daisy Buchanan in *Gatsby*.

He smirked. "Wouldn't we all."

It was one of those conversations that felt like something from *Alice in Wonderland*. A riddle. Circling and circling whatever it was he was trying to say without ever getting to the point. It was maddening.

"Did you know her?" I finally blurted out. "The woman next door?"

He was pouring coffee into my mug. He stopped, looking up at me as if he'd heard me wrong.

"I did find some photos," I admitted. "Like you said."

His eyes widened, and he looked at me with a sort of wild anticipation. Like I was holding onto something he wanted desperately. This kind of need terrified me.

"Of?" he asked, his voice now softened. He was tentative, lacking any of the intellectual bravado he'd been exercising a minute ago.

"*Your* upstairs bathroom," I said. "And a bunch of other things too."

Suddenly, I wished I hadn't told him at all. I felt like I'd just blurted out a secret that didn't belong to me to a total stranger.

"Can I see them?" he asked.

I'd made a terrible mistake.

"I'm sorry," I said. I glanced at my wrist, at a watch that wasn't there, and said, "The ferry will be here soon. I really need to get into town. If I could just get my coat?"

And suddenly, as if a hypnotist had snapped his fingers, Seamus seemed to jerk awake, out of his odd reverie.

"Of course, of course. Hold on. It's probably in the coatroom."

The woman at the information booth at the ferry dock said the ferry Pilar was on was delayed by an hour, which gave me plenty of time to run over to the drugstore with my negatives. I knew I wouldn't be able to print them all, but I could at least do the ones that appeared to have been taken inside Seamus and Fiona's house and make enlargements of a few from the *Epitaphs* collection.

The bells on the door to the pharmacy jingled, and the same

cashier who'd been here my last couple of visits was working again, but he didn't seem to acknowledge any familiarity with me. This was something I'd noticed on the island. It was as if you had to work extra hard to earn your status as an honorary local. I imagine because so many tourists came through in the summers, the real locals didn't bother to remember faces. This is what I told myself so I didn't feel like I was in an episode of *The Twilight Zone,* so I didn't feel like a ghost.

"Happy New Year!" I said brightly and went over to the kiosk. I'd read the directions online so I wouldn't have to ask for assistance. I felt oddly proprietary about the pictures. I didn't want anyone accidentally seeing them. Clearly, she hadn't intended for them to be shared. At least not until someone discovered them in her basement. Though, obviously it wasn't supposed to be me. This was her legacy, I thought, but for whom was it intended?

As quickly as I could, I fed the negatives into the machine and printed 5 x 7s of about ten frames. I found one strip that had no marks on it and almost tossed it aside, but then held it up to the light. My heart stopped in my throat.

I threaded it through the machine and quickly printed every image, then shoved everything into the manila envelope. My heart was pounding hard and fast in my chest as I nodded at the man, who again seemed to be seeing me for the first time.

I still had a half hour, and I was chilled to the bone, so I decided to go to the only restaurant that was open and get a cup of coffee and look at the prints.

The chalkboard sign near the hostess stand said, PLEASE WAIT TO BE SEATED. Surprisingly, the restaurant was bustling with activity. There were no free tables or booths.

"There are some open spots at the counter," the hostess said. So I made my way to the counter and sat down on an empty stool, one with no one immediately next to me. A waitress materialized, coffee urn in hand, turned over the small porcelain mug and filled it.

"You want something to eat too? We've got a nice steel cut oatmeal with apples and raisins?"

"That sounds great," I said.

She returned with a steaming bowl of oatmeal and a sticky pitcher of syrup, refilled my coffee, and then left me alone.

I slipped the prints out onto the counter and picked them up one by one.

The girlie show photos were exactly as I imagined they would be, although blown up, the grit and filth of the midway were amplified. The women were not beautiful, rather crude, the rawness of their expressions acute. They looked distant, their gazes fixated on something beyond the midway. Though it wasn't hope, but rather a sort of sad resignation in their eyes. And the men looked hungry, like animals circling.

There had to be at least a half dozen prints that were absolutely stunning. Almost difficult to look at. How could such violence, such despair be so tremendously, achingly, beautiful?

The series of the teenage couple and the car, as I expected, did not work as a series. But that one photo of them the moment the struggle began was breathtaking.

I felt dizzy as I flipped through the pile.

There were the photos from the negatives I hadn't seen. Confused, I peered closer.

The child. How do I describe the child?

The first photo was taken on a broad expanse of grass, shot as if by someone hovering above. In the center of the photo was a little girl, curled on the grass like a pill bug, eyes squeezed shut in feigned sleep. She was wearing a ratty nylon slip, and her hair fanned out around her. She was maybe four years old. Avery's age. I felt Avery's absence like a blow to my throat.

Barefoot, a Band-Aid on her shin. The detail was incredible. Meticulous. Each blade of grass, each strand of hair, her dirty fingernails, articulated.

In the next photo, the girl had gotten up and was running now, across that large expanse, just a blur.

I quickly sifted through the other prints. She was like a firefly, appearing illuminated in that white nightgown in some shots, and absent in others. I tried to imagine the photographer attempting to capture her. The failure of the shutter. Adjusting then shooting again.

And then, it was twilight. I knew this golden hour. This magical moment before sunset when the world is imbued with a sort of honeyed light. For photographers, it is like a gift. Though the photo, like the others, was taken in black and white, it shimmered with that inimitable soft radiance. It was the same light I'd been seeking in that quiet corner of the duplex back in Queens. The same light that flooded the kitchen of the island house just before sunset.

In this photo, the girl had stopped running and was standing where the grassy field met a line of trees. My heart fluttered. Those were the trees dividing the Fergusons' house from Pilar's. She leaned her cheek against the rough bark of one of the trees, her eyes closed. I could almost hear her counting, "One, two, three . . ." It was a game of hide-and-go-seek, and she was It.

But while this image itself was sweet, the innocence of a child's game captured, it was what I saw in the background that stopped me.

The man was standing in the distance, but he wasn't looking at the child. Instead, he was looking directly at the camera. He had his finger pressed against his lips, telling whoever was holding the camera not to speak. Not to give him away.

Ready or not, here I come!

It's amazing how similar he looked. How absolutely the same. Minus thirty-five years, but undeniable. It was Seamus.

Hide-and-Go-Seek

Clearly Seamus was hiding something, and now I was pretty sure I knew what. He definitely knew the woman who lived in Pilar's house, well enough that he'd played hide-and-go-seek with her daughter. And Seamus didn't strike me as much of a hide-and-go-seek kind of guy. I wondered if it was possible this child might actually be *his* child. But he had insisted the woman, the photographer, did not have any children.

"Happy New Year!" a man said as he sat down next to me, and my hand flew to my chest.

"Christ!" I said. "Sorry, you startled me."

He looked oddly familiar, but I realized it was just the beard. He looked like *Gus*.

"You a photographer?" he asked, gesturing to the prints spread out in front of me.

"Me?" I asked. "Oh, no. I'm just . . ." I trailed off, unsure how to explain exactly what it was I was doing with these pictures. I quickly gathered the prints into a pile and slipped them back into the manila envelope.

"Have you lived here long?" the guy asked.

"No," I said. "I mean, I don't really live here. I'm staying at a friend's. I'm actually meeting her at the ferry dock in just a few."

My oatmeal had grown cold. I pushed the bowl to the side, waiting for the guy to open up his newspaper or something. But he was still grinning at me.

"How about you? Do you live on the island?" I asked, uncomfortable at this sudden interest and attention.

"No. I'm just visiting too."

"In January?" I laughed.

"It's kind of for work," he said.

"Oh, are you one of those bird people?" Pilar had told me there was a puffin colony here, and legions of birders descended on the island each winter.

"No," he said. "Bird people?"

The waitress came over and started to refill my cup. "Actually, can I get my check?" The ferry would be arriving any minute now.

"It was nice chatting with you . . . ?"

"Mike," he said, reaching out his hand.

"Wyn." His hand was warm. I started to put my coat back on.

"Listen, maybe we can get a cup of coffee sometime?" he said.

"I think we just did," I said, gesturing to the coffee mugs on the counter.

His cheeks reddened. "Well, maybe you could show me around the island?"

Was he asking me out?

"Sure," I said, shrugging. "Here's my cell number." I took the pen I'd used to sign for my check and scratched my cell number on the napkin. What was I doing? He had a *beard*. But then I thought of Mia. Of moving on.

"See you later," I said and made my way outside.

I couldn't believe how happy I was to see Pilar. When she drove off the dock back on the island, window rolled down, waving wildly at me, I felt a surge of something I can only describe as relief. I'd been feeling a prevailing sense of unease ever since I'd brought the photos up to Seamus. If he knew the photographer, why would he lie? Even if they'd had an affair, it was thirty-five years ago. And *was* the baby his? I thought of the infant in the photographer's arms, the toothless gums, the agony of the scream. Of the infant in the periphery of those sad portraits of her in the house. But when I'd asked, he'd said there was no baby.

I wondered if Fiona knew. And where the hell was the daughter now? Judging by the dates on the film canisters, she'd be just a little older than me.

Pilar pulled into the parking spot next to the Honda and got out of the car, throwing herself into my arms. "Happy New Year!" she said and planted a fat, wet kiss on my lips. A few fellow passengers eyed her suspiciously.

"Happy New Year," I said, squeezing her hands. "How was your trip?"

"Amazing," she said. "A-ma-zing. I'll tell you all about it when we get back to the house."

And so we got into our separate cars and drove the half mile back to the house.

I helped Pilar unload her suitcases from the trunk and carry them inside. She brought bags and bags of groceries in, as well as a case of wine. I had no idea when she'd had time to pick up all this stuff.

She unfurled a bright red scarf from her neck and peeled off her coat. "Yay!! I am so happy to be here!"

Already, I felt a million times less lonely.

"How long can you stay?" I asked.

"That's the exciting news! I'm here for good now. *Finally.* I'm ready to get back to painting. It'll be so nice to be working here with you."

I nodded, though the idea of returning to the birches was becoming more and more anxiety-inducing every day. I had just a couple of weeks left to finish the painting and get it shipped to Ginger's house in Aspen. I hadn't mentioned Ikea to Pilar.

"How was the visit with Gus?" she asked, rummaging through one of the bags and pulling out a deli container of pomegranate seeds, a box of crackers, and a huge chunk of the stinky cheese she liked. She went to the cupboard and quickly assembled a tray. "And Avery. Oh, Avery! God, when does she come back? I miss her so much!"

"Gus is good," I said. I'm not sure why, but I didn't tell her about what happened in the pool. Or about the way he'd been so cold at Christmas. I didn't mention *Mia*.

She pulled a bottle of champagne out of a bag, unscrewed the wire, and quietly twisted and popped the cork into her fist with a hand towel. The vapor drifted out and she poured us each a glass. "Happy New Year," she said, her cheeks flushed. We clinked glasses and I took a sip. Definitely not the crappy shit we usually celebrated with.

"Oh my God, I totally forgot to ask about the party last night. Did you go? Was the house incredible?"

"So incredible," I said. "But here's the crazy thing. I think I figured out it was a woman who lived here, back in the seventies."

"Yeah?"

"And I think maybe she had an affair with Seamus."

"Who's Seamus?"

"Ferguson. The mansion guy." I felt like I was gossiping about a friend we shared instead of some woman from thirty-five years ago.

"Wow!" she said.

"I think they might have even had a daughter together."

"Holy shit. Then why did she live *here?*"

"I'm pretty sure Seamus and that mean lady, Fiona, were already married."

"Was she like a *kept woman* or something?"

It hadn't dawned on me before. The idea their proximity wasn't accidental. That maybe he'd put her up in this house, "kept" her here.

"I found photos of her with her daughter. And one with him in it. At least it looks like he probably looked thirty-five years ago."

Pilar snapped her fingers, remembering something. "Oh my God. The photo! I totally forgot."

I was confused.

She stood up and went to the dining room where I had set

up my makeshift gallery. Her eyes widened and she walked from photo to photo, agape. "Oh my God," she said. "Are these all from those rolls in the cellar?"

I felt my stomach turn.

"I was going to tell you I showed the photo to my manager. This one," she said, pointing at the one of the hooker on the boardwalk.

"What?"

"I had it on my cell phone."

Nausea swept over me. My skin felt hot, like I might faint. "You shouldn't have done that," I said.

"Why not?" She cocked her head at me. "These are *amazing,* Wyn."

"You just shouldn't. She obviously didn't want to have them developed. They weren't meant to be seen. I found them in the basement, hidden away in a box."

"A *labeled* box," she said. "She clearly intended to get them printed. Why else would she have gone to the trouble to keep them? Hell, to even take them in the first place?"

I regretted showing her. Telling her. Sharing them.

"Anyway, he was blown away. Like seriously bowled over. I told him there were dozens of undeveloped rolls. He said we should get them developed. If the rest of them were anything like the one I saw, we could maybe put a show together. Call it *Epitaphs and Prophecies. Look* at these. She was like some sort of savant."

"*Savant?*" I said. "You don't know anything about her!"

"Hey, why are you so upset?" she asked, reaching out for my hand, which I yanked away before she could touch it.

I thought about how to explain. I felt proprietary about them, as though they had somehow been left behind for me to find. But there had also been something voyeuristic about looking at them, like peering into someone else's life. Like her staring through that peephole in the carnival tent. They *weren't* meant for anyone's eyes. Maybe not even mine. I immediately felt over-whelmed with a sense of guilt. I should never have gotten them printed. Her secrets didn't belong to me.

"They don't belong to us," I said, shaking my head.

Pilar laughed. "Well, you did kind of find them in *my* base-ment," she said, singsongy.

Suddenly all the confusion and remorse I'd been feeling seemed to go through some sort of chemical process, turning into indigna-tion and fury. Every ounce of envy, of jealousy, I'd been feeling for the last year crashed through the floodgates I'd erected to hold them back.

"That's right. I almost forgot, this is *your* house, bought with *your* money. Money you're making because somebody some-where suddenly decided *your* art was worthy."

She was still smiling, but as I continued and she realized I was serious, her smile slipped away.

"It's changing you, Pill," I said. "I know you don't think it has, but it has. Having money makes you feel entitled to more money. It makes you greedy."

Her eyes widened. "I have never been anything but generous with you. With Av," she said.

"Well, thanks for your *charity*. I don't need it anymore."

"What are you doing?" she asked, shaking her head. Reach-ing out for me again. "This isn't about these stupid photos, is it?"

"Of course it is. You can't just sell her out," I said. "You might be okay with that, but . . ."

She stood up, stunned. Her voice deepened. "I'm not the one painting trees to match a goddamned couch," she said.

It felt like a blow to my chest.

Pilar's hand flew to her mouth. "I'm sorry, Wynnie. I didn't mean that."

I shook my head, and my body trembled. "No," I said, anger bubbling acidic. Vile. "You're right. You are. *I'm* the prostitute."

And I thought of those women in the pictures. The girly-show girls, the vacant looks in their eyes as the men leered at them. As they stuffed dollar bills into their ratty G-strings. All that glitter and dust.

Her eyes widened and filled with tears.

Just as with Gus, I'd said something that couldn't be taken back. It was a bell that could never be unrung. I thought about reaching out for her, about apologizing. But I was afraid she'd only recoil from my touch. And I didn't think I could bear that.

We stood staring at each other, neither of us knowing what to do. We'd never, ever had a fight before. Not once in almost fifteen years.

"I think maybe I should go," I said, but then was hit with the shattering reality that I *had* nowhere to go. I couldn't go back to Gus. I couldn't go back to Haven.

"No," she said, her eyes wet. "I actually have a few things I need to do back in the city. It's okay. I'll go."

She stood up and grabbed her old thrift store coat, put on her designer boots.

"That storm in Philly is heading east, they said. I should really get back before it hits. I'd hate to get stuck out here." Her eyes were red, filled with tears.

She gathered her suitcase and small overnight bag from the kitchen floor and opened the door to the blistering cold. I sat paralyzed at the kitchen table.

Outside, the sky had clouded over again. It was disorienting. It wasn't even noon, but it felt like twilight. As she started down the walkway with her suitcases, I stood up and clicked on the porch light, a stupid and futile gesture of thoughtfulness, of apology.

I stood in the open doorway, watching her go and unable to bring myself to make her stop.

She put her bags in the trunk and ducked back into the car. But then the door swung open again and she got out, holding a manila envelope. She walked back up to the house and handed it to me. She seemed suddenly angry now, now she'd had a moment for everything I'd said to register. I could see it in her eyes, hear it in her voice.

"I forgot, your mom wanted me to give this to you. It's mail or something."

"Thanks," I said.

She took a deep breath and turned around again. And she was gone.

It wasn't until after her fog lights had disappeared down the road I felt the sob rising in my throat and let it take over my body.

Alternating between frustration and anger and disbelief, I tried to make sense of what had just happened. I put my mom's envelope on the table and went to the case of wine and opened a bottle, pouring myself a healthy glassful before going to the dining room to look at my painting, at the paint chips and upholstery swatches laid out next to my palette. The blank canvas was leaning against the wall, like the homely girl at a middle school party. I felt sick. I drank the glass of wine in a few swallows and went back for more.

I hoped maybe Pilar would just go cool off and come back. That we could fix this. Whatever this was. In all the years we'd known each other, we'd never had so much as a squabble.

I sat down at the table and looked at the envelope from my mom. It was labeled WYN'S MAIL. I still got a lot of mail forwarded to her house, and she periodically gathered it, opened it, and stuffed it into an envelope. More often than not it was junk disguised as important pieces. "I thought it might be important," she'd say when I shook my head at the offer to consolidate my debts, to refinance my mortgage, the announcements that I'd won contests for cruises and cash.

I tore open the envelope and dumped its contents on the table. I expected my high school's alumni newsletter, credit card offers, maybe someone trying to buy a house I didn't own. But instead it was a thin envelope with no return address. My name and my parents' address written in pencil, the handwriting childlike. For a moment, I thought of Avery, but this wasn't her loopy, happy handwriting.

I tore open the envelope and a sheet of notebook paper slipped out. Torn from a spiral notebook, the edges were ragged.

> *You dont check ur e-mail so I thoght I better rite you a letter. The papers sayin my brother didn't do it. But you know he did. Don't get any stoopid ideas about makin up some other story. You been a good girl. But you do something stoopid and you can forget all about what we said.*

I felt completely hollowed out. Gutted. I read the letter again and again.

> *Don't get any stoopid ideas about making up some other story.*

Questioning

"You like drawing pictures, I understand."

"Objection."

"Just trying to establish an idea of the kind of child she was. Is."

"I'll allow, but make sure this is relevant. You may answer the question, Miss Davies."

"Yes. I like to draw."

"You have a vivid imagination?"

"My teachers say I do."

"Objection. I don't see the relevance here."

"Sustained."

"So, Robert Rousseau followed you into the woods."

"Robby."

It had rained. The air was still heavy with it, thick. It was spring, and the world was blooming. The grass on the playing fields was impossibly green. Electric almost. Like something from a dream. The haze that hung over the field distorted everything as well.

"And in the woods he attacked you."

Jaw snapping, chewing his gum. Tongue clucking. "Come on, you pussy. Fuck her! You fucking coward."

"Raped you."

"Do it, you faggot. What's the matter with you?"

"I don't remember."

The Vanishing Point

One of the first techniques any painter of realistic images must master is one of perspective. That is, how to render a three-dimensional world on a two-dimensional canvas. A drawing must trick the eye into believing it sees that missing dimension, which is depth.

The most simple perspective drawings (a set of train tracks disappearing into the distance, a road funneling into a pinprick on the horizon) have a one-point perspective. This is referred to as the vanishing point.

If this day were a painting, it might be as simple as this. The world as expansive and open as a green, grassy playing field in spring, narrowing, narrowing to that tiny pinprick of light before the world ends.

But of course, nothing about this is simple.

Perspective is illusory in paintings, a dream, a trick of the eye.

Stand here, look up at this fresco. See how it appears the angels are peering down at you through a hole in the roof? Your neck strains, your spine aches as your eyes work to render the figure flat.

Trompe l'oeil, the forced perspective that makes you believe you can reach out and touch The Goldfinch, The Old Violin. Trompe l'oeil literally means, "the deceiving eye." One who views a trompe l'oeil painting is deceived, seeing an invented image as if it were real.

Innocence

I set the letter aside and shook out the next item from my mother's envelope. It was a newspaper clipping dated December 27, the day after the protest. The front page showed a photo of a crowd gathered, holding candles dripping wax onto paper plate candleholders. A write-up about the vigil followed. Below this was a photo of Jan Bromberg. I scanned the article:

> Jan Bromberg, who worked for the New Hampshire Division of Children, Youth, & Families in 1996, has maintained Robert J. Rousseau was not a perpetrator, but rather a victim himself of domestic violence and sexual abuse at the hands of his father. Immediately following the arrest of Rousseau in 1996, the home where he resided with his father, brother, and teenage sister was searched and a stash of child pornography was found. The sister, upon questioning, revealed she had been sexually and physically abused by her father, Richard Rousseau Sr., since early childhood. Mr. Rousseau was arrested and charged with forty counts of child pornography as well as child sexual abuse. He served five years in the state penitentiary before being released. The teenage daughter, Roxanne, was removed from the home and taken into state custody, Richard Rousseau Sr.'s parental rights terminated. Ms. Bromberg,

> who visited the Rousseau house on several occa-
> sions in the years leading up to the crime, was
> working to have the two underage children
> removed from the home when the crime against
> Ms. Davies occurred.

I felt my blood pooling in my knees, in my shoulders. I felt molten.

I poured another glass of wine and began to pace up and down the kitchen floor. I needed to talk to someone, but whom? Gus didn't know this story. Pilar didn't know this story.

> Ms. Bromberg has visited Mr. Rousseau in the
> prison and says he maintains his innocence, insist-
> ing it was his brother, Richard ("Rick") Rousseau
> Jr., who committed the crime. He claims his con-
> fession was coerced by the investigating officers.

I finished the wine bottle and felt sick. I found a crusty loaf of sourdough sticking out from one of the grocery bags Pilar had brought. I ripped off a thick chunk and swallowed it almost whole, hoping it might sop up some of the alcohol. I turned on the faucet, ridiculously thinking a glass of water might help clear my head. I opened the cupboard for a glass and saw Avery's bright red sippy cup sitting there and felt my knees grow weak again.

My phone only had five percent juice, but suddenly I needed to talk to her. I just wanted to hear her voice.

"Hey," Gus said.

"I was just calling to say hi to Av." I knew immediately this was a mistake. My words felt thick, my tongue dry, and my head swimmy.

"It's nine o'clock, Wynnie. She's been in bed for two hours."

"Oh," I said stupidly.

"Are you okay? You sound weird."

"I had some wine," I said, and immediately regretted it.

"Is Pill there?"

The sob I'd been holding down suddenly rose to the surface, bobbing and then bursting.

"I'm sorry," I said, my words now a derailed train. "I didn't want any of this to happen, you know? You're right," I added, nodding. "About the trees. About the goddamned birches."

"Can you hold on?"

I scowled. I was pouring my heart out and he wanted me to *hold on?*

"Wyn?"

I nodded again, but couldn't speak because I knew I would cry.

"Wyn, listen. I'm sorry. Mia is here to look at some of my work."

"At nine o'clock?" I said, feeling my stomach turn again. My legs were trembling.

"I've really got to go," he said. "Are you going to be okay? Maybe get some sleep. I can call you in the morning."

"Fine," I mumbled and hung up the phone. It would have cut out on me anyway.

I felt hopeless. Helpless. What the hell was I supposed to do now? I was completely alone. I'd driven every person who cared about me away. I had no husband, no parents, no best friend, and no child.

I needed to get out of this house. All of a sudden, I felt like the woman who lived here must have felt, the walls closing in on her. I peered out the window at the dark sky. In the small beam of the porch light I could see it was beginning to snow. Below, the waves crashed angrily against the shore. Again and again, perpetual punishment. Pounding, beating.

I opened the door and was met with a howling gust of freezing cold air. I'd need a sweater, a coat. I stumbled up the stairs to my room to find Gus's sweater, to put on a pair of long johns. I banged my hip against the wooden footboard and winced. I walked past Avery's room and felt my body tremble with another wave of sadness. I was wrecked.

I clicked off the hallway light and headed to the stairs.

I felt dizzy; the yellowing wallpaper in its repeating patterns of roses seemed to undulate like waves along the walls. I knew the moment I stepped down, I'd miscalculated the stairs' depth.

But it was too late.

I was tumbling down the hard wooden steps, bones meeting wood, even as I reached out for the banister that wasn't there to stop my fall.

The snap sounded like a gunshot. Followed by so much pain, I thought maybe it had been gunfire rather than the sound of my own bone breaking.

In the aftermath, I lay on the floor in silence. The wind had been knocked out of me.

I stared up at the ceiling, waiting for my breath to return, tears rolling hotly down the sides of my face and into my ears.

"Oh my God," I said when I could breathe again.

I somehow managed to use my left arm to push myself up to a sitting position, wincing at the excruciating pain that emanated from my elbow but radiated all the way down to my wrist. Nausea overtook me, and I turned my head, retching. I vomited, feeling sweat break out across my forehead. My eyes widened as I stared at what seemed to be a pool of blood where I had just thrown up. And then I realized: red wine, pomegranate seeds.

I was too shaky to stand. My entire right side was consumed by pain now, my body pulsing, throbbing. What the hell was I supposed to do? I was all alone. I couldn't drive anywhere; I wasn't even sure I could get myself out the door. And even if I could, where on earth would I go? It was nine o'clock on New Year's Day. The ferry was on a holiday schedule, Pilar had likely caught the last ferry off.

I looked up and saw my phone on the table.

I attempted to cradle my right arm with my left one, cupping my damaged right elbow with my left hand as I rose to kneeling, then standing. The pain made me nearly pass out.

I wondered whom to call. 911? There were no clinics, no

hospitals here on the island. I highly doubted my insurance would cover the cost of getting me to a Portland hospital. Should I call Gus? Mia was with him. Would he even answer? And what would that mean if he didn't? *Pilar*. God, Pilar.

I pressed the HOME button on my phone. Dead. And the charger was back upstairs.

What was I going to do?

Wait. Seamus was home. At least he had been earlier. I didn't know what he could do, but I did know I couldn't stay here in the house overnight. Not alone. Not in so much pain.

I stood up and shuffled across the kitchen floor, feeling all of the other places in my body that had taken the blows of the fall. My head was pounding, but I didn't know if it was the tumble or the wine. I certainly wasn't drunk anymore. I was like a soda can knocked to the floor, all the fizz zapped out of me.

It was dark outside, the sky completely opaque. I opened the utility drawer and grabbed a flashlight. I slipped on my Ugg boots but couldn't put on my coat. It was okay, I could do this. He was right next door.

Outside, snow was falling from the sky but never reaching the ground. It was at the mercy of the wind, which was howling. Angry. I cried out as the door banged shut behind me, startling me. I made my way slowly down the steps and shuddered when another gust of wind ripped across the yard and blasted into me. My ears rang and ached.

I couldn't cradle my damaged arm with my other hand, because I needed to hold the flashlight to see anything beyond the few feet ahead of me. I walked to the edge of the bluff and shined my weak beam of light down the rocks; there was no way I was going to make it down there.

I'd have to take the path through the trees.

I made my way around the side of the house, each step jarring my body into new convulsions of pain. I closed my eyes, felt sick. The nausea washed over me, but the cold, biting wind cut through it. In a strange way, it urged me on.

At the edge of the forest, I felt my knees weaken.

Go, I thought. *You have no choice. Just go.*

The wind rippled through the branches, howled. Warned.

You're already hurt. Nothing is going to hurt you more than you already are.

And one excruciating step after another, I made my way to the path. The one that would lead me to the other side. I was all alone. And terrified.

Inquiry

"Please describe what Robby did to you in the woods. It's okay. Take your time."

He shoved me, and it was just like the time I'd been on the swing and he'd pushed me to the ground. He stole my breath, my words. I landed facedown, felt and heard the crunch of the cold ground against my cheek. And this time there was no teacher with a shrill whistle around her neck to stop him, to make him apologize.

"Come on, you pussy," his brother said. I could see his feet from where I lay, hear him smacking his gum. "Fuck her. You know you want to."

Robby's hands were on my shoulders now, rolling me over, but I could see him glancing back to his brother, waiting for directions. If this were a movie, this shot might be from my perspective, his face surrounded in the golden glow of springtime sunlight. We would see the insinuation of violence, the suggestion of it. Maybe hear the sound of his zipper, of birdsong, before the fade to black.

But there was no fade to black.

There was the metallic sound of the teeth of his zipper and a trembling knee pressed against my stomach, pinning me to the forest floor like a butterfly. There was his soft, hot flesh on my bare stomach. My body stiffened. The sky above him was impossibly blue. Blindingly blue.

There was Rick, hovering over us now. His laughter throaty and hoarse. And Robby, who kept looking up at him, as if waiting for his approval.

I shook my head side to side. No, no, no. But when I opened my mouth to set the words free, there was his clumsy hand pressing so hard against my lips, I could taste his palm. Bitter, salty. Tears stung my eyes.

"Can't you get it up?" Rick goaded. "What are you, some sort of faggot?"

At this, Robby's expression changed. He seemed to snarl, then he was tearing down my shorts, the denim burning my skin. And he pressed his flaccid penis against me, stuffing it between my clenched legs. I gasped. No, no, no.

"Jesus Christ, you freak," Rick said and stomped over to Robby and threw him off of me. Then he was the one standing over me, legs on either side of my body.

He pulled something out of his pocket, and for a minute, I thought it was candy. But then I realized it was a condom. Hanna Lamont had found some in her parents' drawer and brought them to school one day.

Then he was on top of me, the elastic of my panties digging into the tops of my thighs before he finally just tore them off. There were his hands wrapping around my neck, and it went on for so long I thought it would never stop. There was the bass pumping, the music thumping, my heart pounding in my ears, my stomach, and my head. The sky above him was so blue it made my eyes ache, but I was afraid to close them, afraid that in blackness I might disappear. There was his breath in my ear, the smell of Big Red gum, the sweet cinnamon so strong it made my stomach turn. I watched as his eyes rolled back into his head, his jaw slackened, his mouth fell open.

There was no fade to black and a new scene where I awoke in a clean, bright hospital surrounded by the loving faces of my family. There was only his heavy body still, like death on top of me. And his heart beating against my chest. And me thinking that his heart was just like mine. That mine did the same thing after I ran or rode my bike up a steep hill. And how could this be that our hearts beat the same?

There was no fade to black and a cut to the next day when the police combed the woods for clues about who had attacked the girl. Instead, there was him scrambling off of me, yanking his pants up by the belt loops, throwing his head back and howling. Like a dog.

My pelvic bones throbbed, and I was certain I had somehow ignited. I was aflame. Burning from the inside out.

"We gotta get out of here, Rick," Robby said. He was standing with his hands in his pockets, head hung low.

Rick reached into the pocket of his Windbreaker, the Windbreaker that had been pressed so hard across my mouth at one point I thought I might suffocate, and pulled out a knife. It was the same kind of knife I'd seen Robby show some other boys at recess once. A small one. The kind you might whittle a stick with, or maybe use to cut twine.

"We gotta go," Robby repeated.

"You think we can just leave, you retard?" Rick said. "She'll have the cops here so fast. Take care of it." He tossed the knife at Robby, who jumped back to avoid it, and it landed at his feet. "You fucking deaf?"

Robby picked up the knife but stood motionless. Paralyzed.

I started to push myself up onto my hands and knees. The sky burned blue, and I felt like I was two people. Me and not me. Cold and hot. Whole and broken. I couldn't get the smell of Big Red gum out of my nose. My stomach turned as I began to crawl. Rick stomped on my back, pushing me back down into the wet leaves.

"Where do you think you're going?" he said to me, and then to Robby, "I said take care of it."

Robby dropped to his knees next to me and fumbled with the knife. He turned me over onto my back, and I shook my head again. No, no, no.

I could hear Rick walking away. "Hurry up, asshole."

He stabbed at my shoulder, my arms. I squeezed my eyes shut, and felt the cold blade against my throat. And I could feel it shaking in his fingers even as it sliced. I kept my eyes closed as the warm blood ran down the sides of my neck, into the wet leaves.

From the ground I watched his knife fall, and his sneakers crushing the wet leaves.

"Oh, Jesus," Rick said, and then he was next to me. He picked up the knife.

"Please," I said again. "I promise . . . I promise I won't tell anybody what you did. I promise. It's okay. I won't tell anybody. Just don't kill me, and I'll keep it a secret."

And even then, there was no fade to black. There was only his ragged breath as he pondered the bargain I was proposing. And the cold blade against my throat, and the fire between my legs and the ache behind my eyes. And the sound of the church bells in town ringing five o'clock.

"You better not be lyin'," he said. "Cause if you're lyin', I'll come back and kill you again."

What did he mean? Kill me again? I remained conscious. As slowly and as carefully as I could, I rose to my knees. But the pain in my chest felt like he'd stabbed me in the heart. And I was awake, my eyes open wide, the whole thirty minutes it took me to crawl through the woods to the other side, where my mother was on the phone with Mrs. Lamont asking if she'd seen me.

"Miss Davies, without your testimony, we're taking a big chance. Can't you please just tell us exactly what happened?"

I was alive. He'd kept up his end of the bargain. Now it was my turn to keep mine. And so I shook my head. Kept my promise.

"No, no, no."

Fade to black.

Into the Woods

I stood at the tree line now, staring into the dark woods that separated me from the safety of Seamus's house. My blood pounded in my ears. And in my peripheral vision, I saw movement. My body tensed.

I stood still, holding my breath, my arm throbbing.

In the distance, I heard the crush of leaves and brittle ground. Footsteps.

A small cry escaped my mouth when the footsteps stopped. It was so dark, I could barely see. There was only the faint bit of light from Seamus's house shining through the forest, the weak beam of my flashlight. I just needed to run through the woods and get to his house. My ears were playing tricks on me. I was in so much pain, I was delirious.

Crunch.

The whisper of something, the sound of pant legs brushing against each other? Wind?

I took a deep breath, and holding back tears, plunged into the woods.

The footsteps followed me.

When did you realize he was following you?

Who?

Robert Rousseau.

In the dark forest, I was vertiginous. The sky black, the ground beneath me black. The trees cast no shadows. The whole world was a shadow. *Bone black.*

The footsteps grew louder and closer, and I pressed my hand against my chest to keep my heart inside.

"*Wyn,*" a male voice said.

Oh my God. How did he find me?

This time I wouldn't let it happen; this time I wouldn't plead. This time I would run.

Cradling my elbow with my hand, I charged forward, running as fast as I possibly could. Branches and twigs snapped beneath and around me. Scratched my face. I was sobbing as I emerged from the other side of the trees onto the Fergusons' lawn, my heart lodged in my throat.

I glanced behind me. No one was there.

The pain, from which the trees seemed to have offered a momentary reprieve, returned. My knees were weak as I staggered across that enormous lawn to the front door.

The porch lights were on, but they were always on, even when Seamus was not home. I swallowed hard and pressed the doorbell. The sound rang out in the night. "Seamus!" I screamed.

I leaned against the wall next to the door, pressed my ear against the wood. As if I might be able to hear some sort of evidence of life inside. I worried momentarily Fiona might be back and wondered if she'd simply slam the door in my face again.

I peered into the darkness, the thick wall of trees beyond.

The wind snapped at me again; it had teeth, this cold, snapping jaws.

Jaw snapping, chewing his gum. Tongue clucking. "Come on, you pussy. Fuck her! You fucking coward."

I rolled my head back, felt hot tears streaming down my cheeks. I wasn't even aware I was still crying. I rang the doorbell again. And when nobody answered, I felt my legs start to give way.

"Hey!" the voice said.

For a moment, as my knees began to buckle, I had the disorienting sensation I was standing at the top of those stairs again and was beginning to fall. My vision began to darken at the edges, a constellation of stars appearing before my eyes. Stars, or snow? The world was upset down.

My eyes fluttered open at the sound of my name. I started to scream.

"Hey, hey, wait. Please don't be afraid."

The glow of the porch light made him a silhouette, hovering above me.

"I'm sorry," the man said. "I didn't mean to scare you."

"What do you want?" I asked, scrambling across the porch floor, pressing my back against the house.

"I'm Mike, Michael, Ash."

My eyes struggled to focus.

"I met you earlier at the restaurant in town."

His familiar face. Dark beard, brown eyes.

"I'm a documentary filmmaker. I've been following the Robby Rousseau case. I came out here because I hoped I could interview you."

The guy from the paper. Had he followed me from Haven?

"Why didn't you tell me that earlier?" I asked, furious now. "How the hell did you find me?"

"Crazy story, actually," he said. He reached his hand out, and I looked at it. When I didn't accept it, he shoved it back in his pocket. "Your friend, Pilar Santiago, was on *CBS This Morning* and mentioned your name."

"*What?*"

"She was talking about the house she bought out here on the island, and said her best friend, another artist named Wyn Davies, and she were living out here working. If I hadn't seen the show, I'd never have found you."

Goddamn it, Pilar.

"I'm not stalking you. I just really want to give you a chance to tell your side of the story. I know that woman is convinced Robert Rousseau is innocent, but you and he are the only ones who really know, right?"

"So you came to my house in the middle of the night for what reason?"

"I actually called your cell first," he said. "Then I thought maybe you didn't get reception out here on the bluffs. So I came by, and that's when I saw you running toward the woods. You looked hurt, and I was just trying to help you. You are hurt, right?"

I closed my eyes and nodded my head.

And suddenly the front door opened, bright light spilling from the Fergusons' foyer.

"Wyn?" Seamus said. "What happened?"

"I fell," I said, the memory assembling itself like fragments of a broken vase. "Down the stairs."

He helped me up and ushered us both inside. Mike explained he was a "friend" visiting, and I didn't have the energy to correct him. To explain. Seamus brought me to the living room and sat me down on a plush couch.

"It's your arm?" he asked. "Can I see?"

I rolled my head to the right, gesturing to my elbow.

Seamus gently lifted my arm up, and I yelped.

"I think it's broken. You're shaking," he said. And I realized despite being inside the warm house, I couldn't keep my body still. "How long ago did this happen?"

I shook my head. It could have been minutes. It could have been days.

"We need to get you to a hospital."

"How?" I asked. I hadn't heard any planes overhead. After returning the guests to the mainland, they must have stayed there.

"We'll take the boat," he said.

Boat? What boat?

"Stay here with her," he said to Mike, and then to me, "I'll come back for you in just a minute."

I felt myself drifting in and out as I waited for him to return. I sank back into the couch when the pain was too much. I was barely conscious when I felt him wrap me in a soft blanket and lift me up like an infant. And I thought of the little girl. When I closed my eyes to ride out the next wave of pain, I saw the image of him, young Seamus, with his finger pressed against his lips, hushing the photographer. Telling her without words this was their secret.

So many secrets.

I don't remember him and Mike getting me to the boathouse, I only remember waking again as he lay me down on a small bed inside the cabin of the boat, the way the stormy sea rocked us back and forth as Seamus navigated us away from the island. Through the storm. And oddly, instead of feeling terrified, I felt safe. Something about the way he'd carried me, cradled me, the way the boat, the sea itself, seemed to be cradling me, made me feel, for the first time in a very long time, *protected*. And so I let myself fall, again, only this time into a blissfully pain-free slumber.

I woke up twice. Once as Seamus, Mike, and the paramedics were unloading me from the boat and the gurney rolled across the wooden dock, the washboard rhythm of the wheels along the wooden boards. The second time was when the automatic doors to the ER opened and I was greeted by the blinding lights of the hospital. For a single, horrifying moment, I was thirteen years old again. A nurse's face hovering over my own, scowling, oblivious there was a girl behind all the blood and bruises. Unaware I wasn't just a collection of pain.

Exam

"Sweetheart, I am going to explain everything to you as we go, okay? You can just nod or shake your head. I know you are having a hard time talking right now."

Nod.

"Are you currently taking any medications?"

"I take Flintstones Vitamins." My voice sounded ragged, rough.

"No prescription medication? No birth control pills?"

No.

"Do you have any allergies?"

"Cats?" The sound of my voice made me think of a serrated knife.

"Next I'm going to need to take some samples and swabs from the areas where he hurt you. And if you're uncomfortable or scared or need to stop, you just let me know."

"Okay."

"Are you comfortable?"

I was covered in mud. And leaves. And blood. I wasn't allowed to take a shower, and all I could smell was the cinnamon. I reached to my hair and felt something sticky. Stifling a sob, I gestured to the wad of gum in my hair.

"Oh, sweetheart, let me get that out for you. You have such pretty curls; I hate to have to cut it though. Maybe we could get some peanut butter from the cafeteria to loosen it?"

Tears rolled down my cheeks. I shook my head.

"Cut it," I managed.

"Is this *his?*" she asked, her eyes wide and sad.

Yes.

And so she took the tiny pair of scissors, snipped the lock of hair, his wad of gum stuck to it, and slipped it into the plastic envelope.

"Okay. Here we go. Remember, you stop me if any of this hurts or is too scary, okay?"

I closed my eyes.

Broken

"Good morning, sunshine," someone said, and I fought against the pull of sleep.

I opened my eyes and saw a guy with red hair smiling over me. He was in green scrubs and he had a stethoscope around his neck. He was carrying a tray with what I assumed from the smell was breakfast.

"Nice ink," he said, setting down the tray.

"Thanks," I managed, looking down at my right arm.

The tattoos were still there, of course they were, but they disappeared inside the cast.

"You took quite a tumble," he said as he helped me sit up. The pain was strange, not sharp and agonizing as it had been the night before, but somehow muted. Submerged under what I could only assume was a painkiller haze.

I felt very, very foggy.

"What's the damage?" I croaked.

"Broken elbow, a hefty concussion," he offered. "And probably a pretty bad hangover?"

"Shit," I said.

He set the tray down, and the smell wafting up to my nose made me nauseated.

"My insurance?" I started to panic.

"Don't worry about that now," he said.

While Gus and I had only catastrophic health insurance for ourselves, we had made sure Avery's plan was more comprehensive. And I thought of Avery. My God, what if it had been Avery who had fallen down the stairs? What if it had been her instead of me out there on the island? Whatever these bills ultimately were, at least it hadn't been Avery.

Thinking of money made me remember the commission. The birches. Ginger. Ikea. My right arm. Oh my God.

"How long am I going to be in this?" I asked, gesturing to my immobile arm. My useless limb. "I'm a painter. Right-handed. I have a deadline."

The nurse smiled sadly and shook his head.

"I'll let the doctor talk to you about that," he said. "But it was a pretty nasty break. You're lucky you don't need surgery."

"Shit," I said again and sighed. "Shit, shit, shit."

I wondered what happened to Seamus. To Mike. I had no phone number for either one of them. I had no *phone*. The night was hazy; like the pain, it was just out of reach, a gauzy film separating me from it. I remembered running through the dark woods, the beam of my flashlight bobbing through the darkness, the terrifying realization I was being followed. That goddamn filmmaker freaking stalking me into the woods. I recalled the sound of the waves crashing against the side of the boat. The way the snowflakes landed on my hot face as they wheeled me into the ambulance and later through the hospital doors.

"Have you seen the guys who brought me here?"

"Yep. The older one said to tell you he'd be back this afternoon. He was going back to the island and would catch the early afternoon ferry," he said. "I didn't speak to the other guy. He your husband?"

"No," I said. *Gus*. He was going to be so pissed.

He lifted the plastic lid from the plate, revealing pale eggs, limp toast, and three slivers of anemic cantaloupe.

"Thanks," I said, grimacing.

"It tastes better than it looks," he offered.

After breakfast I fell asleep again; whatever painkillers they had me on made it impossible to stay conscious for very long.

"Knock, knock," Seamus said, leaning into the room. He was holding a bouquet of flowers. He seemed tentative. As if I might not remember who he was, what had happened.

"Hi," I said. "Thank you for bringing me here last night."

He shrugged and sat down in the chair next to the bed, setting the bouquet of flowers on the radiator.

"You okay?" he asked. "I didn't realize how hard you'd hit your head."

I nodded.

"Can I call somebody for you? Pilar? Your family?"

I shook my head. Of course, I'd need to let them know. But not now.

"My phone?" I asked.

"Right here," he said. "I went back to the island this morning and grabbed it. I was going to try to find Pilar's number, but it was dead. I used my charger in the car, but you have it locked."

"You went in the house?" I asked.

"I hope you don't mind. I figured you'd need this."

"No, of course not." I thought of what sort of mess I had left behind. Pomegranate puke and a bunch of empty wine bottles. Who knew what else.

"I saw the photos," he said.

The photos. That odd little exhibit I'd curated.

His eyes looked sad. I imagined him in my makeshift studio, studying the woman's face. The hide-and-go-seek photo of himself and the little girl.

"Who was she?" I asked, the question that had been plaguing me since I'd printed that first picture.

He looked past me to the window. I waited as he seemed to gather his thoughts.

"Her name was Sybil Reid. I met her when she was in Skowhegan, at the art school there, for the summer program."

I'd heard of the program before. It had been around since the forties. An artist colony of sorts on a farm in Maine.

"When?" I asked.

"Nineteen seventy-seven."

"What were you doing at an artist colony?"

He laughed. "Oh, no, I wasn't at the school," he said. "I had a friend from the island, from growing up, whose parents moved to Skowhegan when he went away to college. He was home for the summer and invited me to come stay. His dad put us to work on the farm. It was such a nice break to be back in the country after all those years in Boston. I was studying for the bar. It was peaceful. No distractions."

"Fiona?"

"Fiona had just graduated college and wanted to get married, start a family." He took a deep breath. "We were so young."

"So it was a summer fling?" I said. "With Sybil?"

"No," he said, shaking his head. He turned away from the window and looked at me. His face was sorrowful. "I loved her. I wanted to leave Fiona and be with her. But Sybil broke up with me right before I went back to Boston. She didn't want to be tied down to some stuffy lawyer. Stuck as some sort of housewife in the suburbs. I didn't blame her. It sounded awful to me too."

"But the baby?"

His eyes grew glassy.

"I didn't know she was pregnant," he said. "I went back to Boston, passed the bar, and started working at Fiona's father's firm. We got married. Fiona knew how attached I was to the island, and so her father gave us the house as a wedding gift."

"Wow," I said, thinking of the palatial estate next door.

"Money was nothing to him. And real estate on the island was cheap."

I shook my head in disbelief. I thought of our own inheritance, the shitty duplex in Queens. An inheritance that wasn't even really mine at all.

"Fiona promised we would bring our children there in the summers, on holidays."

"And then?"

"And then I got a letter from my friend in Skowhegan. Sybil had asked him to contact me, said she needed to see me."

I scowled.

"The property came with a guest house," he said.

"Pilar's house?"

He nodded.

"So you moved her into the guest house," I said, thinking about that photo. The one of her standing in the mirror, the bed behind her. I thought of the baby, the newborn about to scream. "And you left her there?"

He shook his head. "She needed a place to stay. To work. It was supposed to be temporary."

"But . . ."

"It wasn't. Time passed. A year, two years. I was working in Boston, trying to establish myself. Make a career. I came to see her whenever I could. Weekends. Holidays. Fiona hated it here. Said it made her feel claustrophobic. I told her I was visiting my parents."

"What happened? Why didn't you just leave her?"

"She got pregnant," he said.

"Sybil?"

"*Fiona.*"

Boy, this guy was busy.

"But you told me you don't have any children," I said. If I was counting right, this meant he had at least two.

He shook his head. "The baby was stillborn. At eight months. It devastated her. I couldn't leave her. I couldn't abandon her."

"But Sybil. Her little girl?"

"I ended it. Told her she could keep the house; I even deeded it to her. If she sold it, she could have bought something somewhere else. I would have taken care of them. I wanted to be a part of Rachel's life."

Rachel? My head was pounding, my arm throbbing. The lovely haze of the painkillers was lifting.

It was just as Pilar had thought; he'd *kept* her there. And she was trapped. An artist with a small child to care for. No resources, no money. No choice.

"What happened to Sybil?" I asked. Demanded.

Seamus stared out the window. It was twilight, the city lights twinkling like stars.

"Seamus? What happened to her?"

He looked at me, his face red, his expression strained. "She fell," he said, shaking his head.

"*Fell?*" I recalled my tumbling, end over end, Alice down the rabbit hole. "What do you mean? Down those stairs? What happened to the little girl? *Rachel?*"

"I'm sorry," he said. "I really shouldn't have said anything. Ancient history. And you need to get some sleep. The doctors said they want to keep you one more night, because of the concussion, but you can go home tomorrow. Let me know if you need anything? Here's my number."

Falling

"I'm such an asshole," Pilar said.

"No." I shook my head.

Mascara was running down her cheeks now, and *I* felt like the asshole. As soon as I called her from the hospital, she drove straight back to Maine, took me with her on the ferry back to the island.

"I promised I'd get those stupid stairs fixed. Oh my God, what if it had been Avery?"

I didn't tell her the same thing had gone through my mind. I shook my head. "I had too much wine. It was stupid. It shouldn't have happened."

"And I shouldn't have taken off. You're going through so much shit, and I just abandoned you. What if Seamus hadn't been next door? I am so sorry. For everything."

She sat on the edge of the couch where I was lying. She was wearing a sunny yellow housedress I didn't recognize with a fuzzy argyle cardigan. Motorcycle boots and leg warmers. She had draped the cashmere robe over me and covered me with a cozy blanket. My pain pills were within reach, the iPad, a stack of books, and a mug of tea.

"And I'm sorry about the photos. The film. We don't have to do anything with them," she said. "I totally get it. We can just pretend like we never even found the box."

"No," I said. "I want to understand what happened to her."

"What do you mean, *what happened to her?*"

"There was an accident, I think," I said. "Seamus said she fell. But he wouldn't say anything else."

"Oh my God, do you think he pushed her?" Her eyes widened.

I almost laughed. "No," I said. I'd seen the sorrow in his eyes when he was talking about her. He would never have harmed her.

"Did *Fiona* push her?"

Now, that I *could* see. Again, I recalled my own fall down the stairs, the way the world spun, kaleidoscoping around me. Fragments and blur.

"Who knows," I said.

"Can I see the other photos?" she asked tentatively, and I felt my heart snag a little. Distrust lingering like a rusty barb.

She was right. The photos were amazing, beautiful. What if Pilar changed her mind? They *didn't* belong to me. They belonged to *her*. If she wanted, she could bring the collection to her manager. They could be culled through and curated, blown up and displayed. Sibyl's entire life could be exposed.

"Okay," I said. "The newest ones are in that manila envelope in the kitchen."

"What do you suppose it means?" Pilar asked later, after she had gone through the photos. "*Epitaphs and Prophecies?*"

"I think the *Epitaphs* photos are little monuments to her life before."

"Before what?"

"Before Maine. Before her baby. She was really trapped here. She came here to work, to be with Seamus. But he left her here. Look at how sad she looks in these photos," I said.

Pilar studied the images of her, the self-portraits. And strangely, viewing them with Pilar made me look at them differently, as if I were seeing them through Pilar's eyes. I had identified with Sybil as a mother. After Avery was born, there were several weeks when I felt like my world had somehow collapsed. It was like one of those plastic folding cups you use for camping. It had once been wide open, waiting to be filled, and after Avery was born, it felt like it had folded in on itself, my days that had been so broad and filled with possibility, now suddenly trapped inside the walls of the duplex, into a routine so dull and domestic I worried it might never open up again. I could understand the ennui, the exhaustion, the boredom of motherhood. I felt the despair of blistered nipples and a body taken over by a child's needs. But Pilar had no children. What did she see? A woman. An infant. A house. *Her* house.

"She's beautiful," Pilar said.

I hadn't thought about Sybil's beauty. I'd only considered the beauty of the photos. Of the images themselves.

"Why call these *Prophecies?*" she asked. "Isn't a prophecy a prediction for the future?"

"Yes," I said. "I think these are clues."

"Clues about what?"

"About whatever happened to her."

Pilar peered at the photo of the little girl playing hide-and-go-seek. She touched her finger to the man standing in the background, young Seamus, with his finger pressed against his lips.

We Googled her.

Hunched over the iPad, we typed her name, *Sybil Reid,* into the search box. Looked for her on Facebook, as if she might just appear, a sixty-year-old woman posting photos of her cat. People searches, ancestry.com, divorce records. Finally, I clicked on a link to public death records. There were four Sybil Reids. But the last one on the list, Sybil R. Reid, born January 4, 1953, died November 25, 1981. It said she had died at the age of 28 on Bluffs Island, Maine. It was *her.*

Of course it didn't say how she'd died, didn't offer a photo. And the fact she had been reduced to this, to a couple of dates and her place of death, made me feel sad. There was no obituary, no epitaph at all.

"What do you think happened to her daughter? If her

mother died, wouldn't he have taken her in? He clearly had the money."

"Well, I highly doubt Fiona would have let him bring his illegitimate daughter into that house," I said.

"How long did you say this house was in probate?" I asked.

"Well, it's been empty since the eighties. But it didn't go up for auction until I bought it."

"Who set that into motion?" I asked.

"I have no idea. It was apparently abandoned. Maybe the city?"

"What city?" I laughed, thinking of the little cluster of shops and restaurants in "downtown" Bluffs Island.

"Maybe Seamus can tell you."

"I doubt it," I said. He'd been so elusive. Withholding. And I, if anyone, could understand this reticence.

"We really need to find her," I said.

"Who?"

"His daughter," I said. "She's the one who deserves to have these photos."

"Look her up," Pilar said softly. "She would probably be our age, right?"

Rachel Reid, I typed. There were a zillion Rachel Reids. The profile photos on Facebook showed a hundred different Rachels. Black, white, Asian, Native American. Children, teenagers, young women, middle-aged women. There were death notices and LinkedIn profiles and Twitter handles. There was a Rachel Reid who wrote children's books and a Rachel Reid who'd been arrested for drunk driving in Kentucky. Rachel Reid had Pinterest boards with knitting patterns and recipes for Christmas cookies. Searching for her was like searching for a grain of sand on a beach.

I couldn't paint. It would be at least six weeks, up to twelve, for my elbow to heal. As late as the beginning of April. I had to call Ginger and let her know what had happened. That there was no way the painting would be ready by the end of January. So much for Ikea. So much for *Bjorkar.*

I also wouldn't be able to take care of Avery. Not like this. Pilar would be here to help me, to take care of her after Gus brought her back to the island, but I wasn't even sure if I wanted to be here anymore.

Pilar had set up shop in one of the guest rooms upstairs. I could hear her above me every now and then, the creaking of the wooden floors. Once, I heard the swing in Avery's room and pictured Pilar swinging.

When I looked out the window toward the ocean, there was a heavy marine layer that obscured the view. It was quiet in the house, so quiet I could hear the distant lowing of a foghorn. Had I actually thought I'd come here and be inspired to paint? If so, what? I'd been painting trees for other people for so long now, I wasn't even sure if I had any idea who I was as an artist anymore. That wild spark that used to ignite in my chest whenever I hung a new canvas, when I opened a tube of paint, was nothing more than a barely burning ember.

Had I thought coming here, getting away from the duplex, from that horrible, divided life, might somehow help make things better for Avery? Clearly, that wasn't working either. Instead, she was wetting the bed every night. Not knowing where she belonged anymore. What kind of selfish person was I?

And had I thought coming here would somehow protect me from the day in my life that changed everything? That I could somehow flee from Robby and Rick Rousseau? Forget them? Rick Rousseau wasn't going to let me forget.

I knew the DNA evidence would show Robby was not the one who raped me. Despite his confession and my silence, there could be no physical evidence linking Robby to the woods that afternoon. To me. Rick seemed to think I still had the power to keep his secret, but was that true? I had no idea if his DNA would resemble Robby's. I didn't even know if they had the same mother and father. And he'd used a condom. My head spun with what this all meant.

Robby had been a model prisoner. He'd found Jesus. Been saved. And Jan Bromberg and the Innocence Project were hell-bent on proving me a liar. If I refused to testify, would the evidence speak for itself? And what would that look like? Rick would go to prison, but would Robby be released? They'd never recovered the knife he'd used to cut my throat. And Robby *had* cut my throat. He'd been the one to stab my shoulder, my neck. He wasn't innocent. He'd *tried* to rape me. He'd *tried* to kill me.

But there was every possibility in the world that if I kept my silence, this insistent silence, he would be set free. If I didn't speak up, if I didn't tell the truth, then they would open the doors and send him out into the world. As a mother of a little girl, how could I allow someone like Robby Rousseau to walk free?

But if I told what he did and he still got out, he might come after me.

My mind was buzzing, connecting to one thought then shorting out. But when I squeezed my eyes shut, all I could see were the images, the photos Sybil had taken. The epitaphs to a life she gave up. To a life that was stolen from her. Those images, the truth obscured for thirty-five years.

I gathered the stack of prints I'd made before the accident, spilled them across my lap. I realized I hadn't finished going through them. I'd been so caught up in the hide-and-go-seek photos I hadn't gone through the rest.

I knew exactly where these photos were taken: on the bluff at the edge of this property. They were dizzying. Because rather than focusing on the panoramic view of the ocean, instead, she was fixated on the earth below. I felt dizzy as I looked at them, at the rocks and sand. It was like the series of boardwalk pictures, a study. But what sort of study was this? What was she waiting for this time?

"You don't think, maybe she . . ." Pilar said.

I startled. Pilar was standing behind me. I felt like she was looking over my shoulder, reading my diary.

She fell, he'd said. "I need to talk to Seamus."

I reached for my cell phone but then realized I needed to ask him in person. I'd be too easy to dismiss over the phone.

"I'll go with you," she said.

I shook my head. "No. It's okay. But can you help me?"

She helped me slip on my Ugg boots and put my parka halfway on, one empty sleeve draped over my damaged arm. She opened the back door for me, and I made my way across the small backyard toward the woods. I could feel her eyes on me as I stood at the tree line. I stared at the path that cut through the woods. This would have been the path Seamus took to see her, in the middle of the night, perhaps. The dark woods between their two lives.

And I wasn't afraid anymore. There was no one following me. Not Robby, not Rick, not even Michael Ash. And so I entered the woods. I concentrated on my breath and followed the short path through the cold foliage to the clearing where Seamus and Fiona's house sat quietly, almost expectantly.

Emboldened, I marched across the expansive yard and up the stone steps, the cold air burning my face, my elbow throbbing.

I rang the doorbell and then knocked with my good hand. Loudly.

Nothing. Where the hell was he? How could he just leave? *How could he just take off and leave her here, leave them here?*

I squeezed my eyes shut and saw him standing in the background of the photo, little Rachel playing hide-and-go-seek. *Shhh,* he seemed to say to the camera. "Don't tell her where I'm hiding."

When the door opened, I caught my breath. I was crying.

"Please tell me what happened to her," I said. Imploring.

He hung his head and reached for my good hand, ushering me inside.

"There was another roll of film," he said. "I have it."

The Magic Hour

On a bright Sunday morning in November near Thanksgiving in 1981, Sybil got up, made the bed, fed her three-year-old daughter breakfast, and started a load of laundry. She cleaned the refrigerator, the stove, the floors. She sliced apples, coated them in cinnamon and sugar, maybe let Rachel eat the sweet, curly peels. And she photographed all of this:

Breakfast dishes, dirty clothes, linoleum, apples.

Later, she made her daughter a tuna fish sandwich for lunch, gave her a glass of grape juice, and sat at the kitchen table with her, where they colored in a Snoopy coloring book. They took a walk that afternoon, along the beach, gathering sea glass for the collection Rachel kept in an old jelly jar on her windowsill.

Jelly jar, broken crayons, mermaid tears.

Later, when Rachel grew sleepy, Sibyl took her upstairs to her room and tucked her in bed for a nap. "Sleep tight, don't let the bed-bugs bite," she might have said, and tickled Rachel's toes through the heavy blankets.

Downstairs, she pulled the hot pie from the oven, set it on the counter to cool, and took her camera outside.

A child's closed eyes, steam blown through the beak of a ceramic pie bird.

To Seamus's surprise (and dismay), Fiona had suggested they spend Thanksgiving here. Seamus had told Sybil he'd be arriving before Fiona, to get the house ready for guests. That he would come see her. Come see Rachel. She wouldn't be alone for long.

He missed her, he said. He had made a mistake. They would figure out what to do.

She slung the camera around her neck, so grateful for the
weight of it. Sometimes it felt like the only thing keeping her
from floating away. She took photos of the house where Rachel
was sleeping. She took photos of Seamus's house, quiet and dark
as a catacomb.

She walked to the edge of the bluff and studied the sky. The
days were so short now, they seemed to be tumbling, cartwheeling
like a child across a vast expanse of grass.

The light would be perfect in just a few more minutes. That
golden hour, that magical hour that comes before dusk. She was
only moments away from beauty. But she didn't take any photos,
not this time, and when she lifted the camera from her neck, she
felt untethered. Capable, even, of flight.

When Rachel came running outside, having woken from her
nap, she shook her head . . . *no, no, go back inside.* But it was too
late.

"Mama?" Rachel must have said, running to her. And Sybil
picked her up in her arms, dizzy, already tumbling in her mind.

This was the coveted moment, the golden hour. The sky was
gilded when she stepped off the edge of the cliff, Rachel clinging
to her, face buried in her neck. But there would be no photo to
capture this moment, she thought. And it filled her with sorrow.

But the universe was awash in gold as they fell.

Seamus arrived, as promised, just as the sun set. The door was
open, and the pie was still hot on the counter, the laundry still
spinning in the dryer. He searched the tiny house and then headed
toward the bluffs to see if they had gone on a walk on the beach.
Instead he found the camera sitting at the edge of the rocky cliff
and knew before he looked what he would find below. And on
the roll of film captured inside.

Epitaphs

*I*n art history, I memorized the suicides.
American photographer Diane Arbus (1923–1971) was wracked by "depressive episodes" her whole life, purportedly exasperated by symptoms associated with hepatitis. On July 26, 1971, she swallowed a lethal dose of barbiturates and slashed her wrists with a razor. She wasn't discovered until two days later. She was forty-eight years old.

Dora de Houghton Carrington (1893–1932) was a British painter and member of the Bloomsbury Group. During her lifetime, her work was never exhibited at the urging of her lover, the gay writer Lytton Strachey. When Lytton died of stomach cancer, Carrington borrowed a gun from a friend and shot herself. She was thirty-nine years old.

Frida Kahlo (1907–1954), the Mexican painter, was crippled in a bus accident as a teenager, and suffered ill health as a result for most of her life, including the inability to carry a child. Her marriage to her mentor, Diego Rivera, was plagued by mutual infidelities. At forty-seven years old she died of a pulmonary embolism (officially), though the rumored cause of death was an overdose.

Constance Mayer (1775–1821), a French portraitist, carried on a long affair with her mentor, Pierre-Paul Prud'hon. When his wife finally died, she expected he would marry her, but he did not. And so she took the artist's knife and slit her throat. She was forty-six years old.

Jeanne Hébuterne (1898–1920) was also a French painter. The lover and muse of Modigliani, she bore him a child. However, soon after *she became pregnant with a second child, Modigliani died of tubercular meningitis complicated by substance abuse. The day after his death, she flung herself, carrying their unborn child, out of a fifth floor window. She was twenty-two years old. Her epitaph read, "Devoted companion to the extreme sacrifice."*

The Bluffs

"What did he say?" Pilar asked as I came back into the house.

I shook my head. He'd pieced the story together the same way I'd pieced together her life, from the artifacts she'd left behind. He'd developed that last roll and had hidden those images for thirty-five years. He hadn't known about the box of photos in the basement.

I went to the living room and gathered the prints, the negatives, everything she'd left behind. I tore down the prints I'd hung. The idea of these images, these photos, hanging on some cold gallery wall seemed ridiculous to me. The beauty of them was that they were not exposed but rather protected, coddled. She couldn't protect her own daughter, apparently, but she could protect this.

"What are you doing?" Pilar asked.

I was crying now, my heart slivering. I was so angry at Sybil. How could she have done this? To herself? And to her little girl?

I clumsily made my way to the door, my arm a bundle of pain as I went outside to the rocky edge of the bluffs. Pilar was behind me, but she didn't say a word.

I looked down at the dizzying sight of the rocks and sand below. I wanted to scream at her, *How could you do this? God, you selfish, selfish bitch.*

But as the sun dipped into the trees behind me, the air took on that quality of light she must have seen that afternoon, and for a moment, I understood.

She'd already died once when she left her life behind and came here. She'd written her own epitaphs.

But she didn't have to die *again*. This had been her choice.

The tide was high, the wind violent. I thought about tossing the negatives, the prints. Releasing them, letting her name be *writ on water*. But each of these frames was the truth of this woman's life. Of what happened to her. Hiding them hadn't done anyone any good. I owed it to her to preserve them, not to destroy them. I wouldn't be complicit in another lie.

I walked slowly back to the house, clutching the prints, the negatives. Trembling.

Inside, Pilar was waiting for me. Her face was pale, and her eyes were wide.

"I'm okay," I said. "I'm sorry. Everything's okay."

She shook her head, reached for me.

"What's the matter?" I asked, feeling sick, my heart plummeting. Something was wrong.

"Your dad just called."

"My dad?"

"Yeah. There's been some sort of accident," she said, her mouth twitching nervously. "A fire."

"*What?*"

"Everybody's okay," she said. "But you need to call your dad."

Ash and Ember

The fire started in the cellar.

My father said Husky smelled the smoke moments before the alarm went off and went and woke him and my mother; the little dog saved their lives.

My brother was on duty, and when the dispatcher announced the address, Mark said, his heart stopped. But then muscle memory kicked in. In a small town like Haven, this was bound to happen one day: somebody he knew. A fire engulfing a place he loved.

My father and mother got out just as the flames were climbing the cellar stairs. I picture them standing in their nightclothes on the front lawn, pale as my mother's chicken wire ghosts in the firelight. Ash falling like snow on their shoulders and hair.

My brother said when the fire truck roared down the street where we grew up, it felt like every moment of the last few years had been in preparation for this. "Do you believe in destiny?" he asked.

The firefighters were able to keep the fire from destroying the house, but the kitchen was gutted. The basement flooded.

"How did it happen?" I asked when my brother put my mother on the phone.

"It must have been something electrical. That goddamned furnace? Oh my God, all your artwork, Wynnie. From high school. College. It was all down there." My mother sobbed.

"It's okay, Mom. I don't care. I'm just so glad you and Daddy are okay. Can you put Mark on again?"

"What happened?" I asked my brother.

"It doesn't look like an accident," Mark said softly. "It looks intentional."

"Intentional?"

"Arson."

Trembling after the phone call, I opened my laptop, logged onto my business e-mail account.

> Lissen. Maybe I need to git your attention some other way. You got a responsibility. If you think you can just start blabbing your mouth off you got another thing comin.

I clicked PRINT, opened the earlier e-mail and clicked PRINT as well.

"What are those?" Pilar asked.

I felt my stomach bottom out.

The only person in the world who could help now was Pilar. If only to keep me from combusting. From turning to ash.

I sat down at the kitchen table. My legs were shaking too hard to support me. It made me think of the charred walls of my parents' house. The foundation ravaged.

"Talk to me, Wynnie." She reached out and took my good hand.

"It's not the way I said it," I told her, my voice and throat aching.

"What's that?"

I shook my head. "I was scared. I was just a little girl."

Pilar sat down across from me and took the e-mails from my hand, read them. Tears ran down my face in hot streams.

"Who the fuck wrote these?" she asked.

"His brother," I said, feeling like a valve inside my heart had been released. "His brother was there too. He made him do it."

Unspun

This is the thing about a lie: over time, it not only obscures the truth but *consumes* it. Those who pursue veracity (those do-gooders, those seekers) see truth not as an abstract thing but something concrete. Strong, vivid, with an unassailable right to prevail. But those who fight for it, who fight in the *name* of it, do not understand that truth is anemic, weak. Especially in the hands of an accomplished liar. Especially over years. A lie, in collusion with time, can overpower the truth. A good lie has the power to subsume reality. A good lie can *become* the truth.

However, lies are also precarious things. I picture my own like the shimmery filaments of a web. The truth is that fat insect ensnared in the delicate strands, imprisoned, struggling to break free. Each twist and turn, each flutter of wing, each protest threatening to tear the intricate construction apart.

It had been twenty years since I'd cast out that first lie, that fine thread. And foolishly, I'd believed my design was infallible. That the winged beast, the one wrapped in the silken fibers of my own making, had succumbed. That I was safe.

But what *was* the truth?

Robby and Rick Rousseau followed me into the woods intent on hurting me. When Robby couldn't follow through, Rick took over. His rage and violence, his sickness, both calculated and spontaneous. Whatever had happened to them both as boys twisted them, turned their concepts of right and wrong upside down. *Upset down.* The sky became the ground, the earth became the heavens. But Robby was not innocent. He pressed the blade to my throat; he wanted my silence as much as Rick had.

I thought of Seamus, of Fiona. The secrets, the lies. Seamus had used his money to purchase the silence of law enforcement, of the newspapers, to quietly hide Sybil's suicide (with her baby, God, with that poor little girl). And Rick and Robby had used their knife to purchase mine.

But the funny thing about the truth is, it always seems to have a way of getting free. For two decades, I could practically hear the beating of wings against those invisible threads, gossamer snapping, coming undone. I had a feeling Seamus had simply been waiting for his own lie to come unraveled too.

I would need to tell my parents. Gus. And I would need to talk to Larry. The police. There would be accusations. Cruel and awful things said about me. That wound I thought had healed would be opened again and again and again.

But I couldn't keep his secret anymore. I couldn't keep my own.

Testimony

"So the DNA tests probably showed there was no match be-tween the samples taken and Robby's DNA," Larry said. I'd returned to Haven, shared everything with my parents. And now I sat in his dim office as he paced.

He looked flustered, his white hair long and unruly. "Which casts doubt on whether or not he was the perpetrator of the rape."

"He *tried* to rape me," I said, my throat tight, the old wounds made fresh.

"But he *didn't* rape you," Larry said. "And he's been sitting in prison for twenty years on a rape conviction."

"And attempted murder," I said. Whose side was he on?

Larry continued shuffling back and forth across his office floor. There was a faded path in the Oriental rug, likely from years of such fevered pacing.

He continued, "The knife was never found, but Robby was covered in your blood. There was a confession, which the defense is going to try to show was coerced. Your new testimony is going to call all of this into question. They're going to try to get the original verdict overturned."

I nodded. I knew this. I also knew if it was, if Robby was freed, he might come after me. I took small comfort in his having found God.

"The defense is going to use you as their key witness. To defer the blame from Robby to Rick."

I nodded. I knew this as well. Between the devil and the deep blue sea.

I had forwarded Larry the e-mails, the letter. I had told him about the phone call on our landline.

"He set the fire," I'd told him. "Rick. He thought I was at my parents' house. He was trying to kill me again."

"But you said he used a condom? Then there might not be any of Rick's DNA in the kit either. No physical evidence to link Robby *or* him to you?"

I closed my eyes, forced myself back into the woods again. Recalling every awful moment in excruciating detail. I recollected waning sunlight, the green of leaves. Felt the pounding of the bass in my heart. This same heart beating inside my chest now. I heard birdsong, the crush of leaves, wind, his voice. *Come on, you pussy.* I squeezed my eyes tight, until that blue sky of my imagination turned to stars. I smelled mud. Cinnamon.

"The *gum*," I said to Larry, my heart thudding. "It was in the rape kit. Rick was chewing it, and it fell in my hair. They clipped it out at the hospital. It's got to have his DNA on it. Maybe that's what they found? Maybe that's their new evidence?"

"Okay," he said, nodding. "That's good, Wyn. That's an important detail. Enough to establish he was there. That he was involved somehow."

I nodded. I was still there, in those woods, scrambling to my knees after they were gone. Rick probably didn't remember the gum. Because he had used the condom, gotten rid of the knife, he must have thought he left no trace behind. He must have figured this, coupled with my silence, had been the key to his freedom.

Larry sat down behind his desk and steepled his fingers together. "What we're going to need to work on is proving Robby was equally culpable. That he was an active participant in both the rape and attempted murder."

I nodded. I had no idea how he would do this. I couldn't

worry about it though. I needed to trust the truth, that sluggish, winged thing, would prevail.

"Wyn, this time you have to take the stand," he said. "Will you testify?"

No, no, no.

"Yes," I said. "I will."

Prophecies

"You sure you're going to be okay for a couple of days?" Pilar asked.

I nodded. I'd returned to the island after meeting with Larry. My parents had wanted me to stay in Haven, to wait for the re-trial, which had been granted in light of the "new" evidence. But I still wasn't ready to go home. Life on the island didn't feel finished yet.

Pilar had gotten a call from her manager that a big collector from Sweden wanted to meet her, see her work. I thought of Ikea. About what almost was, but, perhaps thankfully, wasn't.

"When do Gus and Av get here?" she asked as she stuffed her clothes into her suitcase, again.

"Saturday," I said. "Don't worry."

"What did you tell Gus?"

I looked out the window at the sun rising over the water.

"I told him I want to come home," I said.

"To the duplex?"

"No," I said, shook my head, "to him."

Pilar smiled, her eyes wide and wet with tears. "And the trial?"

I nodded. "It'll start in about a month."

"I want to be there with you."

I nodded again. I *wanted* her there. I wanted my parents there. I wanted Gus there. To give me courage. To bear witness. Silence had been easy, and I knew this would be difficult.

As my mind reeled at the thought, I had to calmly talk myself down. Rick and I had made a deal; I'd sold my soul that day to save my life. But he wouldn't kill me again. I wouldn't let him.

Gus and Avery arrived on Saturday evening.

"Mama Llama!" Avery squealed and ran to me, hugging my legs. I bent down and clung to her with my good arm, not even minding the pain of her embrace.

"I missed you!" I said. And as she buried her little body into me, my heart reeled. She smelled of paste and cocoa and shampoo. Her little fingernails with chipped pink polish, her tiny teeth and tangled hair. I missed every inch of her.

"Oh, don't cry, Mama. You're not a mermaid!" she said. "You're not bamished anymore!"

I smiled at Gus. He'd shaved his beard; his face looked vulnerable this way.

"Hi," I said, and moved to hug him.

He gently hugged me, careful of my arm. "This looks awful," he said. "But you look good. You look happy."

After dinner, after Avery fell asleep in her upside-down room, it began to snow again.

It snowed all night.

Gus and I sat together in the living room. We didn't talk about the swimming pool, the kiss. We didn't talk about what that meant, what was going on with us. What had happened before or what would happen next. We didn't talk about what had broken us apart and whether or not it was something that could ever be repaired. We didn't talk about what I'd left behind or what it meant for me to return. We didn't talk about separation, divorce, or reconciliation. We didn't talk about Mia. Or Avery. Or art. Or where we were now.

Instead, we sat on the couch, not touching, with all the lights out, watching the snow fall on the ocean. In the small glow of the porch light, the filaments fell and fell. And we sat, together, mesmerized.

We also didn't talk about Robby Rousseau. We didn't have to. Because he resided in those woods Gus had been pulling me through for the last fifteen years. I looked at him as he started, finally, to fall asleep (hypnotized, anesthetized by the snow on the sea). And I knew without him I would never get to the other side.

"I miss you, Wynnie," he said, just as I was drifting off to sleep too.

"Even though . . ."

"I miss you even though."

In the morning, before Gus and Avery woke, I went to the dining room and watched the sun as it rose pale and soft on the horizon. Slowly, that beautiful morning light filled the room. The walls were empty now, Sybil's photos carefully packed away. Pilar had told me I could keep them, the negatives too. I didn't know what I would do with them, whether or not they should ever be shared. But I would take care of them. I would make sure they were safe.

I had pulled out the print of Seamus and the little girl playing hide-and-go-seek, though, and given it to him.

His hands trembled as he studied the image. "You're leaving soon?"

I nodded.

"Will you ever be back to the island?"

"I think so," I said. "Maybe in the summer."

"Good. I'll see you then." He'd smiled and nodded. "Thank you. For this. For everything."

Mike Ash had called my cell phone a half dozen times, apologizing again and again for the night I broke my elbow. For frightening me. He was hoping he might talk to me after the trial. He'd be there, he said. He, like all the others, just hoped the truth would, finally, come out.

I looked at the birches. Gus had told me not to worry about the commission. That he would take care of me. Of Avery. That I should just work on healing for now. But still. I put the canvas on my easel. It was tricky with only one good arm, but I managed to get it propped up. I stared at those trees, those lies, and wondered if I'd be able to do it. To wander back into those woods again and tell a group of strangers what happened to me. What Robby did to me. What *Rick* did to me under that impossibly blue sky.

Outside the window, I watched a seagull swoop down, its beautiful, controlled flight. And I thought of Sibyl.

Using my teeth, I unscrewed the cap of a tube of bone black and squeezed out a fat, greasy blob onto my palette. I took the largest brush I had and gripped it with my left hand. It felt awkward and uncomfortable. But it didn't take any skill. It only took patience. *A painter should begin every canvas with a wash of black, because all things in nature are dark except where exposed by the light.* And slowly, I began to paint over the trees, to begin again. To tell the truth this time, to not be afraid. Later, when my arm was healed, I would paint the haze that surrounded me that afternoon. The mist that hung both weightless and oppressive in the trees above my head. With meticulous, ridiculous, detail. I would craft those blades of grass, the green of the leaves. Everything unfurling. Everything reaching for the waning sun. I would paint the darkness in the distance.

If this day were a painting, it would take a special brush, one to both paint and erase. To both articulate and obliterate. It would have to carry every color and no color at all. Opaque and transparent. Vivid and subdued.

If this day were a painting, it would be both an epitaph and a prophecy. An end and a beginning.

The Golden Hour

T. Greenwood

The following discussion questions are included
to enhance your group's reading of
The Golden Hour.

Discussion Questions

1. Wyn sees her life as divided between Before and After the attack. Discuss the idea of divisions in this novel (both literal and figurative).

2. Gus accuses Wyn of selling her soul. Is this fair? Why or why not?

3. Wyn struggles with the choices she has made as an artist. How does the discovery of Sybil's photographs help her change her perspective?

4. The town where Wyn grew up is called Haven. Discuss the ways in which the name is accurate and the ways in which it is ironic.

5. This is a novel about friendship, but Wyn's friendship with Pilar is threatened by Pilar's newfound success. Have you ever experienced a similar rift with a friend?

6. This is also a book about secrets. Discuss the secrets each of these characters keep: Wyn, Sybil, Seamus.

7. What do you think will happen between Gus and Wyn now?

8. Do you think that there will be justice with regards to Rick Rousseau? How about Robby?

9. Wyn worries that she has failed as both a wife and a mother. Do you agree with her?

10. Wyn has been living a lie for twenty years. Do you understand why she has never told the truth? What would you have done? Do you forgive Wyn for her lie?

11. Talk about the power of art, both in *The Golden Hour* and in your own experience. Do you have a creative outlet, and if so, what are the therapeutic benefits of it?

Don't miss any of T. Greenwood's critically acclaimed novels!

WHERE I LOST HER

Eight years ago, Tess and Jake were considered a power couple of the New York publishing world—happy, in love, planning a family. Failed fertility treatments and a heartbreaking attempt at adoption have fractured their marriage and left Tess edgy and adrift. A visit to friends in rural Vermont throws Tess's world into further chaos when she sees a young, half-dressed child in the middle of the road, who then runs into the woods like a frightened deer.

The entire town begins searching for the little girl. But there are no sightings, no other witnesses, no reports of missing children. As local police and Jake point out, Tess's imagination has played her false before. And yet Tess is compelled to keep looking, not only to save the little girl she can't forget but to salvage her broken heart as well.

Blending her trademark lyrical prose with a superbly crafted and suspenseful narrative, *Where I Lost Her* is a gripping, haunting novel from a remarkable storyteller.

"*Where I Lost Her* is a spellbinding tale about finding what we most want in the places we least expect. A touching story of one woman's loss and heartache, coupled with the electrifying search for a young girl in the remote woods of rural Vermont, the novel features the eloquent prose of T. Greenwood, indelible characters and an edge-of-your-seat mystery. I loved everything about *Where I Lost Her*."
—Mary Kubica, Bestselling author of *The Good Girl* and *Pretty Baby*

"Greenwood crafts believable relationships with searing, heartbreaking realism. Showcasing the power of friendship and of hope, this mysterious, suspenseful exploration of the human psyche will keep readers turning pages and losing sleep."
—*Publishers Weekly*

"Greenwood's fascinating tenth novel is sure to have readers riveted, as a distraught Tess struggles to learn the truth."
—*Library Journal*

"Intricate drama unfolds as the author provides, in the first-person, Tess's back story of her time in Guatemala relating her fears and anguish. For readers who love the in-depth description of locations, *Where I Lost Her* will not disappoint."
—*The New York Journal of Books*

"This intoxicating blend of women's fiction and psychological thriller is the perfect platform for Greenwood's exquisite prose and masterful storytelling."
—*RT Book Reviews*, 4.5 Stars Top Pick

THE FOREVER BRIDGE

With eloquent prose and lush imagery, T. Greenwood creates a heartfelt story of reconciliation and forgiveness, and of the deep, often unexpected connections that can bring you home.

Sylvie can hardly bear to remember how normal her family was two years ago. All of that changed on the night an oncoming vehicle forced their car over the edge of a covered bridge into the river. With horrible swiftness, Sylvie's young son was gone, her husband lost his legs, and she was left with shattering blame and grief.

Eleven-year-old Ruby misses her little brother, too. But she also misses the mother who has become a recluse in their old home while Ruby and her dad try to piece themselves back together. Amid all the uncertainty in her life, Ruby becomes obsessed with bridges, drawing inspiration from the strength and purpose that underlies their grace. During one momentous week, as Hurricane Irene bears down on their small Vermont town and a pregnant teenager with a devastating secret gradually draws Sylvie back into the world, Ruby and her mother will have a chance to span the gap between them again.

"Set against the backdrop of an impending hurricane, a mother, her young daughter, and a pregnant teen find themselves caught up in their own emotional storms fraught with loss, guilt, and shards of fractured families. Greenwood deftly captures the complicated and subtly volatile situations of these three women at three very different stages of their lives with sensitivity and a stark honesty that makes for a compelling read."
—Tawni O'Dell, *New York Times Bestselling* author of *Back Roads*

"In *The Forever Bridge,* about a family reeling from the death of a child as they face Hurricane Irene, T. Greenwood adds another enticing, lyrical novel to her body of work. Greenwood's facility in bringing fictional Quimby, Vermont to life—which she has now done in 7 of her novels—is reminiscent of Faulkner's evocation of Yoknapatawpha County; a created place so thoughtfully rendered that it lives and breathes even when the book is closed."
—Miranda Beverly-Whittemore, *New York Times* bestselling author of *Bittersweet*

"I loved *The Forever Bridge* from its first beautiful sentence to its breathtaking final one. T. Greenwood delves into the pain of grief, the complex navigations of family in the throes of loss, and brings the reader to a place of hope and, yes, even joy."
—Ann Hood, author of *The Knitting Circle* and *An Italian Wife*

"Amidst a body of extraordinary work, T. Greenwood's latest is her best. Set against the violent backdrop of Hurricane Irene, *The Forever Bridge* tells the affecting, evocative tale of three damaged women all fighting to find a road home. Written with acute humanity and depth, the beauty of the novel is in its complex story and, ultimately, its heartbreaking and redemptive end. Or, in Greenwood's own words: 'That something stolen has been returned to her. That something lost has been found.' "
—Michelle Gable, author of *A Paris Apartment*

"T. Greenwood's *The Forever Bridge* is full of palpable emotion: both the pain of unbearable losses, and the indomitable human connections that somehow allow us to bear them. Essentially an excavation of the fragile bridges we build towards hope, this lyrical and poignant novel will appeal to fans of Caroline Leavitt's *Pictures of You* and Jonathan Evison's *The Revised Fundamentals of Caregiving.*"
—Gina Frangello, author of *A Life in Men*

BODIES OF WATER

In 1960, Billie Valentine is a young housewife living in a sleepy Massachusetts suburb, treading water in a dull marriage and caring for two adopted daughters. Summers spent with the girls at their lakeside camp in Vermont are her one escape—from her husband's demands, from days consumed by household drudgery, and from the nagging suspicion that life was supposed to hold something different.

Then a new family moves in across the street. Ted and Eva Wilson have three children and a fourth on the way, and their arrival reignites long-buried feelings in Billie. The affair that follows offers a solace Billie has never known, until her secret is revealed and both families are wrenched apart in the tragic aftermath.

Fifty years later, Ted and Eva's son, Johnny, contacts an elderly but still spry Billie, entreating her to return east to meet with him. Once there, Billie finally learns the surprising truth about what was lost, and what still remains, of those joyful, momentous summers.

In this deeply tender novel, T. Greenwood weaves deftly between the past and present to create a poignant and wonderfully moving story of friendship, the resonance of memories, and the love that keeps us afloat.

"A complex and compelling portrait of the painful intricacies of love and loyalty. Book clubs will find much to discuss in T. Greenwood's insightful story of two women caught between their hearts and their families."
—Eleanor Brown, *New York Times* bestselling author of *The Weird Sisters*

"A wrenching look at what happens when two people fall in love in the wrong place at the wrong time . . . Beauty and tragedy at the same time, darkness then light—those are Greenwood hallmarks. She's terrific with characters, with the multiple textures that make someone seem human on the page. She has some interesting things to say here about memory, and the ending is as moving as anything she's written."
—*The San Diego Union-Tribune*

"*Bodies of Water* is no ordinary love story, but a book of astonishing precision, lyrically told, raw in its honesty and gentle in its unfolding. Here is a complex tapestry of lives entwined, a testimony to the fact that a timeless sort of love does exist. T. Greenwood has rendered a compassionate story of people who are healed and destroyed by love, by alcoholism, by secrets and betrayal, and yet she offers us a certain shade of hope that soul mates can and do find each other— sometimes more than once in a lifetime. A luminous, fearless heart-wrenching story about the power of true love."
—Ilie Ruby, author of *The Salt God's Daughter*

"Greenwood's [seventh] novel, a tale of love and loyalty, owes its success to the poetic prose, as well as the compelling chronology she employs . . . This compassionate, insightful look at hope and redemption is a richly textured portrait. This gem of a story is a good choice for those who enjoy family novels."
—*Library Journal*

"T. Greenwood's *Bodies of Water* is a lyrical novel about the inexplicable nature of love, and the power a forbidden affair has to transform one woman's entire life. By turns beautiful and tragic, haunting and healing, I was captivated from the very first line. And Greenwood's moving story of love and loss, hope and redemption has stayed with me, long after I turned the last page."
—Jillian Cantor, author of *Margot*

BREATHING WATER

Three years after leaving Lake Gormlaith, Vermont, Effie Greer is coming home. The unspoiled lake, surrounded by dense woods and patches of wild blueberries, is the place where she spent idyllic childhood summers at her grandparents' cottage. And it's where Effie's tempestuous relationship with her college boyfriend, Max, culminated in a tragedy she can never forget.

Effie had hoped to save Max from his troubled past, and in the process became his victim. Since then, she's wandered from one city to another, living like a fugitive. But now Max is gone, and as Effie paints and restores the ramshackle cottage, she forms new bonds—with an old school friend, with her widowed grandmother, and with Devin, an artist and carpenter summering nearby. Slowly, she's discovering a resilience and tenderness she didn't know she possessed, and—buoyed by the lake's cool, forgiving waters—she may even learn to save herself.

Wrenching yet ultimately uplifting, here is a novel of survival, hope, and absolution, from a writer of extraordinary insight and depth.

A poignant, clear-eyed first novel . . . filled with careful poetic description . . . the story is woven skillfully."
—*The New York Times Book Review*

"A poignant debut . . . Greenwood sensitively and painstakingly unravels her protagonist's self-loathing and replaces it with a graceful dignity."
—*Publishers Weekly*

"A vivid, somberly engaging first book."
—Larry McMurtry

"An impressive first novel."
—*Booklist*

"*Breathing Water* is startling and fresh . . . Greenwood's novel is ripe with originality."
—*The San Diego Union-Tribune*

GRACE

T. Greenwood's extraordinary novels deftly combine lyrical prose with heartrending subject matter. Now she explores one year in a family poised to implode, and the imperfect love that may be its only salvation.

Every family photograph hides a story. Some are suffused with warmth and joy, others reflect the dull ache of disappointed dreams. For thirteen-year-old Trevor Kennedy, taking photos helps make sense of his fractured world. His father, Kurt, struggles to keep a business going while also caring for Trevor's aging grandfather, whose hoarding has reached dangerous levels. Trevor's mother, Elsbeth, all but ignores her son while doting on his five-year-old sister, Gracy, and pilfering useless drugstore items.

Trevor knows he can count on little Gracy's unconditional love and his art teacher's encouragement. None of that compensates for the bullying he has endured at school for as long as he can remember. But where Trevor once silently tolerated the jabs and name-calling, now anger surges through him in ways he's powerless to control.

Only Crystal, a store clerk dealing with her own loss, sees the deep fissures in the Kennedy family—in the haunting photographs Trevor brings to be developed, and in the palpable distance between Elsbeth and her son. And as their lives become more intertwined, each will be pushed to the breaking point, with shattering, unforeseeable consequences.

"*Grace* is a poetic, compelling story that glows in its subtle, yet searing examination of how we attempt to fill the potentially devastating fissures in our lives. Each character is masterfully drawn; each struggles in their own way to find peace amid tumultuous circumstance. With her always crisp imagery and fearless language, Greenwood doesn't back down from the hard issues or the darker sides of human psyche, managing to create astounding empathy and a balanced view of each player along the way. The story expertly builds to a breath-taking climax, leaving the reader with a clear understanding of how sometimes, only a moment of grace can save us."
—Amy Hatvany, author of *Best Kept Secret*

"*Grace* is at once heart breaking, thrilling and painfully beautiful. From the opening page, to the breathless conclusion, T. Greenwood again shows why she is one of our most gifted and lyrical storytellers."
—Jim Kokoris, author of *The Pursuit of Other Interests*

"*Grace* is a masterpiece of small-town realism that is as harrowing as it is heartfelt."
—Jim Ruland, author of *Big Lonesome*

"This novel will keep readers rapt until the very end . . . Shocking and honest, you're likely to never forget this book."
—*RT Book Reviews*

"*Grace* amazes. Ultimately so realistically human in its terror and beauty that it may haunt you for days after you finish it. T. Greenwood has another gem here. Greenwood's mastery of character and her deep empathy for the human condition make you care what happens, especially in the book's furious final 100 pages."
—*The San Diego Union-Tribune*

"Exceptionally well-observed. Readers who enjoy insightful and sensitive family drama (Lionel Shriver's *We Need to Talk About Kevin*; Rosellen Brown's *Before and After*) will appreciate discovering Greenwood."
—*Library Journal*

NEARER THAN THE SKY

*In this mesmerizing novel, T. Greenwood draws readers into the
fascinating and frightening world of Munchausen syndrome
by proxy—and into one woman's search for healing.*

When Indie Brown was four years old, she was struck by lightning. In the oft-told version of the story, Indie's life was heroically
saved by her mother. But Indie's own recollection of the event, while
hazy, is very different.

Most of Indie's childhood memories are like this—tinged with
vague, unsettling images and suspicions. Her mother, Judy, fussed over
her pretty youngest daughter, Lily, as much as she ignored Indie. That
neglect, coupled with the death of her beloved older brother, is the
reason Indie now lives far away in rural Maine. It's why her relationship with Lily is filled with tension, and why she dreads the thought
of flying back to Arizona. But she has no choice. Judy is gravely ill,
and Lily, struggling with a challenge of her own, needs her help.

In Arizona, faced with Lily's hysteria and their mother's instability,
Indie slowly begins to confront the truth about her half-remembered
past and the legacy that still haunts her family. And as she revisits her
childhood, with its nightmares and lost innocence, she finds she must
reevaluate the choices of her adulthood—including her most precious
relationships.

"Greenwood is an assured guide through this strange territory;
she has a lush, evocative style."
—*The New York Times Book Review*

"T. Greenwood writes with grace and compassion about loyalty
and betrayal, love and redemption in this totally absorbing novel
about daughters and mothers."
—Ursula Hegi, author of *Stones from the River*

"A lyrical investigation into the unreliability and elusiveness of
memory centers Greenwood's second novel . . . The kaleidoscopic
heart of the story is rich with evocative details about its heroine's inner
life."
—*Publishers Weekly*

THIS GLITTERING WORLD

Acclaimed author T. Greenwood crafts a moving, lyrical story of loss, atonement, and promises kept.

One November morning, Ben Bailey walks out of his Flagstaff, Arizona, home to retrieve the paper. Instead, he finds Ricky Begay, a young Navajo man, beaten and dying in the newly fallen snow.

Unable to forget the incident, especially once he meets Ricky's sister, Shadi, Ben begins to question everything, from his job as a part-time history professor to his fiancée, Sara. When Ben first met Sara, he was mesmerized by her optimism and easy confidence. These days, their relationship only reinforces a loneliness that stretches back to his fractured childhood.

Ben decides to discover the truth about Ricky's death, both for Shadi's sake and in hopes of filling in the cracks in his own life. Yet the answers leave him torn—between responsibility and happiness, between his once-certain future and the choices that could liberate him from a delicate web of lies he has spun.

"In *This Glittering World*, T. Greenwood demonstrates once again that she is a poet and storyteller of unique gifts, not the least of which is a wise and compassionate heart."
—Drusilla Campbell, author of *The Good Sister* and *Blood Orange*

UNDRESSING THE MOON

Dark and compassionate, graceful yet raw, Undressing the Moon
explores the seams between childhood and adulthood,
between love and loss . . .

At thirty, Piper Kincaid feels too young to be dying. Cancer has eaten away her strength; she'd be alone but for a childhood friend who's come home by chance. Yet with all the questions of her future before her, she's adrift in the past, remembering the fateful summer she turned fourteen and her life changed forever.

Her nervous father's job search seemed stalled for good, as he hung around the house watching her mother's every move. What he and Piper had both dreaded at last came to pass: Her restless, artistic mother, who smelled of lilacs and showed Piper beauty, finally left.

With no one to rely on, Piper struggled to hold on to what was important. She had a brother who loved her and a teacher enthralled with her potential. But her mother's absence, her father's distance, and a volatile secret threatened her delicate balance.

Now Piper is once again left with the jagged pieces of a shattered life. If she is ever going to put herself back together, she'll have to begin with the summer that broke them all . . .

"This beautiful story, eloquently told, demands attention."
—*Library Journal* (starred review)

"Greenwood has skillfully managed to create a novel with unforgettable characters, finely honed descriptions, and beautiful imagery."
—*Book Street USA*

"A lyrical, delicately affecting tale."
—*Publishers Weekly*

"Rarely has a writer rendered such highly charged topics . . . to so wrenching, yet so beautifully understated, an effect . . . T. Greenwood takes on risky subject matter, handling her volatile topics with admirable restraint . . . Ultimately more about life than death, *Undressing the Moon* beautifully elucidates the human capacity to maintain grace under unrelenting fire."
—*The Los Angeles Times*

THE HUNGRY SEASON

It's been five years since the Mason family vacationed at the lakeside cottage in northeastern Vermont, close to where prize-winning novelist Samuel Mason grew up. The summers that Sam, his wife, Mena, and their twins, Franny and Finn, spent at Lake Gormlaith were noisy, chaotic, and nearly perfect. But since Franny's death, the Masons have been flailing, one step away from falling apart. Lake Gormlaith is Sam's last, best hope of rescuing his son from a destructive path and salvaging what's left of his family.

As Sam struggles with grief, writer's block, and a looming deadline, Mena tries to repair the marital bond she once thought was unbreakable. But even in this secluded place, the unexpected—in the form of an overzealous fan, a surprising friendship, and a second chance—can change everything.

From the acclaimed author of *Two Rivers* comes a compelling and beautifully told story of hope, family, and above all, hunger—for food, sex, love and success—and for a way back to wholeness when a part of oneself has been lost forever.

"This compelling study of a family in need of rescue is very effective, owing to Greenwood's eloquent, exquisite word artistry and

her knack for developing subtle, suspenseful scenes . . . Greenwood's sensitive and gripping examination of a family in crisis is real, complex, and anything but formulaic."
—*Library Journal* (starred review)

"A deeply psychological read."
—*Publishers Weekly*

"Can there be life after tragedy? How do you live with the loss of a child let alone the separation emotionally from all your loved ones? T. Greenwood with beautiful prose poses this question while delving into the psyches of a successful man, his wife, and his son . . . This is a wonderful story, engaging from the beginning that gets better with every chapter."
—*The Washington Times*

TWO RIVERS

Two Rivers is a powerful, haunting tale of enduring love, destructive secrets, and opportunities that arrive in disguise . . .

In Two Rivers, Vermont, Harper Montgomery is living a life overshadowed by grief and guilt. Since the death of his wife, Betsy, twelve years earlier, Harper has narrowed his world to working at the local railroad and raising his daughter, Shelly, the best way he knows how. Still wracked with sorrow over the loss of his life-long love and plagued by his role in a brutal, long-ago crime, he wants only to make amends for his past mistakes.

Then one fall day, a train derails in Two Rivers, and amid the wreckage Harper finds an unexpected chance at atonement. One of the survivors, a pregnant fifteen-year-old girl with mismatched eyes and skin the color of blackberries, needs a place to stay. Though filled with misgivings, Harper offers to take Maggie in. But it isn't long before he begins to suspect that Maggie's appearance in Two Rivers is not the simple case of happenstance it first appeared to be.

"In *Two Rivers*, T. Greenwood weaves a haunting story in which the sins of the past threaten to destroy the fragile equilibrium of the present. Ripe with surprising twists and heart-breakingly real charac-

ters, *Two Rivers* is a remarkable and complex look at race and forgiveness in small-town America."
—Michelle Richmond, New York Times bestselling author of *The Year of Fog* and *No One You Know*

"*Two Rivers* is a convergence of tales, a reminder that the past never washes away, and yet, in T. Greenwood's delicate handling of time gone and time to come, love and forgiveness wait on the other side of what life does to us and what we do to it. This novel is a sensitive and suspenseful portrayal of family and the ties that bind."
—Lee Martin, author of *The Bright Forever* and *River of Heaven*

"T. Greenwood's novel is full of love, betrayal, lost hopes, and a burning question: is it ever too late to find redemption?"
—Miranda Beverly-Whittemore, author of *Bittersweet*

"Greenwood is a writer of subtle strength, evoking small-town life beautifully while spreading out the map of Harper's life, finding light in the darkest of stories."
—*Publishers Weekly*

"T. Greenwood's writing shimmers and sings as she braids together past, present, and the events of one desperate day. I ached for Harper in all of his longing, guilt, grief, and vast, abiding love, and I rejoiced at his final, hard-won shot at redemption."
—Marisa de los Santos, *New York Times* bestselling author of *Belong to Me* and *Love Walked In*

"*Two Rivers* is a stark, haunting story of redemption and salvation. T. Greenwood portrays a world of beauty and peace that, once disturbed, reverberates with searing pain and inescapable consequences. A memorable, powerful work."
—Garth Stein, *New York Times* bestselling author of *The Art of Racing in the Rain*

"A complex tale of guilt, remorse, revenge, and forgiveness . . . Convincing . . . Interesting . . ."
—Library Journal

"In the tradition of *The Adventures of Huckleberry Finn* and *To Kill a Mockingbird*, T. Greenwood's *Two Rivers* is a wonderfully distinctive American novel, abounding with memorable characters, unusual lore

and history, dark family secrets, and love of life. *Two Rivers* is the story that people want to read: the one they have never read before."
—Howard Frank Mosher, author of *Walking to Gatlinburg*

"*Two Rivers* is a dark and lovely elegy, filled with heartbreak that turns itself into hope and forgiveness. I felt so moved by this luminous novel."
—Luanne Rice, *New York Times* bestselling author

"*Two Rivers* is reminiscent of Thornton Wilder, with its quiet New England town shadowed by tragedy, and of Sherwood Anderson, with its sense of desperate loneliness and regret . . . It's to Greenwood's credit that she answers her novel's mysteries in ways that are believable, that make you feel the sadness that informs her characters' lives."
—*Bookpage*

Connect with Us

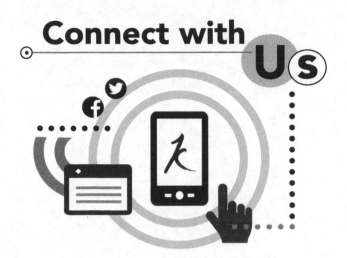

Visit us online at
KensingtonBooks.com
to read more from your favorite authors, see books
by series, view reading group guides, and more.

Join us on social media

for sneak peeks, chances to win books and prize packs,
and to share your thoughts with other readers.

**facebook.com/kensingtonpublishing
twitter.com/kensingtonbooks**

Tell us what you think!

To share your thoughts, submit a review,
or sign up for our eNewsletters, please visit:
KensingtonBooks.com/TellUs.